On the Brink of Shards

NANCY RIVEST GREEN

Nancy R. Green

2015
Dearest Ginny –
    To a moon group
soul sister & lover of nature –
hope you enjoy the story!
    Love,
        Nancy

On the Brink of Shards

NANCY RIVEST GREEN

Moonlit Press
Fiction

Williams, AZ

First Published December 2014

On the Brink of Shards
by
NANCY RIVEST GREEN

Printed in the United States of America

Cover Design by
Al Brown
al.brown@moonlitpress.com
in cooperation with:
Web Dust World: Designing, Developing and Delivering Usable and Sustainable Tools, Techniques and Technologies

Original artwork by ValJesse O'Feeney with permission
Cover photograph by Terryl Warnock

Published by Moonlit Press LLC
P. O. Box 126
Williams, Arizona   86046
moonlitpress.com

ISBN-13: 978-0-9894698-2-1
ISBN-10: 0989469824

Library of Congress Control Number: 2014920671

DEDICATION

This book is dedicated to my long suffering husband who always makes me feel like a goddess, to the mother whom I've lost, but will always love, and to the spirit of Arizona, which fills my heart.

AUTHOR'S NOTE

I have lived in Arizona for most of my adult life, long enough that the canyons, rivers, mountains and forests sing in my soul. This magnificent landscape and the people who have lived here over time inspire my respect, admiration and awe. I have tried to bring realism and facts into this story, but I also have molded the people, ceremonies, and even the landscape into a work of fiction to carry this story forward. During my life I have immersed myself in this land and these cultures, living and breathing in many of these places in the Great American Southwest. I lived at Walnut Canyon where this story begins, spent many years living at the Grand Canyon, and passed quiet hours of contemplation at Keyhole Sink. I have wandered, absorbed and relished these places. So dear reader, when you find inaccuracies, as I'm sure you will, just enjoy the story, keeping your own love for this region as ballast for any foibles on my part.

Nancy Rivest Green
December, 2013
In my beautiful log home,
watching the snow fall

Journey From Afar

Kaiya Kayko

Cañon Grande

Drok's Journey

I

Kaiya was jerked awake by a shriek which shattered the night. She had been lulled to sleep by the chanting of the nearby women. Her heart now pounded as the cry died away. But the chanting had stopped, the sudden silence more ominous than the shriek.

Then the air filled with a high, ear-splitting keening, rising and falling as the women filled their lungs and threw back their heads to mourn the loss of beloved kin. Their cries echoed and re-echoed throughout the canyon, until the rocks and stones seemed to join in the chorus. Kaiya knew her mother was gone forever, and the baby she labored so long to bring forth had died with her.

Kaiya struggled to remember the previous evening. Her mother said she felt ill, and had gone to her sleeping furs early. Kaiya stayed up with Jumac, the old woman from the chamber next door. Jumac was the clan's oldest woman, round and slightly bent at the shoulders. But her bright dark eyes sparkled with humor and liveliness. Although her steps were halting, her voice and heart held the stories of the clan.

Kaiya crept out of her sleeping furs into a strange room. Then she remembered her mother's startled gasps, and Jumac hobbling in. Amid a flurry of activity, Kaiya was scooped up and carried off, waking just enough to see if it was her father. But it was only Bertok, her father's younger brother. She started to protest, but Bertok gently placed his hand over her mouth and laid her on a pallet in another room. He tucked her in and stirred the fire's coals before slipping back into the night.

All of this Kaiya remembered in a rush as she reached the T-shaped doorway and thrust the deerskin aside. The canyon below held shapes and shadows cast from the crescent moon. The stars twinkled, so many, so bright. The sound of the wind in the pine trees comforted her now that the keening had faded. Then, the drums started to thump, signaling the clan to assemble.

Kaiya was finally awake enough to allow the truth about her mother to sink in. She slumped against the doorway and curled up, shivering in the pre-dawn cold. Her sobs were as soft as whispers.

Jumac had been the first to respond to Saratong's cries, and was also the first to check on Kaiya. She found the little girl, held her close, rocked her, and pushed Kaiya's black hair away from her hot, tear-streaked face.

"Come with me, little one, to the gathering," Jumac said.

Kaiya stood. She shook out her deerskin dress and made futile passes at her tangled hair. Putting her small hand in Jumac's leathery one, they walked slowly into the flow of people on their way to the ceremony.

Dawn broke just as the entire clan gathered. People huddled, then made way for the arrival of Saratong's body. She was wrapped in a clean deerskin so that only her head showed. The tiny baby, wrapped in a soft rabbit fur, was placed on Saratong's belly.

A space was cleared at the edge of the village's trash midden to make room for the bodies. Everyone in the clan had picked up something to contribute to covering the bodies; twigs, pinecones, pine needles, leaves, stones. Each man, woman and child approached the midden and deposited their offering. People close to Saratong lingered a while, tears streaming, every line in their faces etched with grief. People brought more juniper and pine branches to cover her. When all was covered, the People stepped back and bowed their heads.

He seemed to appear from out of nowhere, floating above the crowd. When the two men who carried him lifted him onto a tall stump near the edge of the canyon, the illusion of floating remained. Sunlight glowed on the stump. His voice filled the air.

"Blessed Spirit, we come before you to pass over one of your own, Saratong, and an unnamed infant. We know your cycles of birth, death and rebirth. But our own pain is great as we contemplate the loss of this cheerful young mother. We know her greater good is to be with you, Creator of All, but we mourn her because her nature brought us joy."

There was absolute silence in the crowd. A long, long silence. As Kaiya leaned against Jumac, she dozed. She was startled awake by the hiss of a rattlesnake – but there was no snake near her. She looked up. Four dancers sidestepped forward. The shells on their leggings rattled and hissed. The leader of the ceremony started a chant, picked up in turn by the People. The chant seemed like a wail to Kaiya, as she stood and sang, feeling the burning emotions arise in her heart. She felt the pain of loss, despair and loneliness. More tears made hot streaks down her cheeks. Through her tears, she looked toward where her mother lay. It seemed that her mother called to her. Kaiya twisted free of Jumac's grasp and tore through the crowd. There were startled gasps as people tried to restrain her, but Kaiya broke free and headed straight toward the mound. She was but a breath away when a large form blocked her way.

"Let me by! I want her!" Kaiya sobbed.

"No, Kaiya—your mother isn't really in that mound, look!"

The man who blocked her way was the same man who had led the ceremony. He picked her up, held her tightly, and walked away to the edge of the crowd. He pointed up to the blue sky. There, between the wisps of clouds, and only for an instant—Kaiya could see her mother looking down peacefully at them. Then she was gone.

"Kaiya, did you see her?" the man asked.

Kaiya turned to gaze into his eyes. She had only seen this man from a distance, but she knew he was Moochkla the healer. He was old, not as old as Jumac, but still old. His face was textured with deep wrinkles born of sun, time and hardships. But his eyes were bottomless, shiny black pools of energy.

"Yes, I saw her in the clouds," Kaiya said. "Did you make her into a cloud being?"

"No," Moochkla said. "That really was your mother's spirit, rising up to begin her journey. But only you and I saw her."

"Where did she go?" Kaiya asked. "Why were we the only ones who could see her?"

"She went to that place between worlds, where she will review what she learned in this lifetime, and design what she needs to do next. The reason I saw her is I am a healer. Now, why could you see her? Perhaps it is because you are young, or because she was your mother. Or perhaps," said Moochkla, "it is something else." He backed away from the mound and returned Kaiya to the ground, still holding tightly to her hand. "Perhaps it is because one day, you too will be a healer."

Kaiya looked into Moochkla's eyes. For the briefest second, she had a glimpse of herself as a grown woman--- happy and self-assured. Then it was gone.

"You are a magic man," Kaiya said.

She slowly pulled her hand from his and walked to Jumac, turning back once to look at Moochkla. He stood with his arms outstretched to the sky.

"Great Spirit of the Earth, you have shown me the one I am to teach," the healer whispered.

A little less than a moon later Kaiya stood before another going away ceremony. This time it was for her father, Borhea, who had never returned from a hunting expedition in mid-winter. He had been the best hunter in the tribe and a likeable young man. He knew Saratong was due to bring forth another child during the last moon of winter. When he didn't return, the clan remained hopeful and continued to look for him.

A hunting party found him on the first warm spring day when Winter loosened its icy grip on the land and air. The signs around Borhea clearly told the story of his death. He had been stalking a deer up a steep, ice-covered, rocky ravine when he slipped. He straightened up, trying to regain his balance, but lost his footing, and plunged backwards to the canyon floor. The rocks underneath the surface of the snow shattered his spine.

Kaiya listened solemnly to Moochkla presiding over her father's going away ceremony. After everyone had contributed to covering the pile, she slunk away into the trees. She slipped silently to a rock where she felt hidden, but where she could gaze into the canyon.

"You feel alone now."

Kaiya jumped at the sound of the nearby voice and turned to see Moochkla standing close to her rock.

"But you are not."

"I didn't even hear you! How can you sneak around like that?" Kaiya exclaimed.

Moochkla chuckled. "I am an old man who moves slowly and quietly in a place I have known for many years. You are a young girl lost in her own thoughts." Moochkla hunkered down beside her and hefted a piece of limestone in his hand.

"How old are you?" she asked.

"I have seen many winters," replied Moochkla.

"You must be tired from trying to keep warm all that time."

Moochkla threw back his head and gave a hearty laugh. "Yes, there are times when I thought I would never feel warm again. And you, Little One, must be tired of seeing so much death in your short life."

"Why didn't my parents get to be old like you?"

Moochkla sat next to her on the rock. He gazed out over the canyon and followed the path a turkey vulture carved out of the deep blue sky.

"Kaiya, there are many things I need to tell you. Some things won't make any sense until you are older. But know now and for always, that the Beloved Spirit has a life planned for each and every one of us. Nothing is by chance. We who live in this one small place on our Bountiful Mother may not be able to see or understand all reasons for all things. But you must believe that there is a reason."

"Will I have people in my life who stay with me and take care of me?" asked Kaiya, tears spilling down her cheeks.

He pulled her close and she nestled into his lap, sobbing softly. He tried to straighten her tangled hair with his fingers, then sighed, realizing it was a hopeless task. Moochkla waited until the racking sobs faded, then lifted her up to sit beside him.

"Kaiya," he said, taking her small hands into his large, gnarled ones. "Look into my eyes."

She gazed directly at him.

"You will be admired by many and feared by a few. You will have a love that defies all bounds of time and space. But know that this love will not come quickly or easily. When it comes, after much hardship, you will know it was worth the wait."

As she gazed deep into his eyes, for the briefest moment she caught a picture of the back of a strong young man, like her father's brother, Bertok. Then it was gone. She gave his old hands a squeeze, then let them go and stood. She turned and ran lightly between the pines and over the brambled shrubs. As she ran, she felt Moochkla's energy flowing and surrounding her, as if to remind her that she wasn't ever really alone.

II

Drok awoke with a jolt of pain across his thighs.

"Get up, you worthless waste," growled his father.

Drok scrambled to his feet and backed away. His mother cowered in a corner against the wall, trying to make herself invisible. She would offer no refuge from her husband's wrath.

"The day is half over, and you have done nothing," barked his father.

In fact, the sun was just beginning to warm the walls of the city-state of Tula.

"Go tell the pulque maker to fill this," thrusting a jar into Drok's hands. "And you'd better not spill a drop on the way back."

Drok bolted through the doorway, and kicked an ancient dog lounging in the sun against the mud wall of the house. The poor animal howled with pain and limped off along the face of the building. Drok's face twisted into a grin. But it would appear to others a look of rage. Over a year ago, his father had hurled hot oil at his son in a drunken rampage. Drok's face was horribly twisted and scarred. His lips, mouth and chin had taken the brunt of the oil's fiery heat, but puckered scars were on his cheeks as well. The mottled white, pink and brown colors cast his right cheek in stone. That was the only time his mother had attempted to help him by running to fetch the shaman. But despite the healer's best efforts, Drok's face never returned to normal. Just seeing him reminded people of their nightmares. The other children learned quickly to stay out of Drok's path, for his bullying was boundless. Even the older children learned to avoid him, as his anger seemed to instill him with an unexpected strength. Although smaller than other boys his age, he frequently launched vicious attacks.

Drok's path to the marketplace of Tula was not the most direct. He veered from one side of the road to the other, crashing into an old woman balancing a big bundle of sticks on her head. He laughed when the old woman knelt and groaned, gathering scattered sticks.

Later, Drok jumped into the way of a small girl trying to herd several turkeys toward the marketplace, causing the frightened birds to shoot out in as many directions as there were turkeys. She gasped when she realized who had caused her birds to disperse. Drok slowed down long enough to place his flat palm against her chest and shoved her backwards into the dirt. There she lay, a pool of her tears in the dust. Drok's face contorted once again.

Tula, the "Place of the Reeds", nestled in the valley of the Tula and Rosas Rivers. 30,000 people resided within the city walls, while another 60,000 lived in the outlying areas. The heart of the city was on the southern end of a high ridge. It boasted several open plazas, temples, palaces and two ballcourts. In the surrounding area were thousands of single-story buildings with flat roofs. The pulque maker was in a popular store near the city center.

He arrived at the stall of the pulque seller hot and out of breath, but feeling better. Shoving others helped. The man in the stall filled the jar and grunted to Drok that he would be by later for payment. Drok knew that when the pulque maker showed up, his mother would pay. She would be used again.

He hated the walk back with his slow, measured steps so as not to spill any of the precious liquid. Drok's return path pulled him away from the bustling center. He didn't want any encounters on the way back which would interfere with the delivery of his cargo.

In the distance, he could see and hear the training of the city's soldiers. Today was hot enough that they wouldn't be wearing their warrior garb. Even with loincloths only, the warriors looked the part. In order to get this look, many parents, hoping their sons would be chosen as soldiers, forced the flattening of the soft heads of their babies against a hard cradleboard. This caused a high, wide forehead associated with most warriors.

Warriors' cries, followed by the crash of bodies practicing combat, sent a shiver of delight through Drok. He liked to hang around these men, longing to be invited to join them. Even within their own city, people dodged the ranks when the army marched through the streets. Drok imagined the thrill of conquering a city, dressed in a feathered helmet, quilted armor, with piercings in his nose, mouth and ears. A conquered populace would be truly afraid.

Drok's father was gone from their dwelling upon his return. After carefully setting the jar down, Drok turned toward his mother. She had been a pretty young girl, with bright black eyes and straight black hair. But her life with her husband had snuffed the spark from her eyes. Her hands trembled as she attempted to weave a basket. Her eyes touched Drok's face with warmth and love as she whispered, "Go now while he is gone."

Drok nodded and returned outside. He ran back to the place where the soldiers were training. Sometimes he retrieved arrows or spears thrown by the soldiers and was rewarded with scraps of food. He was cautious when handling those sharp, bifacial obsidian blades.

Today the goal of training was to create confusion for the enemy. Over and over again, a line of soldiers would form. On command, they flung themselves forward, yelling wildly. The men were drenched in sweat and exhausted. Drok ached to be among them. Since there were no weapons to retrieve today, he just lurked along the sidelines for a while. He grew tired of being in the sun and decided to go see what was happening by the temples.

In the center of the town plaza rose a great pyramid. Countless slaves captured during wars had been forced to build this monument to Tlaloc, the Rain God. It had taken years of slave labor to complete. It was an impressive structure, built from the plentiful limestone rock found in the area. The imposing triangle dominated the skyscape of the city. It was visible for many miles distant and from anywhere within the city. Beyond it Jicuco Mountain could be seen away in the distance.

Minor priests stood at the base of the pyramid, tallying the tributes and tithes brought from outlying areas or from merchants within the city. Summer and fall were the busiest times, when most people were supposed to pay up. Payments were crops of corn, beans, squash, and cotton. Pottery, basketry, woven textiles, jewelry or obsidian weapons were also accepted. Some taxes were taken in the form of work performed. The work of sculptors, painters and other artisans also had value.

Other tax payments were made in the form of human cargo.

There was a constant need for slaves for the pyramids. People who failed to provide their payments on time learned to expect a visit from the temple soldiers.

A group of girls just slightly older than Drok was being delivered to the temple. Drok was close enough to see that a few had budding breasts, which the priest grazed with his fingers as he examined the girls and bartered with the man. Drok knew that some of the girls would wind up as virginal sacrifices, while others would serve the priests in the temple. Drok noted the ornate jewelry the priest wore around each bicep and wrist. Around his neck was a pendant of a jaguar. Even his cotton loincloth was painted with the face of a jaguar. The man delivering the girls wore only a tattered loincloth.

Also approaching the temple were slaves who needed attending, carrying loads of raw cotton. Annoyed by the interruption of his more enticing task, the priest looked around for assistance. Spying Drok nearby, the priest raised his voice and his bony finger simultaneously, and boomed at Drok.

"You there, temple boy! Go in and get Beeta. Tell her I need help down here, hurry!"

Drok's first reaction was a scowl at being mistaken for a lowly temple boy. Then he jumped into action, realizing this could be a chance to see inside the pyramid. Repeating the name Beeta so he wouldn't forget it, he scooted along the side of the temple. He knew enough of the ceremonial aspects to know that the use of the front steps was only for the priests. There must be an entrance either at the side or in the back, Drok thought. Drok ducked inside a curved stone entryway at the back corner. He stopped still, confused by the darkness and feeling the cool emanating from the stones. Waiting a few moments for his eyes to adjust, he inched down a long corridor. When no one else appeared, he continued along the dark passage. Abruptly a narrow staircase began. Tripping over the first step and cursing quietly, he picked himself up and began the ascent. Like the stairs on the exterior of the pyramid, these were only big enough to step sideways with the toes and the ball of the foot. It was disrespectful to show face or rear to the gods of the Temple of Tlaloc and Drok did not want to dishonor the gods.

Drok came to a landing where light streamed in from slits in the stones above. With it came some fresh air into the damp dark.

Drok heard a slapping of flesh and the scrambling of footsteps echoing away from him down the hall. A priest suddenly appeared in front of Drok out of the darkness. His harsh voice called out, "Boy, what are you doing here? You know you aren't allowed in this chamber!"

"I-I-I was sent here to find Beeta. The priest at the entrance collecting tithes—I forget his name—says he needs some help," Drok blurted out.

"I'll send her. You go now. You should not be here," the priest scolded.

Drok backed away, then turned and fled from the imposing figure. From behind the wall he heard a peal of female laughter followed by a low male chuckle. Drok tried retracing his steps back to where he entered the temple, but nothing seemed familiar. As he turned yet another corner, he collided with a girl just slightly older than he. She swayed from the impact and thrust out her hand to push against the wall for support. Her breasts were bare and close to Drok. She wore a belt with a jaguar head to hold the gathered folds of her skirt. Both arms had gold bangle bracelets at the wrists which clicked together as she moved. Her eyes were glazed and unfocused, but she finally figured out what had caused the collision. She reached down and cupped Drok's genitals and gave them a squeeze. Drok was surprised at the pleasure of the touch. The girl laughed and drifted off down the corridor. Now Drok leaned against the wall for support, his heart still pounding from the encounter with the priest, and now faster still from the touch of the girl. When his breathing slowed, he inched along the wall toward a sliver of light. The sliver widened as he approached. He stepped into the light and found himself in a large chamber lit with flickering torches. The cavernous room held piles of ceremonial robes tossed carelessly on the floor. The colors were rich burgundy, vibrant indigo, royal purple—colors that only high officials were allowed to wear. Ornate headdresses were heaped alongside the robes, shimmering gold with touches of silver and copper glittering in the torchlight. Drok started across the room to examine these treasures but stopped cold when he heard a small sound behind him.

He twirled about to face the most enormous man he had ever seen. In the flickering torch light, the man's features were crossed with shadows and light. His towering height wavered in the light, making him appear even taller. His head was shaved and gleamed, shiny with oil. His muscular arms crossed his chest across a long robe with billowing sleeves. He glared down at Drok.

"Who are you?" he demanded.

"I am Drok. I was sent to find Beeta to help the priest collecting tithes at the front of the temple. But...but I got lost on my way back out."

"That must surely be true, as no one would enter this room without permission if he knew better."

The man stepped closer, and Drok could now see that his eyes were the color of the sky and rimmed in red. His skin was pale, pale white. The hair on his arms was pure white. He's not old, Drok thought. Why is his hair so white?

"I prefer to live here in the darkness of the temple," said the man, reading Drok's thoughts. "I was born this way." He paused, eyeing Drok's disfigured face carefully. "You're not a temple boy, are you?"

"No," stammered Drok. "I was just walking by the temple and the priest thought I was and sent me on this errand."

"So, without any knowledge of where to go or whom to see, you just entered the temple and started exploring?" To Drok's surprise, the man tilted back his head and let out a peal of laughter.

"We could use someone around here like you. Let me talk to the high priest. Wait here."

Drok was relieved to be left alone in this great chamber. He continued across the room to the piles of robes and fell to his knees in front of them. Fingering the luxurious fabrics, he let them fall against his thighs. The sensation left his skin tingling. These textiles were woven to create a softness that was foreign to Drok, used to his coarse, homespun cotton clothes. He leapt to his feet as he heard footsteps in the corridor. The enormous man reentered the room, accompanied by a priest. This one was obviously a man of high standing, as his jewelry was the most ornate Drok had ever seen. A copper breastplate dotted with turquoise and jade covered his chest. It hung by two chains which reached from the breastplate's corners around the priest's neck. He wore only a loincloth, but it was held around his waist by a sash decorated with a snarling jaguar. Even his sandals had decorations of silver.

"Drok, bow to Cumani," the taller man ordered.

Drok immediately crouched on the floor, head down.

"Loka tells me you entered the temple without permission," the priest said sternly.

"No." Drok shook his head vehemently. "The man at the entrance to the temple told me to find Beeta."

"But he must have thought you were a temple boy, and you never informed him you weren't."

"I was scared," mumbled Drok.

"What?" the priest demanded.

Drok lifted his eyes to the priest's face.

"I said I was scared," Drok repeated.

Loka asked, "Is it all right for a young man to admit fear?"

Drok replied, "It's all right to feel fear, but not to show fear to your enemies. Then they will know that you are weak."

Cumani and Loka exchanged glances.

Cumani said, "We are short of temple boys right now. Do you have any desire to work in the temple?"

Drok considered this. Before him flashed the images of soldiers drilling in the hot sun. Then he recalled the temple guards, fearsome with their painted faces, piercings and armor. He nodded to the priest. "I have always wanted to be a temple guard," he lied.

Cumani stared down at this strange boy. He did need more workers in the temple just now. He liked this boy's grit and his damaged face. He would be no temptation to any of the temple girls.

"Very well," the priest replied. "Loka will accompany you to notify your family. Then you will return here and begin your training."

Drok couldn't believe his ears. Escape his father? He felt a pang of regret about leaving his mother. She was the only person who had always been kind to him.

As Loka and Drok left the temple, Loka donned a large, woven straw hat with a wide brim to keep his eyes safe from the sun's glare. Drok had to race alongside the tall man just to keep up. The day's shadows were lengthening in the tight passageways through the city streets. Drok noticed that Loka always kept to the shadowy side of the alleyways.

They arrived as day slid over into dusk. Before setting foot on his own street, Drok spied his father standing with a group of men hunched around a table. The men were intent on a gambling game, hooting and scoffing at each move. Drok's father was drunk, loudly boasting and jeering at the foolishness of each man's play. Drok stood back, and pointed out to Loka which man was his father. Loka strode toward the group, towering over all the men. He waited until the men one by one noticed his presence. A hush ensued as the men waited for Loka to speak. Loka gestured to Drok's father, and motioned for him to follow him back to where Drok stood. Drok's father looked startled, but lurched after Loka. He swayed in front of Drok, looking down at him in anger. He raised his arm and swung a backhand in Drok's direction. His balance was off, and the blow only glanced Drok's shoulder.

"What did the boy do?" he demanded.

"Your son is needed at the temple. He will no longer live with you," Loka stated.

Drok's father's eyes narrowed. "Oh, but he is my only son. I need him to help me with my ah . . . business."

Loka opened his fist and held it out. "This will compensate you."

Drok's father cupped his palms toward Loka's hand. Cacao beans clicked as Drok's father greedily counted them. Loka turned to leave and Drok's father turned away.

"Wait," Drok said. Both men turned back toward Drok. "Say goodbye to my mother for me."

Drok's father spat on the ground and staggered back to the game without a word.

Drok stood a second longer watching his father's back retreat. He turned back to Loka.

"I hate pulque," he blurted. "I will never drink it."

"Good," Loka replied. "There are enough temptations in life without that."

"What do you mean?"

"Well, humans as a whole are weak. People always want to do what feels good now. It takes a stronger person to put aside something that feels good now in favor of waiting until later for something better. Your father likes the feeling of pulque and gambling. I'll bet that money never makes it back to your mother."

Drok nodded. "So many times we wouldn't have enough money for food, but there always seemed to be a way to get pulque."

Loka said, "The successful people in life put aside temptation until their goals are met. Then they make sure that temptation doesn't interfere with their success. You want to be a temple guard. Then you must keep that thought in front of you. Whatever opens before you, keep that thought as your guiding light."

Drok pondered this as they made their way back to the temple. He had never thought about life in the long term. Day to day survival was all that previously mattered to him. Now he realized the gods had dropped an incredible opportunity into his lap. Surrounded by the powerful men of the temple, all he had to do was work hard, gain their favor, and he could have anything he wanted.

III

The sun hung longer in the sky each day as spring moved on. Kaiya was living in Jumac's chamber, uncomfortable about taking up space in the old woman's cramped quarters.

Her clan chose this place wisely. Most of the dwellings were on the west side of an island of rock jutting out over the canyon. The cliffs had deep, recessed, limestone caves. The overhanging lip became the roof, while the cave wall was the back of the room. The eroded, scooped out center became their living quarters. The People need only construct the front wall. Rocks were abundant, and could be built into a substantial partition held in place with clay and soil daubed with mud. The T-shaped doorways allowed easy entry for someone carrying a large load of wood or a deer haunch slung over their shoulders. It could easily be covered with a hide in inclement weather.

Kaiya pushed aside the deerskin and slid out into the cool of the morning. She loved looking along the ledge as the village awoke, seeing heads pop out and hearing chattering voices. Across the narrow chasm, Kaiya could see other households rousing, too.

Before she got assigned her chores, she went to douse her face in the creek. She jump-stepped down the nearly vertical slope, and soon was at the creek, splashing her way noisily into mid-stream, the cold water stinging her skin. Flinging back her long hair, she ran her wet fingers through it, pulling it back into a long tail. Securing it with a twisted piece of yucca twine, she turned and scrambled up the steep slope to the first ledge without stopping for breath.

Moochkla and Jumac sat with their backs against the wall of Jumac's dwelling, one on either side of the doorway. Kaiya approached uneasily, suspecting she was the topic of their conversation.

"Greetings, Kaiya," began Moochkla. "I have something important to discuss with you. I have been alone in my house for many moons since my wife died. She used to help me with all of my herbal work. I am getting old and need to teach my herbal skills to a younger member of our clan. I think that should be you." Jumac nodded encouragingly.

"Can't I just stay here with Jumac and go help you sometimes?" Kaiya asked.

"No, Kaiya, I need you to come to my house to live. You need to see and understand how everything works together for the greater good for all the People."

Kaiya knew where his house was. Everybody in the clan knew where it was, but few people had been in it. The thought of actually living there made Kaiya shudder.

"But, I like it in the canyon," Kaiya said. "I help lots of people. I gather wood and clay and help grind. I get water and I'm learning how to weave yucca cords. And how could I play with Akeela?"

"Ah, but there is beauty and work to be done in the forest as well," Moochkla said. "You will spend time in many different places during your lifetime, Kaiya. Let me help you gather your things."

Kaiya shuffled inside and began tugging at her sleeping furs. She heard Jumac and Moochkla speaking quietly. Kaiya's belongings were few and most were in her basket, her prized possession. Bowl-shaped, with a lid which fit exactly in the top of the bowl, it had a little loop on top to slide a finger through to easily remove the lid. Kaiya recalled her mother's fingers braiding and weaving pine needles and yucca cord. She fought back tears. Moochkla entered, noticed the trickle of tears, and kindly patted Kaiya on the shoulder.

"It is important that you get training, Kaiya, for yourself and for the clan. Jumac and Akeela will still be here to greet you."

"I know," Kaiya said. "I just miss my Mother. She made this basket." Kaiya thrust the basket toward Moochkla, who took it from her, nodding gravely.

"Yes, I remember her working on this. She made it in honor of you. See that zigzag design? That was the lightning storm that happened the night you were born."

Kaiya looked up in surprise. She had heard this story from her parents, but how did the healer know?

"Do healers know everything about everybody?" Kaiya asked.

Moochkla coughed and glanced sideways toward the doorway where Jumac stood holding her hand over her mouth to suppress her laughter.

"No, we don't. But it's important that I keep track of what's going on around here. Come now." Moochkla scooped up Kaiya's sleeping furs.

With a few odds and ends trailing over her arms, Kaiya slowly followed Moochkla out of the canyon to the forest floor above.

The healer's dwelling stood alone in a clearing just past a trailhead seldom used by the villagers to access the canyon. His house was the only one of its kind in the vicinity, built before Moochkla's time and used by each successive healer. Rocks created four rectangular walls, about as high as a man's head. The roof and ceiling were made from trimmed logs laid across the shorter span. The purpose became clear as soon as Kaiya stood on the threshold and peered inside. After blinking a few times to adjust her eyes to the darkness within, she saw dried plants suspended from the rafters—leaves, stems and stalks tied together in bunches. The whole left side of the house was devoted to herbs, while the smaller, right side was set up as tidy living quarters.

Moochkla settled Kaiya's sleeping furs neatly in one corner and stirred the coals of the fire. Kaiya inched her way into the dwelling, overcome by the profusion of aromas. How could this jumble of herbs ever be used to heal? Settling uneasily on her sleeping furs by the fire, she watched Moochkla. He bustled about, pulled down leaves from one bunch, then stems from another, and added these to a pot simmering on the fire. He chanted softly as he stirred the mixture together.

"What are you chanting?" Kaiya asked.

"I always ask the Great Spirit for guidance when I am creating medicines. I never want to do any harm. I want only the highest and the best to enter the person who is sick."

"How do you know what herbs to use for which sickness?"

"Ah, Kaiya, that is what you will learn. But it will take years to learn it correctly, because you don't want to make mistakes. Some are easy remedies, others complex and dangerous. Always, you need to be guided by the Great Spirit. You will become healing hands on Earth. Come closer to me, Kaiya."

Kaiya stood before Moochkla. He cupped her chin in his hand and looked straight into her eyes. Kaiya returned the stare. Surprised by something moving in his eyes, she realized it was the two of them, out in the woods gathering herbs. They were both older, and Kaiya recognized herself as she would look as a young woman. He dropped his hand and his gaze and stood back.

"What did you see?" he asked softly.

"Us. We were out in the forest gathering plants."

"Kaiya, sit down here by the fire."

She sat with her arms wrapped around her knees, curious to hear what he had to say.

"You have a special gift from the Great Spirit," Moochkla said. "You are able to see things that others can't. Things which may be in the future, or things that a person might be thinking about. Remember when your mother became a cloud being at her going away ceremony? You and I were the only ones who saw that happen. I think you may have noticed this happening before. This is not to be taken lightly or used to spy on people's private thoughts. It is a gift to be used only for good."

"Yes, it sometimes happens when I look into a person's eyes."

Moochkla nodded. "I think you are grown up enough to realize what a serious thing this is. You are blessed, but in some ways this gift is also a burden. Guard it and use it well."

Resuming his soft chanting, Moochkla returned to his potion. Kaiya huddled by the fire, thinking about eyes, about seeing. She remembered seeing the love pour out of her mother's eyes. She remembered her mother and father, the special way they looked at each other, as if there was a yucca string attached between them. Eyes were more than seeing a rock before you tripped or helping you put the right amount of water into the pot. Eyes were a way of signaling. Now she realized she had another, deeper layer of seeing, without the other person even knowing. Moochkla was right, she must use it carefully. She shivered.

Sometimes images came to her unbidden. She could not stop the scene from unfolding before her. It was like the acting out of a hunt before the actual hunt. She could no more stop it than she could stop the hunters from hunting. Even if she shut her eyes, she saw the deer dancer raise his arms and continue dancing inside her head.

It was all so confusing. Why did she have this gift? Was it the Great Spirit's way of making up for the loss of her parents? Kaiya decided she must pay attention to everything around her when this happened.

Their days passed pleasantly. As the days grew longer, Moochkla used every moment of daylight to show Kaiya the emerging plants. Until now she had never paid attention to all the things growing around her. They were to hide in or gather for the fire. She was amazed at the intricacies of each plant. Moochkla, too, was delighted with Kaiya. She was a willing and interested student, often bringing a grin to Moochkla's weathered face.

"What are these?" Kaiya asked, pointing to a low lying bloom, with green leaves and purple and white tubes.

"Ah, wood betony, the first sign of spring," Moochkla replied. "This is always one of the first plants to arrive after winter. Break off the blossom and suck the tube."

Kaiya tried it and was surprised by its sweetness.

"It's to remind us of Mother Earth's sweetness, which is easy to forget during a cold winter like the one we've just had."

"What medicine can it be used for?" Kaiya asked.

"Use it for persons with a bad headache or stomachache. It will help them relax and feel sleepy, which sometimes is all they need."

"How about the paintbrush flower?" Kaiya pointed to the red fringy flower, proud that she already knew its name.

"The flowers are good to eat, but the roots and green parts make you sick. The flowers can be used to help with the twisting sickness."

"What's that?" Kaiya asked.

"It's when people's joints become inflamed and swollen. It's usually in the older people of the clan. Their hands get gnarled, or their knees get twisted and they have trouble walking. It's from aging and constant use. The paintbrush tea helps with the pain."

"Why do people get sick at all?" Kaiya asked.

"Oh, Kaiya, I only wish I knew. I'm sure people have been asking that question as long as there have been people. I don't understand why some people die young, like your parents, and then others, like me, seem to live forever. Some people, like Jumac, get old without having anything seriously wrong with them, while others have so many things go wrong. Why do some people get sick and then get better, while others get sick and die? I wish for just one day I could see the world as the Great Spirit sees it and know all the answers."

They walked side by side through the forest, aware of the world around them of sky, canyon and creek, each with its own spirit. Kaiya could feel the burden of Moochkla's place in the village as healer trying to keep the People all healthy and alive. She realized that this burden would slowly be transferred to her. She straightened, thrust her chin up and stopped.

"I will help many and save some," she said.

"I have no doubt that you will." Moochkla's voice was warm.

Kaiya and Moochkla developed their rhythm of life together. Moochkla always rose first, stirred the coals of the fire then coaxed them back into life with his breath. He then added a few more sticks to begin the new day's fire. He made their tea from the twigs of the ephedra plant. Shoving rocks into the hot fire, he later removed and placed them into a pottery vessel. He poured water over these hot rocks, slowly heating, then finally pouring the water into small cups for Kaiya and himself. Tea spikes floated in them. After a few moments of steeping, he brought the aromatic cup to Kaiya's sleeping furs. The rising steam usually brought Kaiya to consciousness. Sometimes she played at sleeping, but Moochkla saw through this, lowered the cup, and tickled Kaiya's cheeks and chin with a feather. She stood it for as long as she could, then burst from beneath the furs, shrieking with laughter. Moochkla, who had never lived with children, was always amazed at the exuberance Kaiya exhibited at the simplest parts of life.

Breakfast was a small meal, usually some piki bread which Kaiya had proudly learned to make. Using the ground blue corn meal, she added some water and a little juniper ash from their fire. She used an oil made from squash, watermelon and sunflower seeds to smear on the flat baking stone, heated with the fire. Kaiya dipped into the batter and spread it onto the sizzling stone. The batter mixed with the oil and cooked almost immediately. She peeled up the crinkly sheet and rolled it into a log-shape, easy for storage. They broke small pieces off for breakfast, along with any nuts or berries which happened to be at hand.

Then it was off into the forest to search for whatever plant remedy Moochkla needed at the moment. He spent his days making his way through the village, stopping to chat and check how people were doing. After this long, cold winter, many people were weathered and beat. Although there was little snow last winter, the extreme cold had killed quite a few people and weakened others. Some were worried about the lack of snow, which was affecting the flow of the creek. This in turn, affected the fish as well as the deer, elk and antelope the people depended upon in the hunt. Moochkla tended to the sick, and tried to instill hope in the people whose spirits were low.

Spring was always a hard time for the People, as they waited impatiently to plant and harvest the crops. But this spring seemed worse than most because it followed three brutally cold winters with little snow. Some people seemed lethargic with just enough energy to find a place to sit in the sun. It was as if their bones were still cold from winter and needed thawing before beginning the tasks of spring.

IV

Drok's training in the temple was relentless. Accustomed to obeying his father, he learned quickly from a young age to assess his father's moods and act accordingly. But this new life was different. The tasks of a temple boy were more complex than anything he'd ever witnessed and the rituals intricate.

Although the priests and Loka were stern, never did they strike him. Their displeasure was clear, though, in their expressions. Their eyes flashed and their mouths tightened. Sometimes there would be a sharp exhale, followed by the correct action repeated. Drok cringed, waiting for their blows, but they never came. He redoubled his efforts to please them. Their pleasure was shown just as inscrutably as their displeasure. A faint light came into their eyes, and a slight twitch of the corner of a mouth showed Drok he had performed correctly.

There were a few older temple boys who made it clear from the beginning they would not befriend this new boy with the disfigured face. If Drok approached this group, they simply looked at him in disgust and walked away. Although Drok never had many friends before, in this strange, new environment, he wished he had some. He knew bullying wouldn't work here.

The temple girls were another story. They doted on Drok. Since he was young, he was no sexual threat to any of them and they seemed to delight in parading in front of him barely dressed. He was agog, as he had never seen a completely naked woman before, so he spent as much time as he could in their chamber. These young girls were being groomed for sexual sacrifice on the altar of the pyramid. Before the sacrifice they were quite indulged, given as much fruit, meat, fish, breads and pulque as they wanted. The priests spent time with them, too. There was much laughing, teasing and flirting among the priests and the temple girls. Sometimes the wafting scent of burning hemp drifted out from their chamber.

One time Drok tiptoed to the doorway to peek. A priest had a temple girl on top of a mound of soft robes. Her legs were spread wide, with his face buried between them. The girl writhed and moaned as the priest licked and kissed her. She lifted herself up on her elbows so she could watch the priest. Drok was shocked by the feelings which arose within him, unable to tear his eyes away. At home he had witnessed the hurried thrusts of his father on his mother. It seemed joyless, except for the one moment when his father would go rigid, cry out and collapse on top of her. He was sure his mother hadn't derived any pleasure from that act. Yet, here was this girl moaning and moving in a way that made his own heart race.

Moving his hand to the cleft between her legs, the priest pushed his fingers inside, and she rocked in rhythm to the tempo of the priest's fingers. Her sounds reminded Drok of birdcalls he heard from the jungle; rhythmic, short notes. Finally she let out a loud cry of pleasure, and pushed the priest's hand away.

Less than a moon after Drok had lived in the small set of huts behind the temple, there was to be a ceremony to summon the rain god, Tlaloc. Drok was chosen to assist, and all of his attention was taken up with his training.

Life was difficult for the Toltec Empire at this point. The lack of rain caused many problems for the people of Tula. 30,000 people lived in and around the city. The arable farmland near the riverbank was getting drier each year. In the past, spring floods from the upstream rains would bring rich new soil and leave moistened dirt perfect for planting. But the rains had diminished. Both the land

and the people cried out for rain. Crops were failing, and the city's food reserves were lower than ever before. Even the reliable crops of corn, beans and squash were withering in the fields. People living in areas which typically grew cotton had given up on that water intensive crop. The rivers surrounding the city were low, causing the many canoes of goods heading up and down the river to bottom out. Disgruntled river men were constantly getting out of their canoes to push out from the mud and back into what little current remained. Tensions ran high in the city as it was harder and harder to find clean water for drinking and all other important purposes.

Drok felt his part in this ceremony was critical because of the crippling lack of rain. The day had been a hot, sticky one. As the sun finally faded behind the jungle horizon, the full moon slowly rose on the other side of the plaza. From his vantage point in the chamber, Drok could see the crowd through the slit in the stones. They gathered below him in the space around the front of the pyramid. He was nervous about performing his part in the ceremony, which was to walk around the perimeter at the top of the pyramid carrying copal incense held in a shell.

He gathered the copal resin himself once he was chosen for the ceremony. At the time of the new moon, he hiked out into the jungle alone to search for sappy trees he could cut with his stone knife. He laid the resin out in the hot sun in the temple courtyard to dry. Breaking off a small piece, he managed to light it and keep it lit. After much practice he thought he could repeat this act for the ceremony. Now he wasn't so sure.

Loka made sure Drok dressed appropriately before he appeared above the crowd. The new loincloth was the first piece of clothing Drok could remember receiving for a long time. Loka approached Drok with hot oil to rub on his chest. Drok recoiled, remembering what his father had done to his face with hot oil. Loka didn't notice Droks's fear and applied the oil. To Drok's relief, the touch was warm and even soothing.

"This will make your skin shine so the people can see you easier," Loka stated. Loka also combed Drok's long, black hair for him. Drok reached to pick up his ceremonial shell and resin when Loka stopped him.

"Here, you will need this." Loka handed him a belt with a jaguar head fastener.

Drok looked up in astonishment. He had long coveted this object as most of the temple workers had one.

"A person can't have one of these until participating in an official ceremony, and now you are," explained Loka.

Drok's eyes showed his thanks and he proceeded to the platform on top of the pyramid. He stepped out of the doorway and over to the edge of the pyramid platform, his breath catching momentarily at the distance down to the plaza. It was a long, long way down. It never seemed that far when he looked up from the base. But way up here, the air seemed to shimmer as he looked out over the jungle canopy. It was so exposed up here, no trees or vines to slip between and disappear. Here, all was seen by the gathering crowd below. Drok took a deep breath and began his slow walk around the perimeter of the platform. He coaxed as much smoke as he could out of his swinging shell of puffing incense, watching it waft around him. The more smoke, the better. This would summon the rain clouds to bless the ceremony. Step. Bring other foot even. Step. Bring other foot even. His measured paces brought him from the crowded plaza side to the jungle side to the settlement side, around to the jungle and back again.

Meanwhile, the ceremony unfolded in the center of the platform. Cumani emerged, resplendent in his glittering cape. The edge of the cape was stitched with strands of gold, and strong, black geometric designs ran around the border. Arm bands of copper circled each bicep, emphasizing the jaguar head fastener holding up his loincloth of jaguar fur. His tall golden crown, decorated with the rare feather of the quetzal bird, caught the last rays of the setting sun, shooting light beams as he turned. He offered a silver pulque chalice studded with stones of jade and turquoise to each of the four directions. He chanted, quietly at first, then louder and louder until the crowd below took up the chant with him.

From the interior chamber, one of the temple girls was led toward the altar, supported on each side by a temple boy. She was wrapped in a shimmering violet cloth tied over one shoulder. Her headdress was heavy with gold. Drok could see her out of the corner of his eye as he walked his path. Her eyes were unfocused and her neck swayed as she was escorted forward. In one swift move, Cumani reached for the cloth at her shoulder and pulled the garment away. He gathered her up and laid her out upon the altar, legs splayed. Jumping up near her feet, his arms thrown wide to the heavens, he implored the gods for a return of the rain. Then he thrust aside his loincloth in order to enter the nearly unconscious girl. She moaned loud enough for the crowd below to hear her. The audience moaned with her, swaying with the rhythmic movement of the couple high above them. Cumani gave one loud moan, which was echoed by the crowd. He pulled himself off the girl, and jumped to the platform to finish the ceremony.

"We give you new life, that you may reward us with rain!" he bellowed. "RAIN. RAIN. RAIN." The crowd took up the chant.

Drok continued with his incense smoke until Cumani left the platform. He noticed the girl seemed dazed as she struggled to get off the platform and rewrap the cloth around her. She just now seemed to understand what had occurred.

The drugs must be wearing off, thought Drok. He walked past her into the chamber, eyes greedily taking in her curvy body. Someday I want to be the priest leading this ceremony, Drok thought.

After the ceremony when rain did not appear, the people murmured among themselves that the priests seemed to be losing their powers. With so much tribute being demanded by the temple, and their crops failing, what were people supposed to do? The farmers were doing their part, but the priests weren't doing theirs. Some villagers hid small amounts of their meager crops for their families. If the temple guards found out, those people met with a severe beating, sometimes death.

Even in the cocoon of the temple, some of the discontent of the people reached Cumani's ears. He wanted to find out how serious the animosity was against the temple. Because he was too recognizable to the general population as the head priest, he chose Jamex, a young priest in training, and Drok, to mingle in the marketplace and listen to what people were saying. The boys left the temple together, but Jamex soon pulled Drok aside.

"Look, Drok, you are small enough to hide in places. Go down by the river where the men work loading and unloading the boats. Stay hidden, as people might remember your scars. I will be in the marketplace, but I think it's important to know what people who are coming into or leaving the city have to say."

Drok hurried down the trail towards the river. His city was situated on a high ridge on the north side where the Tula and Rosas Rivers met. There was a trail heading sharply downhill toward the dock. From the top looking down, it reminded Drok of intestines, a long serpentine gash on the side of the cliff. He loved to run downhill, jumping switchbacks when he could, annoying the uphill hikers with huge packs fastened to their backs by wrapped cloth. Some of the heaviest of the hikers' loads were stabilized with tumplines around the carrier's forehead and down each side to the fully packed baskets on their backs.

Drok finally slowed his headlong dash, remembering he was supposed to be blending in, not sticking out. He reached the bottom hot and sweaty and dove off the side of the dock into the water. He was surprised how much more shallow the river had become. Some of the boatmen strained to push their heavy cargo boats upstream. Even some of the boats going with the feeble current moved ponderously. Drok swam over by the dock and realized this might be a great place for him to eavesdrop. An upstream boat was just arriving at the dock.

Immediately a man sprang out. He was well-dressed and obviously used to giving commands. Drok heard his feet hit the dock and watched him stride over to the landing. The man's strident tone rose above the whole area.

"What do the priests expect us to do?" the man fumed to the worker in charge of the dock. "No one in my village has any crops to spare for the temple! We barely have enough to feed my villagers. I am bringing this boatful, and no more. The temple guards can come and search our area for hidden food, but they won't find any. If the priests would do their job and bring us rain, I could bring more."

With that, the man huffed his way up the trail, with his bearers bringing a paltry load of foodstuffs from the boats. Drok watched the man disappear from sight.

People leaving the city were grumbling as well. Drok overheard some people talking about the armies conquering new lands, and bringing the captured slaves to the city.

"There isn't enough here to feed our own people, let alone all these foreign slaves," shouted one man going upstream at another boatload of slaves heading in to dock at Tula.

Drok spent most of the afternoon listening to the disgruntled boatmen and their passengers. No one seemed to be in a good mood. He headed back up the trail when the afternoon sun crawled up the ridgeline so that only the top of the cliff remained in the sunlight. Drok appreciated the cool shadows as he trudged back up the trail. When he reached the top, he saw just how much the river had receded. He remembered as a youngster not being able to see the opposite shore. Now it was just a narrow trickle in the center with high cutbanks on either side showing where the water had coursed before.

Back at the temple, Cumani gathered the priests-in-training to hear what Drok and Jamex had to say. Jamex echoed many of the same complaints that Drok overheard. People were frustrated, poor and hungry. Many blamed the priests for the lack of rain. After Jamex finished speaking, Drok brought up the one different complaint he had heard. "I heard one man say that there wasn't enough to feed all of their own people, never mind all these new slaves from conquered lands."

Cumani cocked his head and looked sharply at Drok. "Yes, we do have many more slaves than we used to," Cumani mused. "Too many, really, to be able to feed them all." He continued to look intently at Drok. "Since our regular temple ceremonies don't seem to be working anymore, I wonder what would better please the gods and the people. I will retire to my chamber to speak with the gods. I must not be disturbed." He rose and left with a swirl of his robes.

V

Kaiya delighted in her new duties as Moochkla's apprentice. She was free to explore the surrounding forest as long as she wanted, provided she returned with the correct herbs for Moochkla's remedies. She still had to collect firewood, but it was much easier to do that in the forest than it had been in the steep canyon. Getting water was a tougher task. Not only did it still have to come from the creek at the bottom of the canyon, but it had to be carried through the forest to their home.

My home, Kaiya thought. At last she felt comfortable there. She still returned to the village from time to time to grind corn, but that was an opportunity to catch up with her friends. She especially missed seeing Akeela every day and loved every moment they spent together.

The grinding stones were placed side by side in a row so the women and girls could turn toward one another and chat over the rasping of grinding stone against grinding trough. Akeela pelted Kaiya with questions about life with Moochkla. Kaiya in turn asked for the latest village gossip.

Kaiya felt less awe-stricken now around Moochkla. As their days blended together, he made her feel more like she felt with Jumac. He frequently chuckled at her many questions.

One day she wandered farther from the house than she ever had before. Alerted by something twitching above her, Kaiya stopped. The ropey tail with the black tip could only belong to a cougar. Kaiya inched her way backwards to the closest big tree and hid. Peering around the reddish bark of the old pine, she got a better view.

Two spotted cubs gamboled about the feet of their mother, her opinion of their hijinks displayed by the twitching of her tail. As the kittens' antics moved closer to their mother, her ropey tail began to jerk about in outright annoyance. Finally, able to take it no longer, she rose to her feet and stalked into the cave at the back of the ledge, stepping over the tumbling, mewing kittens on her way. Kaiya delighted in this unexpected family scene. She kept her hand over her mouth so her giggles wouldn't spill out. If they smelled Kaiya's presence, they ignored it.

Each day thereafter, Kaiya found herself drawn back to the ledge with the cave to watch this forest family. She always remained hidden, observing daily life from a cougar's point of view. Some days she didn't see them at all. Other days were wonderful, watching play fights, practice for real life. Once, as Kaiya watched the cubs, the mother ran across the clearing with the haunch of a fresh deer kill in her mouth. The little kittens eagerly tore into the meat and soon were streaked with its blood. The mother patiently cleaned each cub with her big grainy tongue. One of the cubs squinted its eyes and yowled in disgust, much to Kaiya's amusement.

As the spring days passed into summer, villagers reported seeing many dead prairie dogs. Children were warned to stay away from animals they had not actually killed. Moochkla explained to Kaiya the reasoning behind this rule.

"The kill may belong to another animal, Kaiya, and it will be coming back to get it for its young. If the animal died of old age, Coyote, Fox, Thunderbird or Raven will take care of it. But if it died of disease, none of the forest creatures will touch it. That's the bad thing about the prairie dog villages—they live so closely together that if one gets sick, many will die. It's a good lesson for our people to live together in small groups to stay healthy."

Kaiya was away from her forest family for several days before returning to her watching place. But as she approached, apprehension seized her. Something was very wrong and out of place. She crept closer than usual to the family's ledge, stopping in disbelief when she saw the tawny lump at the base of the ledge. The buzzing flies confirmed her fears—the mother cougar was dead.

Where were the cubs? Kaiya ran around to the place where she had first seen the mother leap gracefully onto the ledge. But it was a hard, scrambling climb for Kaiya. She grabbed a boulder and hoisted herself to a point where her feet could gain a toehold. Several more precarious moves got her higher up the rock wall. Panting from the exertion, she finally collapsed on the ledge. One still body of a cub lay a few yards in front of her.

Carefully, Kaiya got to her feet and took several steps to the opening of the cave. She hesitated, then tiptoed slowly inside, allowing her eyes to adjust to the dim light. From way at the back, she heard a scuffling sound, followed by a sharply exhaled breath. Suddenly, a spitting, snarling ball of fur lunged at her feet. She leapt backwards and stumbled over a rock, crashing on her back. The kitten pounced into Kaiya's hair, thrashing at first. After being alone for several days, hungry and frightened, it was grateful for the faintly familiar smell of Kaiya. Liking the soft warmth of her hair, it curled up close to Kaiya's head and licked her ear. Kaiya gasped as the raspy tongue continued to lick. The kitten broke into a contented purr.

Kaiya reached around her head to disentangle the cub and brought it close to her face. The two motherless youngsters stared into each other's eyes. Sliding the little creature inside her bodice, Kaiya ran all the way back to Moochkla.

Moochkla listened as Kaiya breathlessly told what happened on her visit to the ledge, pulling forth the sleeping kitten. Moochkla frowned and shook his head.

"Kaiya, if this animal has the same disease that killed the mother and the other cub, it could be passed on to you. Return it to the cave now. And then, go wash yourself and your clothes thoroughly in the creek. Go."

Kaiya turned and started toward the door, but turning back, countered, "But Moochkla, when I looked into his eyes, I felt the same way when I look into your eyes and can see things about the future. I saw us older and still friends. I feel there is a reason I found his family in the first place, and that I returned in time to save him. And I've already thought of a name for him. Tal, meaning strong friend. Strong enough to survive the loss of his mother and sister and disease and being alone and..."

Overcome with emotion and exertion, Kaiya plopped down in the doorway with Tal in her lap, bent over him and tucked her hair in around him. Moochkla sighed, feeling a pang of sympathy for Kaiya's affinity with this motherless being.

"We will have to watch Tal carefully for any sign of disease," Moochkla said softly. "And—he was born free and cannot be held here against his will. As soon as he is old enough to be on his own, we can do nothing to keep him here."

Kaiya smiled up at Moochkla. She pointed down to where the kitten was breathing loudly, sound asleep.

The days passed quickly as the household adjusted to its newest member. Kaiya chewed small pieces of meat and then tore off an even smaller piece for Tal. He followed her everywhere, tumbling over his own feet in his excitement to keep up with her. He barely tolerated Moochkla, keeping his distance even inside their small house. He snarled and leapt away from any stranger, but always returned to Kaiya, once the others had left.

His play amused them on their herb hunts—pouncing on grasshoppers, stalking little snakes and trying to catch birds as they flitted to the ground. Once he pursued a squirrel up a tree and then froze as he realized he had left the ground far behind. Kaiya stood at the base of the tree for a long while coaxing him into coming back down.

Kaiya and Tal learned to avoid conflicts with the other villagers by visiting an uncrowded part of the creek to get Tal his daily drink of water. He learned to lap water out of a pottery bowl which Kaiya placed just outside the door of their house.

As the seasonal wheel turned toward autumn, Kaiya realized Tal must learn to hunt for himself to survive the winter. She could not continue to provide for him during the time when food was scarce for all the people. She took him out into the forest with the thought of trying to teach him to hunt. A chipmunk took the lesson out of Kaiya's hands by jumping down from a tree branch directly into Tal's path. He gathered up his gangly legs and pounced all four right on top of the chipmunk, biting into its back.

She leaned down to pet him, but he snarled and hissed at her. She abruptly stepped back, but could still see his eyes glaring directly at her. In them she could see him as an enormous mature adult. Things had shifted. He was the wild animal that Moochkla warned her he would become. But she caught a glimpse of herself in his eyes that told her he would often be in her life.

Tal never slept in the house with Kaiya and Moochkla after that. But he would surprise them both by stealthily appearing in the house at odd intervals. Although Kaiya called for him as she left for her walks, it was up to him whether he would show up and come along or not. Sometimes out in the forest appearing abruptly, he startled Kaiya into shrieking. He seemed to enjoy it if she yelled, and danced about her legs as she scolded him. Each time he reappeared she noticed how much bigger and heavier he was. She watched his spots fade away completely, and noted that his movements were much more fluid and graceful, his fur darker and more luxuriant. She longed to run her fingers along his back as she had done when he was little, but she knew she couldn't do that now. He was grown up, wild and free.

VJO

VI

Cumani was worried. His lifestyle as head priest of the main temple of Tula was being rocked by the discontent of its citizens. People were desperate enough to air their doubts about the power of the temple in public. Fortunately, the New Fire Ceremony was approaching. This usually revived the spirits of the city.

The ceremony followed the fall harvest. After the cross quarter day, the Seven Sisters would rise high in the sky by midnight, signaling Cumani to begin the ceremony. This year, he would be adding a new element.

He observed Drok, this curious boy who entered into temple work as if born to it. He sensed a power in him, just below the surface, restless and wild, as well as a talent to lead, a trait yet unknown to the boy. This boy would bear close watching. But for now, Cumani needed him for this ceremony as the one temple boy who would do as he was told and not question the change in the ceremony.

People bustled throughout the city. All buildings must be cleaned thoroughly before the ceremony. Everywhere stick and grass brooms were being vigorously wielded by women sweeping the dirt and cobwebs out into the streets. Buckets of water were brought up from the low river to wash walls and floors, women were seen on their hands and knees scrubbing with reed brushes.

Cooking had to take place before dark that day. At nightfall, every single fire in the city was extinguished. Instead of the quiet glow of hearth fires, flickering torches on the city walls, or small brush lights, the city would become as dark as the vastness of space. Some people used this cover of darkness for sinister reasons. This was a good time for revenge or theft. It was also a time for lovers in illicit affairs to grope in the shadows. People gathered, hunkering in the darkness, awaiting the sound of the conch shells calling them to the base of the temple.

Toltec warriors roamed the city to keep order and to make sure everyone complied with the edict to extinguish all fires. Appearing suddenly, the soldiers were fearsome in the dark. Even in the gloom it was easy to make out their outline; the feathered helmet, loincloth, sandals and spears. As they marched through the narrow alleyways of the city, their high helmets made them seem impossibly tall.

From the small set of huts behind the temple where Drok lived with the other temple boys, he watched the city fall into darkness. Without sight, sounds seemed more acute, sounds usually not heard. A woman called out, answered by a man's voice, then raucous laughter. Running footfalls ahead of the marching steps of the soldiers. A low hum of voices. Water splashed on the street.

Drok stepped outside the hut and leaned against the wall. He thought about what Cumani discussed with him. The gods had spoken to Cumani about the new path which ceremonies must take to bring back the rains.

Back in the priests' chamber, Cumani and Loka sat alone. Around them were the vestments and robes needed for the ceremony. Cumani shared his vision from the gods.

"I swallowed the peyote and meditated. I cleared my mind of all earthly matters and concentrated on opening a channel to receive help in solving this problem of drought. Last year's failed crops made us hungry, I told the gods. But another year like it will cause famine. Please help us. Then I started to feel sick. I held back as long as I could, but eventually the food came up. As soon as my stomach was empty, my mind filled with colors. Twirling reds, yellows, oranges, blues. Then all colors drifted away, except for red. Everything became red. The red flowed in and around my head. Then it flowed from the top of the temple's altar down the stairs out into the plaza."

"Why red?" Loka asked.

Cumani looked at the floor, fingering the robe he would wear for the ceremony.

"Blood," he replied. "It was the blood of sacrifice. Human sacrifice. Slaves from faraway lands."

Loka looked solemnly at Cumani, then stood and walked to the chamber doorway, gazing out through the hallway to the plaza where some people were already gathering.

"This will change everything," Loka said. "The people will demand more sacrifices if they think this will bring more rain. Right now we have plenty of slaves. But what if the supply of slaves diminishes? Will we kill each other?"

"Then there are all the people who keep pouring in from the countryside because their crops failed," Cumani said.

Loka stared hard at Cumani. He couldn't believe what he had just heard.

"Those are our people," Loka said. "They are Toltecs, just like us."

Cumani stood. "I fear there won't be any more Toltecs unless the rains come," he said quietly. "I hope what I am about to do will please the gods."

There was tension throughout the city. The people heard the conch shell blast and made their way to the temple plaza. It was an eerie walk through black streets and alleyways. People startled as they were surprised by others or sometimes by shadows.

Drok stood in the chamber next to Cumani. Loka assisted each with their garments for the ceremony. Outside and below them they could hear the increasing murmur of the crowd, like the rumbles of a thunderclap.

Loka finished helping Cumani and Drok dress, then stepped back to survey their appearance. Cumani looked resplendent in a hooded robe doused with orange, yellow, and purple splotches of fabric. His tunic underneath was yellow with black splotches like the coat of a jaguar. Loka polished Cumani's armbands, bringing out the shine of the worked gold and emphasizing the jade inlay. He reached under a pile of fabric and pulled out a different armband, a cuff of silver with a repeating pattern of a curled wave in an endless circle. In the center of the cuff was a large island of turquoise. He took Drok's arm in his hand and twisted the cuff above Drok's elbow. Drok gaped in astonishment.

"This is a special and important ceremony," Loka said. "I want you to realize what an honor it is for you to assist."

Drok could not take his eyes off this shining band with its turquoise island. He couldn't believe that it was actually his. He knew the jaguar skin loincloth he wore belonged to the temple, and could only be worn by the temple boy assisting in the ceremony. His own jaguar head belt held up the fur around his waist. His black hair had been washed and combed out by Loka. Finally, he remembered to look up at Loka and express his thanks.

A hush fell as the sound of marching soldiers approached the plaza. In the midst of the soldiers was a naked slave. One soldier grabbed his shoulders and spun him away from the regiment. Another grabbed his arm. The two pushed him to the base of the of the pyramid and gestured to the slave to bow low and begin climbing the steps. In case the terrified victim attempted escape, a third soldier stepped in behind. The quartet slowly began the ascent to the high platform at the top of the pyramid.

From the stamping of feet on the stairs of the pyramid, Cumani knew the soldiers and the prisoner were approaching the platform. Throwing his hood over his head, he nodded to Loka, and motioned Drok to follow him.

The absolute darkness surprised Drok. He had forgotten that all of the city fires were extinguished. Inside the chamber they had used a small torch to prepare for the ceremony. Fortunately, Drok had attended several ceremonies, so he had a feel for the size, length and width of the platform. It would have been easy to step off the edge and plummet to the ground far, far below.

Cumani uttered a sharp command to the soldiers to take the slave off to one side of the platform. Meanwhile, Drok carried small pieces of wood, kindling and fire starting tools to the statue of Chacmool. It was twice the size of a man. The seated figure's torso angled back, while the knees bent up, feet flat. On the belly section between the bent knees and the upright head was a flat plate. On this, Drok began to build a nest of twigs so the fire could flare up in a blaze easily seen by the crowd below. Drok knelt beside the statue, waiting for Cumani's signal to start twirling the fire starting sticks.

"Citizens of the city of Tula, we gather here this night to begin anew. New Fire. New times. These times have been hard for us. The gods have not heard our prayers for rain. Our corn, beans and squash crops are dying, our Tula and Rosas Rivers are drying up, and our people fear what misery lies ahead. But, the New Fire time comes just as things feel the most dire. Look overhead, see the Seven Sisters? They hold the promise of rain."

Necks in the crowd leaned backwards, looking into the black sky at the star spectacle above.

"I have spoken to the gods, and the gods have spoken to me," Cumani thundered to the stars.

That was Drok's signal. He rapidly rubbed the fire sticks together, then twirled them in his small bowl filled with dried grasses and small strips of bark. As the sparks flew out from the whirling sticks, wisps of smoke arose from the bottom of the bowl. Drok breathed gently on the sparks and a tiny fire burst forth. Cumani glanced at Drok, who nodded to him that the fire was ready. Cumani continued his speech.

"We have swept the city clean of all evil," he shouted. "We now purify our beautiful city with the New Fire and a new ceremony, one that turns our lives toward abundance and prosperity."

Cumani leaned down towards Drok's bowl with a small torch, waited for the fire to catch, then transferred it to the wood on the stomach of Chacmool. Since Drok had doused the twigs with oil, the fire went up in a dramatic whoosh. The audience gasped in wonder, involuntarily stepping back from the sudden brightness above. Temple guards came forth to catch their torches in the New Fire so people would be able to see the rest of the ceremony.

Cumani turned his attention to the slave and motioned the guards to bring him to the altar. There they placed him on his back. Cumani threw back his hood and tore the robe from his body. Illuminated by the flickering torches, Cumani's oiled skin gleamed and his jewelry sparkled. He seemed larger than life. He stepped up on a small platform at the head of the altar by the trembling slave. Guards stood on each side, grasping an arm and leg. Drok stood close behind Cumani, hidden from view.

"The gods have spoken to me," Cumani shouted to the assembly below. "They are displeased with us. We have ventured far, conquered new lands, returned with spoils of war, but offer nothing to the gods for all their favors in battle. Limiting our rains is their way to get our attention. Finally we cry out in hunger and despair— what is it you want from us? What should we do to bring you pleasure, Tlaloc?"

He paused, faced the edge of the platform, throwing his arms wide to the stars above. "It is not enough to bring us your virgins, the gods said to me in a dream. We want blood. Human blood. Blood from the people we helped you conquer. The gods have helped you become so powerful because they want this blood. This will be payment for the gods to bring the rains. This young man from far away must die. Then our gods will be pleased."

The slave held down on the altar could not understand Cumani's language and didn't know what was coming. Drok came forward and handed Cumani a bifacial knife made of obsidian. Cumani held it above the head of the slave, who then realized his fate and began to howl. The blade rested, then plunged into the belly of the victim, ripping all the way up to the throat, stopping the chilling shrieks of terror. Cumani suddenly seemed spent, and dazedly backed away from the altar, dropping the knife to the floor with a clatter. Drok looked at the implacable faces of the guards, back to the shocked face of Cumani, his tunic and hands splattered with blood. This was not how Cumani had told Drok the ceremony would end. Someone had to finish the ceremony correctly, or this man had died for no reason, and the gods would be displeased.

Drok spun around and grabbed the knife. Before anyone could stop him, he jumped onto the altar to finish the ceremony. He cut into the victim and pulled out the still beating heart. The damp, warm organ in his two hands seemed to pulse with a power, a power that entered Drok's consciousness with the ferocity of a bolt of lightning. He felt a tingling throughout his body, and swayed from the impact. Thrusting the heart high over his head, he yelled, "For Tlaloc! For Tlaloc!"

Slowly, the paralyzed crowd below him took up the chant. "For Tlaloc! For Tlaloc!"

Then, Drok felt unmistakable splatters of rain hitting his face. The sky had been clear when the ceremony began, but the ever changing clouds of the jungle had gathered unnoticed during the intensity of the ceremony. It was a few sprinkles only, but the gods must be pleased! Drok had pleased the gods. Not Cumani. Drok had finished the ceremony to the satisfaction of Tlaloc. Feeling as tall as Loka, he motioned to the guards to drag the body over to the edge of the platform. Loudly, he prayed to the gods.

"We thank you for your gift of rain, and hope you are pleased with the sacrifice. I leave the heart on the altar for you, Tlaloc. It is a symbol of our desire to please you."

He kicked the body over the edge, watching it writhe and turn as if it still was alive. He grimaced his lopsided grin and stood, arms folded across his chest and felt the power of the gods ripple through his body.

The crowd roared its approval.

To complete the New Fire Ceremony, Drok signaled the guards to light the torches along the stairs of the pyramid. Two by two, torches blazed as the guards reached down to set each pair on fire, causing the torchlight to make its way slowly down the length of each side of the pyramid. Shadows danced against the stones from top to bottom. As the pyramid glowed, it seemed to breathe in rhythm with the flickering flames. When the guards closest to the bottom received the fire, they each stepped away from the stairs to light the huge fires prepared on the ground.

The twin bonfires sputtered, then caught, a blaze rising from the wood. People shuffled forward to light their own torches and take the new light home with them. The city slowly took on the look of a normal night in Tula.

The people were strangely silent as they dispersed with their new lights. Some weren't sure if this was a night of new light, or the beginning of a new darkness.

VII

Moochkla gave Kaiya a day off from herb gathering to go clay gathering with the women and girls. It took a morning's walk to go down the creek to a special cave. The sediment in this cave was the perfect consistency to mix with water, sand and old, ground up pieces of broken pottery to form the clan's vessels and cooking pots.

The young girls scampered on ahead, boulder hopping alongside the creek. Kaiya and Akeela skipped along together, one challenging the other to jump further or higher along the creek, happy in each other's company. The women walked more sedately, speaking in low tones with occasional peals of laughter as the latest gossip was exchanged. The girls chattered excitedly—darting tadpoles, shimmering dragonflies, swooping blue-grey gnat-catchers occasionally catching their attention.

Each carried a basket especially made for clay gathering. The yucca fiber and pine needle baskets were woven tightly and lined with tree sap to make them waterproof. This allowed clay with water added to be cured in the baskets for a few days before it was usable. The girls turned these baskets into great sources of amusement, using them to mimic life events, from a fat behind to a gigantic pregnant belly to the ordeal of childbirth and the sudden appearance of a baby. Or balancing on their heads and seeing how many steps could be taken before it tumbled, or pretending to poop in the basket and then passing it around for others to partake. Their giggles, shrieks and hoots echoed off the high, narrow walls of the canyon.

Upon arrival at the base of the cliff with the cave visible high above, the girls began to quarrel among themselves who would have to scale the slope and dig out the clay to fill each basket. The women arrived in the middle of this argument and cooled tempers by making an arbitrary assignment that Kaiya be the digger. She sighed, went and rolled in the creek for cooling off, and then looked for the hand and foot holds.

Over time, the people had carved and chipped tiny steps into the cliff face making it possible to grasp a place with each hand, while each foot had a place to keep balanced until the next safe move. Kaiya was actually relieved to be the digger, as the other girls had to spread out over the cliff below, balancing on the tiny footholds, to pass the heavy baskets back down to creek level. Maintaining balance on the steps when passing the heavy baskets was difficult.

Kaiya was strong and light, so she reached the level ledge in front of the cave quickly. From this high vantage point, she turned to look back along the creek and the meandering turns of the canyon. The girls below her spread out over the cliff face looked as small as scurrying squirrels. Parts of the canyon walls were still throwing shadows down to the water. Other sections were in full sunlight, with the moving water sparkling and dancing. The peaks of Sacred Snow Mountain High Place in the distance looked serene on this cloud-free day.

Kaiya poked her head into the cave and was surprised by a long black feather lying on the floor. She pulled it out and waved it to the crowd below. The women sent a message up the row of girls that Kaiya should hand it down. Moochkla would want to see it. Kaiya realized that because of the size, it could only belong to the thunderbird. Moochkla would value it greatly for his ceremonies.

Basket after basket was sent up to Kaiya, who scooped in piles of clay and then handed the full ones back down to the relay team. Finally, all baskets had been filled. The girls scattered over the cliff face lowered themselves down. Kaiya waited until the last head disappeared from view before she began her descent.

She paused long enough to envision that huge bird resting in the cave. The bird would have stood almost as tall as she and was formidable with its big beak and red head. But they had no interest in living humans, only seeking animals that were already dead. Kaiya had seen them up close feeding on elk carcasses on the edge of the forest. They hissed and flapped their giant wings before quickly returning to the dinner before them.

Kaiya reluctantly started her descent, sad to leave her lofty perch with the sweeping views of her homeland. Arriving down from her climb, she eagerly joined the others in sharing dried berries and nuts before starting back. The return trip was harder because of the heavy baskets. Traveling west with the sun in their eyes, many girls misstepped and slipped back into the creek. Cries of dismay arose anytime the valuable clay fell from a basket. Kaiya lost a few handfuls, but otherwise arrived with an almost complete load.

When the women returned to the village, they added water to the baskets of clay before setting them out to cure for a few days. This made the clay more malleable for the potters.

The next few days were busy in preparation for the pottery making. All hands of the clan were needed and the bustling created the high energy of a festival gathering. People chattered and called to one another to make sure there were enough materials. Strands of conversation could be heard all over the village.

"Do we have enough sand?" "Yes, I brought some up from the creek bed." "Go fill these pots with water." "Ugh, I already dragged some up from the creek. Do we really need more?" "We need more old broken pottery to be ground back to grit to show Earth Mother that respect for the old is being embodied in the new."

The weather was marvelous. Three days ago the skies had opened up in a punishing downpour. The cloudburst had caused water to rage down the canyon, raising the creek's level much higher than usual and changing the creek's color to red. Dirt and rocks washed down from the canyon's rim added to the torrent. When the storm faded near sunset, two lines of clouds near the horizon had parted enough to allow sunrays to shoot out between them, making a soft haze in the air recently filled with moisture. Trees, flowers and grasses dripped well into the night, and morning dawned with a feeling of being cleansed. Ever since, the air had a soft coolness to it, dimming the memory of the many dry days before. The elders of the clan remarked how that kind of rainstorm was an every day occurrence during the summer months in years gone by.

Some people really enjoyed the grinding of the clay and old broken pots down to a fine powder. Often those were the gossipy women who positioned the grinding stones close to a friend so the rasping of the rock against stone drowned out any of their sharing of secrets. The grinding took a long time, with women rotating in and out of the line of grinding stones as their arms became tired. When all was crushed, the master potters of the clan came forth to mix just the right combination of water, old material, sand and clay to start the formation of the pots.

Their pottery was highly prized, not only within the clan but also by the traders who came through. Pottery for daily use was simply formed by coiled ropes of clay one on top of the next to form the outline of the pot. The sides were then smoothed both on the inside and out with a stone scraper. Handles were created out of another coil of the red clay.

But pieces meant for special or ceremonial occasions were often breathtaking. Some were created with the sensuous shape of a woman in mind, full of curves and roundness, others tall and straight with a flared lip at the top. Some were big, round, smooth bowls with a small hole at the top, reminiscent of the place of emergence. Others were wide, shallow bowls on a pedestal. Some handles looked like the intricate braids women created in one another's hair. In some, a thumbnail pressed into the clay created little crescents all around the pot. Other pots had texture created by pulling the clay with the fingertips so that the surface of the pot jutted away from the vessel like tiny waves teased upwards by the wind. It all depended on the inspiration and skill of the potter and what special orders had been placed by the traders and people in the clan.

Children loved to hang around the potters to watch the magic of creating something almost alive out of dirt and water. Some interested in perhaps one day becoming a potter sidled up to a kindly adult who might give them a hand in technique and a turn with the clay. Overnight the clay was allowed to harden. The next day was for the painters.

While back in the village, Kaiya looked everywhere for her beloved Uncle Bertok. She so missed him. She had grown up with him sitting at her family's fire, and she couldn't remember a time when he wasn't an active part of her life. He was all she had left now as far as immediate family. He looked so much like her father Borhea from a distance. But closer up, their features were strikingly different. Where her father's face had been chiseled and intense, Bertok had soft, delicate features. He was without a doubt the finest painter of the clan. He had painted pictographs on walls since he was a tiny child, barely able to walk. Coming upon one of his pictures unaware, people were startled by the remarkable images he could create. Cougars snarled, whiskers almost trembling, antelope seemed poised to leap away, and tall, mysterious beings seemed ready to walk out of the walls. His paintings on pottery were much in demand.

Kaiya ducked in and out of the growing crowd, surprised she couldn't see Bertok. Finally she realized why. As usual, he was the center of attention in a small cluster of people. Seeing Kaiya approach, he broke into a wide grin and motioned her to come closer.

"Here's my favorite girl!" he exclaimed. He pulled her into a warm hug, Kaiya's grin matching his. "How have you been? Are you well? Is that Moochkla filling you full of potions to make you grow so pretty?"

Kaiya giggled and settled herself by his side. Bertok continued to chat with a group of other painters, talking about designs. Gesturing in the air, he drew a square within a square with a twist at the corner. Then he turned his attention to Kaiya.

"No, really—are you well?" he asked again.

"Oh, Uncle, sometimes I wish I lived in the village with the other children. But most of the time I'm very happy. It's so beautiful in the forest. Tal and I explore and collect the herbs that Moochkla needs.

Sometimes Moochkla comes with us. But most of the time I'm by myself and it gives me time to think."

"And what is it that fills your head these days?" Bertok asked.

"I worry about the clan because of the drought. I've thanked the Great Spirit over and over again for this wonderful rain we just received. But it's not enough—we need more. And I think about this gift, as Moochkla calls it, of seeing."

Bertok was the only one left from the family who knew and understood about Kaiya's unusual way of seeing. They had talked about it together at length. Somehow, she felt that Bertok truly understood—perhaps because of his innate talent for drawing.

"Does it happen often these days?" he asked.

"It's happened with Moochkla and Tal."

Bertok thought back to the revealing statement from Kaiya when she was still quite young that when she looked into his eyes, she always saw him surrounded by men.

"How about you? What have you been doing?" Kaiya asked.

"Well, I've been trying to hunt. But there isn't much around here that wants to be caught. And you know," he said, glancing around and lowering his voice, "I would always rather draw than hunt. I just learned how to hunt so easily because your father was such a good teacher."

Kaiya thought back to the two brothers, their constant presence at the fire, and remembered their heads close together, then thrown back simultaneously in laughter, her father roaring and pounding Bertok on the back. She smiled at the memory of the love they all shared.

Meanwhile, other children of the tribe wandered through the forest and open grassy meadows in search of beeweed. This plant with the reddish-purple and white blossoms was boiled down into a sticky mess perfect for paint to decorate the pots. It took a lot of plant material, slowly set to a simmer, to create enough paint for many pieces of pottery. And, small fires under the paint had to be tended carefully so the paint would not thicken and solidify, someone always in attendance stirring.

Boys cut off stalks of yucca fronds. Yucca plants were plentiful and highly prized by the clan for their versatile uses. The broad, thick leaves started wide at ground level and tapered to a sharp, pointy needle at the top. Peeling back the green skin at the end exposed bristles perfect as paintbrushes. By whittling and trimming the narrow edge of the new brush, different widths were created to fit the particular stroke needed for a design.

The painters awoke early and gathered, some in groups and some singly, to greet the rising sun. Moochkla raised his arms and bowed his head just as the orange disk rose above the canyon's rim.

"Oh Blessed Spirit of the East, we call upon your new dawn to fill our painters' spirits with light. Guide their hands as they create. We wish to honor you with our work."

Each painter chose several yucca brushes from the array and settled down with a pot of beeweed paint and a blank pot. Unlike the amiable chattering of the day before, this process required silence. People wandered quietly from painter to painter, appreciating the skills of each artist. Small gasps and murmurs of approval were heard as individual designs struck deep chords within the hearts of the onlookers. Children hunkered nearby, practicing with discarded brushes on old pieces of broken pottery. Often they tiptoed toward a particular artist whom they admired, studied the design, and returned to recreate what they had observed.

The designs were as varied as they were beautiful. Spirals, twisted braids, waves of water, geometric patterns of triangles and dots, lightening bolts, thunderclouds, lines that squiggled, godly beings, animal shapes, formations of canyons, rivers and mountains all sprang to life in the hands of the painters. The paint turned from black to a brownish red when it hit the damp clay. After a while, all the pieces of pottery were placed in the sun to dry.

The third day of the pottery-making festival was always an anticipated event. It was the feast and firing. Food preparation had been going on in the background while the pottery held the attention of the people. Now all that was left to do was build the enormous bonfire. The people dug the pit deeper than usual, to show the Spirits their intention to use the pottery well. The potters determined when the pit was big and deep enough to halt the digging. A berm was created around the perimeter of the fire pit to help with the air flow to the pottery. The pit was lined on the floor and walls with rocks to help hold in the heat.

Then everyone went into the forest to return with an armload of wood. Some clan members used the opportunity to follow a person whom they desired. Fires of passion often preceded the pottery fires.

The pottery was carefully carried from the drying place to the fire pit. It was considered extremely bad luck to break a piece of unfired pottery, so great care was given in this task. To drop a piece of pottery before it had a chance to live showed disrespect to the Earth that provided the materials.

In the late afternoon, a small fire to remove moisture from the pit was lit and the pieces of pottery gently placed upside down on the pieces of wood. Layer after layer of pottery was carefully positioned by the painters and potters as Moochkla and a drummer softly kept up a chant of protection.

When all of the pottery had been assembled, old pieces of broken pottery were tucked in, over and around the new pots to act as a protective shield from the bonfire. A small fire burned slow and smoky until the shadows of dusk began creeping through the forest. Then the potters threw small handfuls of dirt on the pottery and placed log after log in a triangle criss-cross pattern above and around the tower of pottery. After creating a torch out of a long branch with matted, dried grass, the huge pile was set ablaze.

Moochkla led the assembly in a chant encouraging the fire to grow higher and brighter. Whoops and yells ended the chorus before it started again. The fire responded to the song of the people by popping, crackling and flickering lustily. Assured that the fire would continue, women brought out the baskets of food. People lounged around the fire, eating and chatting. The fire starters kept a watchful eye on the fire and added more wood.

When everyone had eaten, the food was stored and the best storyteller, Jumac, choose a story of another time of drought.

A long, long time ago, back when the plants, trees, animals and people had no barriers between them, all understood one another. One girl loved the birds, fascinated with their ability to just spread their wings and fly. She longed to be one of them. She learned the languages of hawks, eagles, chickadees, nuthatches, ravens, and jays to be more like them. She collected feathers she found lying on the ground, gathered them into bunches and attached them to her arms. Then she climbed to the tops of hills, trees or boulders and leaped off, hoping to stay airborne, but always crashing to the ground.

The people in that time had many troubles, just as we do now. There were too many people in each village, and not enough food or water. People had to travel far away for game and food to gather. The skies remained free of clouds. No rain or snow fell.

The people tried to plant their crops. But the birds swooped in to eat the seeds, or the squirrels, chipmunks and rabbits ate whatever tender shoots managed to come up. People were discouraged, and didn't know what to do.

Their healer went out into the forest on a vision quest to ask the Spirits for help. When he returned, he gathered the people together and told them what he had learned.

There is a mountain close by that must be climbed to the top. At the top, the seeker will find the rim of an immense volcano. Below will be a boiling, mass of red lava. In the space between the rim and the lava is a shiny red stone. Bring that stone out of the volcano and put it where the sun can shine on it all day long. This stone will heal the earth around your village and make your crops grow again. Then you must have many rain dances to make the rains fall. Send the best person you have to retrieve this stone.

So the people talked among themselves. Finally a young man volunteered. A party of warriors went with him to the base of the mountain, and chanted songs of encouragement as he climbed the flank. Making it safely to the top, he waved to his companions and disappeared. The warriors waited and waited, but their friend never returned. Again and again, many tried to retrieve the stone. But no one ever returned from the depths of the volcano.

Finally, the little girl who loved birds timidly approached the healer and told him of her plan. The old healer listened. Nodding assent, he went to help the girl get ready. The two of them left the village with big burden baskets full of feathers, straps around their foreheads, the baskets hanging down their backs. The two trudged to the top of the mountain and stopped on the rim. Looking down into the frightening volcano, they could see the bubbling, heaving lava. They also spotted the shiny stone.

They worked to attach the feathers to the girl's arms, back, shoulders and legs. The healer offered a prayer of protection. Then the little girl raised her arms and leapt toward the sky. She disappeared below the rim and was lost to view. She felt herself hurtling downward, wind roaring through the bunches of feathers. She aimed the best she could for the shiny red stone, and managed to stop just above it on a small ledge. As she struggled to catch her breath and balance, the shiny, red stone moved. She realized it was not a stone at all, but the head of an enormous bird. The bird unfolded its wings and stood up fully, towering over the frightened girl.

"What is it you seek?" the bird demanded sternly. The girl told the story of the hardships of her village and how the healer's vision had led many to their deaths trying to retrieve the stone.

"I thought you were the stone," the girl said miserably.

The huge bird continued to glower at her. Finally he said, "I can help your people, but what can you do for me?"

The girl gulped, and said, "I have always loved birds and wanted to live among them. I could be your friend."

The bird thought for a moment, and then said, "I don't need a friend, I need a mate. I am the last of my kind in this area. In order to help your clan, I would need you to become my mate."

"What could you do for my village?" the girl asked.

"I am a thunderbird. I can bring the rains. If the rains return, the crops will grow and your people will be free from hunger and want. Will you do that for them?"

The girl nodded. With that, she felt the feathers she and the healer had attached float away from her body. Her clothes, too, fell away. She felt her arms and shoulders become wings, and her feet become claws. She watched her hair fall and felt her face transform into a beak.

With a nod from the huge bird, they both turned toward the rim and spread their wings and soared upwards. They passed by the healer, who had never given up hope. He had waited on the rim and now watched in wonder as the bird-girl and her mate flew overhead and glided off toward the mountain, Sacred Snow Mountain High Place.

Days later the people of the village saw two dark specks headed toward the village, followed by a billowing thunderhead. The enormous birds circled the village, riding the waves of air currents. Clouds then rolled over the village, dropping the precious rain. The people were saved. And that is why we still have the thunderbirds today. One of our own loved birds enough to become one of them in order to save our people."

The crowd showed their appreciation of Jumac's storytelling by offering up a high-pitched cry into the night.

The fire was fed throughout the night. It was important for the firing of the pottery to have the burning be continuous until well into morning. Lovers volunteered to stay up to watch the fire and spend precious time together without too many watchful eyes. The food, storytelling, and the soothing effect of the fire sent most of the people off to bed.

The next morning, the potters dug cautiously through the embers to test various pieces of their work to be sure the pottery had set up hard and strong. Deciding to let it burn for a little while longer, they built up the fire, although not to the bonfire proportions of the night before. When this daytime fire had been reduced to embers, the pottery was deemed ready. By late afternoon, the pottery was cool enough to touch. Many people came forward to help with rubbing the pottery gently with water and sand to help remove the ash and bring out the color and designs.

Moochkla stood apart from the crowd, gazing out over the canyon. He was so grateful for the hard work by everyone in the clan, the camaraderie it brought and the high energy felt from creating all this beautiful pottery. Some pieces would remain here to be used, a constant reminder of this clan effort, while others were traded. Where would some of this pottery end up, Moochkla mused. He heard tales from Kokopelli of a vast body of water to the west, a land of frequent rains and lush vegetation far to the south, and massive mountains to the north. He wondered what the people were like who lived in these vastly different climates. Could they feel the bright sun and dry air when they used this pottery? Could they envision canyon walls plunging deep into the Earth all the way down to the creek? Could they smell the pine trees?

VIII

Cumani staggered back into the interior chamber of the pyramid. He had been so sure of what the gods wanted from him. But when he actually had to perform the deed, it was too horrific for him. Over and over again in his mind's eye he saw the terror in the slave's face and the blood oozing out along the gash which he had made.

"I gave you blood," he called, beseeching the gods, banging his clenched fist against the chamber wall. "But I could not grasp the heart. I just couldn't do it. Not the heart."

He backed into the wall and slumped to the chamber floor, his head on his bent knees. He stayed that way for a while, feeling faint, trying to calm his breathing and his heart. "I couldn't do it, I just couldn't do it," he muttered over and over.

"Drok could," Loka said, as he entered the chamber. He squatted before Cumani, waiting for the priest to compose himself.

Raising his head to meet Loka's gaze, Cumani said, "I saw him. He seemed to enjoy it."

"The time is right. You must train him to be a priest," Loka said. "The crowd saw him perform. They didn't know anything was amiss. Only you and Drok knew something was wrong. I'm not even sure the guards realized you couldn't finish the ceremony. If you are sure from your vision that this is what the gods want, then it really isn't important who performs the ceremony."

Cumani jerked his head up with a glare. "I am the head priest here," he shouted. "Not some deformed boy!"

"Yes, you are. But a smart priest surrounds himself with good aides to help emphasize the ceremony's importance, to give it power. I know of no ceremony which any priest performs completely alone."

Cumani looked carefully at his most trusted advisor. Of all the people in the temple, Loka was the only one who had no motive for subterfuge. Because of his unusual appearance, he was always considered special. Brought to the temple as an infant and raised there, he grew up observing the way the temple worked. Watchful and perceptive, he had an excellent grasp of people and politics. Unruffled under pressure, his logical conclusions helped solve conflicts. His allegiance was to the current head priest, but he never was afraid to speak his mind. He spoke what he saw.

Cumani stretched his legs into a standing position, relieved to feel that the shakiness had passed. He paced back and forth in the chamber under Loka's gaze. Time passed as Cumani thought things through. He recalled the power that he sensed in Drok. Left unfettered, it could be dangerous.

"You will begin training him tomorrow," Cumani announced. With his dignity restored, he strode from the chamber.

Loka watched him leave, realizing he had just witnessed a turning point. The Toltec world would never be the same. He wondered if that was a good thing.

Drok tossed and turned on his straw pallet in the hut he shared with many other temple boys. Going over and over what had happened during the ceremony, feelings of power shuddered through his body. He, Drok, had finished the ceremony, with the gods' reward of rain. It wasn't much rain. But that didn't matter. He kept thinking—I brought the rain. If I were better prepared, there might have been more rain. The gods were pleased with him. He had not felt this good in all his life.

Somehow, he was not surprised the next morning when Loka said, "Gather your things. You are moving into the temple to begin training to become a priest."

Drok grinned his grimace and prepared for his new life.

IX

Moochkla and Kaiya walked along the ledge trail back toward the village. Kaiya loved taking this way to the village, feeling as if she were sneaking up on the houses. Sometimes she heard wisps of conversation not meant for her ears, some funny, some mundane and others quite shocking. She sensed that Moochkla liked this approach to the village as well. News about the well-being of the clan was important to him. She knew that some information came to him intuitively, other through the gossip channels, but sometimes scraps of conversations were overheard.

She once caught Obaho out in front of his house, dancing naked. He stopped in gaped-mouth astonishment when he saw her, and turned shyly to run back into his house. His small dwelling was the first one on this approach to the village. Obaho was a kind but simple-minded young man of the tribe who had been injured in a rock fall. When a cliff suddenly gave way during a rainstorm, an avalanche of rock caught the baby Obaho on his head. He had been placed in his cradleboard by his young mother while she tended the fire, never dreaming that she was placing him in harm's way. Although he had seemed like a normal baby, it became obvious that being buried by the falling rocks had injured his head. Able to do simple tasks, like fetching water or wood, he was hopeless in tending the fire or cooking. He was clumsy on the hunt, but he could carve realistic animals out of a stick of wood. He spent time knapping the obsidian stone for tools and arrowheads for the villagers, and creating his magical animals. After being sure she had enough water and wood, Obaho took his meals at his mother's house, but preferred to live in his own small house for sleeping. Anyone walking by at night heard him telling stories to himself and singing.

As soon as they passed by Obaho's house, they heard voices raised in anger. A man and woman hurled insults back and forth. In the background a small child cried loudly. Moochkla raised his hand to motion Kaiya to stop. They listened intently trying to make sense of the accusations. It seemed that the woman was disappointed in the kill from the hunt. A bowl came flying through the air, followed by a man bursting out of the T-shaped doorway. He stopped abruptly, aghast that the healer stood directly outside his dwelling.

"Come walk with me, son," Moochkla said. The two men started for the village, the younger man gesticulating wildly as he explained his side of the argument.

Meanwhile, Kaiya ventured inside the doorway, pushing aside the deerskin. The woman looked up, startled, but relaxed when she saw it was Kaiya.

"Akeela isn't here right now, Kaiya," said Eika. "I think she went down to the creek." Eika looked tired. She had 2 children, and was large with the third.

"I wasn't actually looking for Akeela right now," Kaiya said. Akeela was Kaiya's closest friend. Eika had been best friends with Saratong, so the two little girls had grown up at each other's fires. Eika was just having the new little one when Kaiya's mother had died. Otherwise she would have been willing to raise Kaiya.

"I was walking by with Moochkla, and I heard you and Marp arguing."

Eika said. "Moochkla heard us? He will have something to say about that, I am sure."

"Marp is walking with him right now toward the village."

Eika clapped her hands over her face. "I'm sure he will make everything sound just fine! How am I supposed to feed this hungry boy who still wants my nipple, and help the new one grow, when Marp won't bring me anything to eat? It's getting too hard for me to get around by myself to the creek and the forest. Akeela helps out as much as she can, but I need Marp to bring me meat. That's the only thing that makes me feel strong."

"I've heard many people complain about how the game is so scarce," Kaiya said, squatting down onto her heels by the fire. "The other day, Bertok only brought home a chipmunk."

"Only a chipmunk?" Eika snorted. "And he is the finest hunter in the tribe, now with your father gone. I guess I shouldn't be so mad at Marp."

"Moochkla says the animals are wandering away to other places that have more water, now that the creek is just running as a trickle."

"I know," Eika responded. "We need more rain. All of our ceremonies have only brought us one good storm. The whole rest of the rainy season we only had sprinkles. How many summers has it been since we have had a really good rainy season?"

Kaiya couldn't answer that question. In her short life, she had never seen what the elders of the tribe called the normal amount of rain. Jumac told stories of day after day of storms coming promptly each afternoon in midsummer. After the lightning time, then the winter snows began. There was snow on the ground during the whole winter. It melted slowly back into the Earth, which would tide them over until the next rainy season began. Now the winter snows had never gone over Kaiya's ankles.

Moochkla told her of a time when the snow came up to his waist more than once each winter. Sometimes big snows fell at the beginning of winter and remained on the ground for several moons. There would be times of melting, but then the big snows came again. Kaiya had never seen anything like the stories she heard.

"Akeela has been working to try to help save the crops. It's been hard work—going down to the creek to fill a pot with that trickle, and then carry it up to the fields. She has been very discouraged, as plant after plant died. I think it is going to be a very long, hard winter."

Eika sighed. "Just like last winter when so many babies died. I only hope this one that I'm carrying will make it through."

X

Drok felt enormously pleased with himself. He arose early each morning to meet with Cumani and Loka, and fell into bed late at night after a long day of training. Being a priest meant memorizing details of ceremonies and temple protocols. The slightest transgression would mean an offense to the gods. Drok did not want to displease the gods.

Drok was most fascinated learning about Tezcatlipoca. Warriors called on this god of evil and destruction during battle. Tezcatlipoca ruled the night sky, including the moon and stars. He also ruled the hearts of young men. Drok had heard of this master of dark magic through whispered conversations when people murmured that bad luck and misjudgments could be blamed on Tezcatlipoca. But as Drok learned more and more about this warrior god, he was mesmerized. He dreamed about the god's face, depicted in so many friezes on the temple walls—large, wide open eyes, flat forehead, tongue protruding, and fingers entwined through the hair of the next victim. Texcatlipoca was a blood-thirsty god.

Since the pyramid honoring the rain god Tlaloc was now the primary focus of worship in these times of drought, the other pyramid in the city had fallen into disrepair. This was the Temple of the Warriors, but the city had lacked the resources to send an invading army out for quite sometime. Drok walked over to it. Slightly smaller than the main pyramid, it was otherwise identical. He squinted up at the altar platform. He could see himself as the head priest performing rituals to honor Tezcatlipoca.

Discussing his plans with Cumani, Drok outlined what he saw as needed to revitalize the old pyramid. He could use the temple guards to supervise the slaves to shore up the limestone blocks, reapply mud mortar in places, and replace some of the bricks crumbling from exposure to the hot sun and splashed with jungle rains. He envisioned the addition of warrior columns, carved in stone, holding up the lintels over the doorways opening out to the platform. These figures would be three times as tall as a man, imposing and fearsome. Serpent columns would stand at each of the corners at the base of the pyramid. Their heads would rest on the ground, eyes bulging, mouths wide open with teeth exposed, and rattles rising straight into the sky. He would add friezes around the crumbling middle of the pyramid—monsters to terrorize the onlookers. He suggested using the skulls of the sacrificial victims to line a pathway up the stairs of the pyramid. He explained all this with fervor.

Cumani listened in silence to Drok's plans. Inwardly he shuddered. This boy, now a young man, saw a world of darkness; Cumani tried to see ways to help. He realized that the blood he saw spill in his original vision was simply a drop in the river that Drok saw flowing in his twisted mind.

Drok took great delight in supervising the guards. Barking out commands, and shouting rebukes, he kept up a punishing construction schedule. He stalked around the bottom of the pyramid, looking for things to criticize. He wanted the pyramid ready for ceremonies in time for the Summer Solstice, six moons away. He did some of the work himself, enjoying using his sturdy and strong young body, watching his developing muscles as they strained to lift the heavy stones.

To look more important, he inserted a silver nose ring into his septum, one that hung down almost to the top of his lip. Since he did not have the flat forehead of so many of the warriors, he tried different ways to look fierce. While getting his nose ring, he had looked at earrings, but none appealed to him. Lounging in his new quarters near the top of the pyramid, he daydreamed about an earring that would distinguish him from everyone else. With the design still fresh in his mind, he hurried down the stairs and out into the streets, headed for the metal worker's stall.

Jorin, the metal worker, was busy helping another customer, and did not see Drok come in. Drok banged noisily on the small table near the front of the store. The old metal worker looked up in alarm, then seeing who it was, rushed over to Drok.

"Oh, my young priest, how good of you to return. I hope there is nothing wrong with the nose ring I sold you last week," Jorin said.

"No, it's fine," Drok said. I want you to make me a special earring."

"When I finish helping this young man, I'll see to it," the metal worker said.

Drok looked dismissively at the waiting man. He was clearly one of the artisans, a sculptor, perhaps. "He can wait," Drok said. I have to return to the rebuilding of the pyramid. It's most important to honor Tezcatlipoca."

The old metal worker shuddered slightly at the sound of that god's name. He murmured apologetically to the artisan and turned to Drok. He had heard of the viciousness of this priest-in-training, and decided not to try his patience.

"Tell me about what you would like, and I will start on it right away," Jorin said.

In detail, Drok described his earring. The metal worker was an artist, and nodded approvingly at Drok's design.

"That is very unusual, and will look handsome on you, I'm sure. Return late tomorrow afternoon and I will show you what I've created that suits your standards."

Drok left the store in high spirits. He loved to be the one to give orders, and watch people jump at his commands.

That night Drok again dreamed he was in sole command, clothed in an extravagant cape fastened around his neck with a clasp of gold. His shiny new earring cast beams of light caught from the sun on the warrior statues as he moved about the platform. The dream faded, but the feeling of power remained with him when he awoke.

The following afternoon as the sun threw shadows of the pyramid over the eastern part of the city, Drok returned to the jeweler's stall. True to his word, the old metal worker had created a silver masterpiece. A small earcuff fit on the side and almost to the top of Drok's right ear. Drok didn't flinch a bit as the old shopkeeper pierced Drok's earlobe three times. Into the three new holes went identical silver balls showing in the front of the ear, with three silver chains behind reaching up to attach to the earcuff. The three chains formed dangling loops which swayed as Drok moved and shook his head, drawing attention away from Drok's damaged face. He felt fierce and in command. It had been his dream, and now it was real.

XI

If only all days could be as pleasantly perfect as these, Kaiya thought. The dawn started off cool and crisp, but lapsed into warm, sunny mornings filled with turquoise-blue skies accented by fluffy white clouds. Just when it seemed that the sun's rays might be getting just a little too warm, one of these lazy floating clouds drifted across the sun, provided cooling shade. The cloud then headed on its journey in the sky stream to reward someone else in a different place.

Kaiya chose outside chores. She knew the time would come, all too quickly, when she would have to stay inside because of winter's chill and harsh weather. When she finished, she would give herself the rare gift of time to sit, contemplate, maybe even doze. To bask in this early autumn weather, after the lightning, before chilly times, was truly to be kissed by the Great Spirit.

The oaks blazed fiercely red, a contrast to the tall grasses in their yellow and brown hues. Kaiya was struck by the unending beauty of the world. No wonder potters created vessels of loveliness, inspired by the Great Spirit's changing display of nature's glory all around them. The soft patterns of dots in the feather of a flicker, the scalloped leaves of oaks, spirals mimicking the swirling movement of water, jagged bolts of lightning, whirlwinds, magnificent animals, blazing suns and shining moons all appeared in her clan's artwork. She looked toward the Sacred Peaks and saw the splashes of yellow aspen groves, creating a jagged hem of a bright skirt at the base of the mountain. What a bittersweet time of year, she thought. So much beauty before so much hardship.

It struck her that autumn was such a fleeting time of year. She thought back through all the phases of her own short life, the carefree and much loved child, the terrified and lonely orphan, the shy apprentice, and now the emerging healer. Now she could understand that there was continuation of life after the transition through death. She had already changed so many times, and knew she would continue to do so.

Life seemed so precious now that she understood the depth of Moochkla's responsibility and her own future as a healer. She appreciated his gentle teachings about herbs and dis-ease of the people. She thought back to the day when a young mother brought her baby to Moochkla. The poor mother had tears in her eyes as she explained how the child had coughed all night, a wracking, chest-heaving cough that seem to rend the child's body. Kaiya watched Moochkla take mullein leaves and other herbs she herself had collected during the summer and crumble them into boiling water.

"Make the baby drink this tea three times a day," Moochkla said to the young mother.

The next day when they went to check on their patient, the little boy was clearly breathing much easier and the mother's face had lost that haunted, anxious look.

Often when people came to him with a complaint, Moochkla was wise enough to know it probably was more than just an aching head. Kaiya was amazed at how the old healer listened, asked a few questions, and then watched the person blurt out what was really wrong. Sometimes it was a true physical ailment which could be treated rather easily. Often it was just a matter of helping the body do its own job with the aid of healing herbs. Like the time when Jumac had pain when she urinated, burning pain that made her afraid to pee. Moochkla made her drink copious amounts of juniper tea, which cleared out her system in a few days, allowing normal elimination. Kaiya fervently hoped that time would allow her to grow into half the healer Moochkla was.

She smiled and felt the warmth she held for him. Tonight she would serve him what little they had left in their food stores, feigning lack of appetite due to her womanly cycle. The clan couldn't afford to lose him, and she felt young and strong. The spirit of beauty in this gorgeous autumn all around her was food enough for her today.

XII

Pobal and Pem paused to wipe sweat from their brows. The jungle humidity weighed heavily on their aching backs.

"If only it would rain, really rain," said Pobal, "instead of being so sticky all the time."

Pem nodded in agreement, too tired to answer. They had been working on this field since early morning. The sun felt as if it were boring a hole in his head.

"We have to stop and rest in the shade," Pem said. "Maybe then we would have enough strength to finish this today."

"You would think these thistles couldn't grow when it's been so dry. It's as if the weeds are gathering all the moisture from the air and the maize isn't getting any. Look how sad and small the corn plants are."

Pem had dropped his hoe and hunkered down in the shade of a big tree nearby. Pobal followed.

"I'm so hungry," Pem said. "I can't keep working so hard with so little to eat."

"Do you think we could find work in Tula?" Pobal asked.

Pem thought for a moment. His older brother usually came up with ideas, but Pem was the one who had to do the organization and follow through.

"We could let the younger children tend the fields while we're gone. It would only take a few days to get to Tula, a few days to see what we could find, and then a few days to get back. And maybe it would be easier to find food along the river. When we get back tonight, let's tell Mama."

Mama listened to her sons' plans. She had been dreading this day for a long time. She knew her sons were restless and bored, and the lure of the city called many young men away from the countryside. She only hoped they would find some safe work and not become a warrior like her husband. She had a feeling they would not return, and blinked back tears as she rummaged through their meager food supply for something they could take with them.

The two brothers rose early the next morning, before any light penetrated the jungle canopy. It had been a long time since they had been down to the river. When they finally reached its banks, they were surprised how low it was.

"I don't think it will be easy to fish here. The river's so low that all the fish must have gone downstream where it might be deeper," Pem said.

The brothers easily crossed the river. The path on the opposite side was well-trodden on the way toward the city. They talked about the only other time they had visited Tula. Their father had brought them when they were much younger. They remembered being amazed at the imposing pyramid temples, the throngs of people and the multitude of shops and stalls. Their father had been killed far away in the fighting, and they hadn't been back since. They debated if they could find the shop of their father's friend, Jorin, the metal worker. Jorin had been like a big brother to their father, and had made a fuss over them when they were just boys visiting the city.

Sleeping on a soft, sandy beach along the river offered a relatively cool spot and the availability of water. Hungry after their long hike, they finished the food their mother had packed for them. The sun hit their spit of sand early, so there was nothing for them to do but rise and begin walking, determined to reach Tula by that evening. In truth it was well after dark when they saw the lights and buildings of the city. Uneasy in the shifting masses of people, they skirted the outside of the city, searching for an out of the way place to sleep. They noticed many young men, faces pinched with hunger, also casting furtive glances around for a place to bed down. Pem put a hand on his brother's shoulder and pulled him into a small space between two stalls.

"I don't like the looks of things in the city. Do you feel the tension in the air? The city seems full of people wandering without any place to go," Pem said.

Pobal looked around him. Young men passed by, sometimes stopping for a while with their backs to the wall, squatting low, watching the rest of the crowd walk by.

Pem continued, "I think we should sleep here and then try to find that stall first thing in the morning. But I think we should take turns, one of us watching while the other sleeps. I'll take the first watch."

Pobal shrugged his shoulders in agreement, and eased himself into the slot. There was exactly enough room for him to lie down while Pem squatted on his toes near the entry. Pem caught snatches of conversation as people passed by, and could sense that the city was in a state of unrest. Apparently theft was increasing, especially theft of food. The temple guards had stepped up their patrols, and anyone caught stealing was sentenced to work on Drok's project. Pem wondered who this Drok was, as that name was repeated in many of the passing conversations. Finally his cramped, tired body couldn't balance anymore, so he poked his brother until he was sure Pobal was awake, then slumped beside the stall into exhausted sleep.

The noise of the city woke both brothers, as Pobal never did stay awake during his turn at watch. In the pre-dawn light, howler monkeys hooted deep cries from the jungle just outside the city.

Inside the city, foot traffic increased and merchants started banging around in their stalls to organize their day's work. Stiffly, the brothers rose from their cramped quarters and asked the first man walking by how to get to the stall of Jorin the metal worker. His directions were complicated, and they had to ask several more people before they found the right street. The shop was closed up tight, so they crouched against the wall in front of it, sleepy, hungry and exceedingly thirsty. Pobal dozed off, but Pem remained alert, taking in the talk and actions of the city people.

The sun was beginning to bake their section of the street when Pem noticed an older man walking toward them. He smiled, recognizing his father's friend. Rising to his feet and poking his brother awake, he stood.

"Greetings, Jorin. I am Pem, and this is my brother Pobal. Do you remember our father?"

The old man stood blinking in the bright sun. He looked the two dusty boys over and his weathered face broke into a smile.

"Oh, Pem, you are the image of your father!" But you've both grown so! You were just little boys when he brought you here. Come in, come in, and tell me what you're doing here."

Jorin took down the planks covering the front of his store and ushered the boys in. Pobal whistled at the amount of silver jewelry spread out along the tables. He fingered some of the items, and noted an unusual earring design repeated in many of the pieces. Three round balls went through the earlobe, attached to dangling chains going up to an ear cuff.

"What's this?" he asked.

"That's one of my best selling items," Jorin responded proudly. "Drok, the young priest rebuilding Tezcatlipoca's temple designed that earring, and now all of his followers want one. I can't keep up with all the orders. Some of the young men would rather have one of those earrings than dinner." He paused, and looked the boys over. "How long are you planning to stay in the city?"

Pem and Pobal glanced at each other. Pem, as usual, took the lead.

"We thought we would come to the city to make it easier on our mother. She has the younger children to feed, and we are now old enough to take care of ourselves. We were hoping to find work and stay in the city. But, we don't want to be soldiers like our father. He died fighting, you know."

Jorin nodded solemnly. "It was a great loss, but your father died bravely in battle. I was there when they brought his body back. He died an honorable death."

"Our mother has never been the same," Pem said. "We were looking for work that would be less dangerous."

Jorin looked carefully at the boys. He did need help, but he couldn't pay them. "How about this? I'll clean out the back of the store so you can have a place to sleep. That would be a great help right there, as I worry about having this much silver with the place unguarded at night. But, I could also use your help with metal working. You could be my apprentices. It would be a tribute to your father to have you working for me."

Pobal started to respond, but Pem cut him off. "That would be good to have a place to sleep in exchange for watching your store. But, if we're going to work for you, you would have to feed us as well."

Jorin thought about this. If he could get away with just paying them room and board for their labor, it would be worth it to have the extra help and added security.

"All right, I can provide you one meal a day. If you work extra hard, two meals a day. That's the best I can offer."

"That sounds good to us," Pem said. Pobal looked like he was about to speak, but Pem shot him a look which stopped him.

"We have heard many people speak of this Drok. Tell us about him," Pem said.

Jorin moved about the store, rearranging clutter to make a space for the boys' sleeping quarters. "He was a temple boy, and he assisted Cumani in the very first ceremony of human sacrifice. Cumani must think a great deal of him, because he's given Drok complete freedom in the rebuilding of the pyramid." Jorin glanced around and lowered his voice, to avoid being overheard by people on the street. "I find him demanding and arrogant for someone of his age. I think he's letting his newfound standing go to his head."

Speaking normally now, Jorin continued, "He has quite a following among the young men of the city. Many of the young men used to be soldiers, but the city is too poor to send out an army now. And, boys like you keep coming in from the countryside. Also, the crops are failing due to the lack of rain, and the city's food supplies are running low. So there are a lot of hungry young men without a lot to do filling up the city. Drok delivers speeches from the pyramid some nights, and the young men love to hear him."

Again, Jorin glanced around. "Personally," he said quietly, "I think his talk is dangerous. Killing is his answer to everything."

"Well, I'd like to hear him talk," Pobal said.

"First I need your help here," Jorin said. He put the boys to work in the shop just as the first customers began to file in.

Pem caught on very quickly to both working with customers and working with metal. Pobal was better suited to more menial tasks, such as sweeping up the metal shavings.

Several days passed by in a blur as the brothers adjusted to life in the big city. Talk drifted through the shop that Drok would be speaking at the partially finished temple that evening. Both boys begged Jorin to be allowed to attend.

"I really want at least one of you to stay in the shop at all times. How about the one who stays gets an extra meal?" Jorin asked.

Pobal salivated, thinking of more food. Pem was always on the edge of hunger, too, but was curious to hear this Drok speak. He let Pobal stay and eat.

Heading out into the street, the first thing Pem noticed was that many young men going toward the temple carried weapons. Normally in the city, the only weapons seen were carried by soldiers, but the streets were bristling with quivers of spears across shoulders and down the backs of many men. He walked along with the crowd, listening, trying to blend in yet remain unobtrusive at the same time. The crowd gathered mass as it approached the temple and spread out along the base, filling the plaza. Pem was amazed to see this many people, mostly men, his age or slightly older. Some leaned on sticks, some were lame. It didn't matter, they all came.

A flash of light appeared at the top of the temple, and then a lone figure stood on the edge of the platform. Torches along the top burst into flame one after the other as a small boy ran along lighting each. The crowd below could now clearly see Drok. He stood in his jaguar skin loincloth held by his jaguar head belt. One upper arm held an armband, and his silver chain earring dangled and sparkled in the light. Two dark tattoo lines started at each outer cheekbone and ended at his chin, partially masking his scars. The crowd gave a roaring cheer when he thrust both fists high in the air above his shoulders.

"Good men of Tula, I welcome you to the home of Tezcatlipoca, the god of the night and all things dark. And dark is the night for all of us now, with our city faltering and failing to provide enough for all."

The crowd shouted in agreement.

"When this temple is completed in time for the Summer Solstice, there will be a ceremony to renew our devotion to Tezcatlipoca."

Deep hoots and cheers echoed through the crowd at this.

"He is the god we need right now to help us return Tula to a land of plenty. We are hungry. We are dry. We are soldiers, but the city won't send us out to fight. There should be food for all, water for all, work for all, money for all, and wars for all soldiers to fight."

Wild applause and shouts echoed through the plaza.

"But first, we have to honor Tezcatlipoca by finishing this pyramid. Then we must provide sacrifices. He will make things right for us!"

Drok thrust his fists into the air again, whirled around and exited the platform. The crowd below continued yelling, clapping, and thrusting their fists in the air. The air filled with the smell of sweat, hemp, and the sticky sweet aroma of pulque. The men milled around, talking excitedly. Pem noticed that many of them wore the same earring as Drok. He suddenly realized the extent of Jorin's work, trying to supply these earrings to all the young men eager to be followers of Drok. Why does this young priest hold such sway over so many? As he turned to walk back to the shop, the crowd parted and the chatter stopped. Drok was walking right by him. Close up now, Pem could see the disfigured face and the arrogant posture. Pem caught a glimpse of his eyes—fathomless black depths with no soul. Pem shivered in the presence of raw power.

XIII

Kokopelli, the god of fertility and music, was said to come into the fields at night and give a tiny tug on the corn seedlings to encourage them to grow. But the more common Kokopellis were the many traveling traders. A visit from any of the traveling Kokopellis was always a treat. Kokopelli was not the wayfarers' real name, but rather a title. These traders traipsed from villages to major centers with goods and most importantly, news. Messages from loved ones, items for trade, reports and gossip from neighboring villages were exchanged for a place to lodge, camaraderie, and meals. This job was for a young man, as it involved long distances carrying a heavy pack. Always handsome and outgoing, these traders were attractive to the young women. The oft-repeated joke was that a Kokopelli had to be strong all day for his travels and strong all night, as he seldom slept alone. The announcement that Kokopelli had been spotted sent women hunting for their best tunics and their finest beads.

There was another who anxiously awaited any word that a Kokopelli was on the way. Bertok longed to see one of these travelers. Sess was the one Kokopelli who made Bertok's heart pound. He often thought about becoming a Kokopelli himself, just so their paths would cross. But, he felt an obligation to his clan, as he was their best hunter. Also, he would not have been able to perform the legendary love-making with the young women as he traveled among the villages. His heart just wasn't in it.

This time barking dogs and cries from a little boy collecting wood announced Kokopelli's arrival. Small children and women trailed behind and alongside of him, with demands for news and what items could be traded. Usually Kokopelli lingered and chatted his way through the village before making his first official stop at Moochkla's house. He acted differently today, made apologies and promised to be back later. But first he had to speak with Moochkla. The disappointed throng fell back, and he continued toward the herb house, arriving at the doorway to see Moochkla bent over the fire.

"Ah, good to see you, my friend," said Moochkla. "Come sit by the fire and join me in a small meal."

Instead, Kokopelli grinned, thrust his hand beneath his tunic and extracted the most startling bird. It was like nothing ever seen in this place. It had a big, curved, black beak, and pinkish-white skin encircling beady black eyes with black stripes under each eye. The feathers could scarcely be believed—some bright blue like the sky, others blood-red, yellow-orange bits of fluff on the chest and green feathers on top of the head. The creature squawked at being treated in such an undignified manner. Both Moochkla and Kokopelli chuckled. The bird's right wing drooped at an unnatural angle. Kokopelli pulled gently at the broken wing to show Moochkla the problem, while the bird tried to peck at Kokopelli's hand.

"I am to bring this bird to Chaco," he said.

"What is it?" Moochkla asked.

"It's from the south where it is warm and humid all the time. This bird is called a macaw, and where it lives there are thousands of them everywhere, like ravens here. But they need a warm climate. This one talks too much. I had tethered it to a tree and was making camp when a red-tailed hawk came to investigate all the noise and attacked it. Before I could ward off the hawk, the macaw's wing had been damaged. Is there anything you can do to help it?"

"I have seen such feathers before in ceremonies, but I didn't know where they came from," Moochkla said. Moving closer to inspect the broken wing, he kept a wary eye on the dangerous beak. The bird sensed Moochkla's calm manner and settled down enough to be examined.

"Yes, I think I can help. But the bird should not go anywhere while it is healing. You should leave it here and get it on your next trip through."

At that moment, Kaiya burst through the doorway with an armload of firewood. "I heard Kokopelli is coming," she began, stopping short as she took in the scene and dropped the wood on the floor.

"What is that?" she asked. As she strode toward the bird, both Kokopelli and Moochkla tried to warn her about the beak. But Kaiya held out her arm to the bird, who wriggled free from Kokopelli's grasp and hopped onto it. Kaiya and the bird stared at each other. The bird tilted its head from side to side so each eye could take in this girl. Kaiya mimicked the bird's motions, cooing and talking softly the whole time. Kokopelli marveled at their instant friendship.

"I think I've found a caretaker," he said. Kaiya remained as enchanted by the bird as it seemed to be by her.

"This would be a good time to work on the wing," Moochkla said. He prepared a poultice and rummaged around until he found a small scrap of soft deerhide. While Kaiya spoke endearments to the bird, Moochkla pulled the wing away from its body and swiftly applied the salve and the bandage. "Go out and find a stump or log that has a sizeable branch sticking out from it. This bird needs to have something to curl its claws around."

Kaiya attempted to place the bird on one of the sticks she had dropped on the floor, but it just dug its claws more tightly into her arm. Kokopelli stole up from behind and grabbed the bird. More squawks. Kaiya tried to slip out the door, but the bird twisted in her direction and strained to follow. Kaiya had remembered the perfect stump and called Moochkla to help her drag it back. Soon they had the bird set up on its perch. It seemed content to just sit there, preen its feathers and watch Kaiya.

"What does it eat?" asked Kaiya.

"Well, its favorite thing is fruit. But it will eat nuts, seeds, flowers, or insects," Kokopelli replied.

Kaiya immediately left to gather food for her new charge.

"I wish this was all that was coming up from the south," Kokopelli said to Moochkla. "I'm afraid there is something far more sinister."

Moochkla settled back on his heels near the fire, where he had been working on a healing potion. "How so?" he asked.

Kokopelli accepted a small bowl of stew and reclined against his pack on the floor.

"I had heard some disturbing stories about how the people of the South are practicing bloodletting and torture during their religious ceremonies. I have just spoken with a fellow Kokopelli who has been down there recently. What he saw is chilling."

Kokopelli halted his narrative long enough to take several bites of stew, then looked up sympathetically at Moochkla, who hung his head.

"I know, that is a very thin stew. The game is all gone from this area. All I had was the last strip of meat from a baby rabbit Kaiya brought home last week. She wanted to keep it for a pet, but I told her it wouldn't live, so she should give it to Tal or me. I guess I must have looked hungrier than Tal because she gave it to me. I am sorry, friend. You deserve better after your long travels, but I don't think you'll find much better fare anywhere in this village."

Kokopelli nodded. "It's the same everywhere I go. People are starving, and it's not even winter yet. People have cut down all the trees nearest their villages, and it makes the soil blow away. Then it's too hard to grow crops with the all the good soil gone."

"So, what did your friend see down there?" Moochkla prompted.

"Oh, yes. My friend had watched one of their ceremonies in the past. Back then, there were ceremonial offerings of harvest foods or small game and fish to their gods. Then they started bringing a virgin to the altar. You know how much the Toltecs like to drink the pulque. They would get the poor girl drunk, and in elaborate ritual take her virginity in front of the crowd. That was sick enough, but then, captives from conquered tribes were brought to the pyramids and shockingly killed upon the altar in a bloody show. They ripped the still-beating heart from the chest of the victim. This ravaging became central to all their religious ceremonies. Crowds couldn't get enough of all that bloodletting. The sacrifice was supposed to ensure a bountiful harvest and keep the rains coming. But these people from Tula are having the same problems we are. Poor crops, scarce game and no rain. So they make more ceremonies in an effort to appease their gods."

Moochkla was stunned. He had never heard of such cruelty, but then remembered stories about the military strength of these people from the South. If they were to gather their armies for a push in this direction, his people and the surrounding clans would be easy targets. In their weakened condition from hunger and thirst, the people of his clan would soon become the victims upon the altar.

He thought of his clan's increasing problems, how quick people were to anger, and how frustrated everyone was. He could envision a charismatic newcomer convincing his debilitated people that these ceremonies would solve their problems. He thought back to the last few trying months, watching his people lose their composure, yell at each other, even hit one another in their misery. Watching a small boy throwing stones at an injured animal one day, he realized that the boy was not trying to kill the animal for food, but instead was enjoying watching the animal writhe in terror and pain. Were his people close enough to the brink of desperation to accept this ritual from the people from the South? He shook his head and sighed heavily.

Just at that moment Kaiya reappeared with handfuls of lunch for the bird. She cooed and cuddled with it on its perch, while offering food.

"Is this a girl or boy bird?" she asked Kokopelli.

"It's a boy bird. They usually have the more colorful feathers."

Kokopelli stood and shouldered his pack. "I think I must go now to trade and visit with my friends in the village. But I had to get the bird to you without the eyes of everyone in the clan. That poor bird needs to get some rest and heal before it will be ready for the curious. I also needed to let you know that news from the south." Kokopelli strode back toward the village.

"What news?" Kaiya queried.

"Not now, Kaiya. Let's get ready for tonight's feast with Kokopelli. We also need to always hang the deerskin in the doorway until this bird is better."

"I will call him Bato," Kaiya said.

"Don't get too attached to him, Kaiya. He belongs to Chaco Canyon and is here only until he is ready to travel."

Kaiya pouted, but worked hard to gather what they could spare for dinner that night.

The gathering could not be called a feast, as no one had anything to spare. People brought a little foodstuff they had hidden away. After finishing their meager meal, everyone sat back in anticipation of Kokopelli's talk. Part comedian, part storyteller, and part musician, Kokopelli didn't let them down, telling the funny and unusual things from his travels. The stories he had heard from others, and reports of what leaders had said as they sat beside their nighttime fires made them all feel closer to one another. His audience sometimes roared with laughter, or wiped away tears at the tender moments. He told of the amazing bird, and then winked at Kaiya as he told them of the safe haven for the bird until the wing healed, and then they could see it. He told some of his story of the people of the South, but left out the frightening news that he had shared with Moochkla. Always, he ended the evening with sweet songs on his flute. As usual, several young women of the clan lingered beside the fire after most people had gone home.

Bertok, too, continued to sit by Kokopelli as he had throughout the evening. But Kokopelli made his preference known, and soon there was only one young woman. He shouldered his pack, and the two slipped away into the forest. Bertok watched them go, feeling as if his heart would break.

XIV

Drok worked at fever pitch as the days narrowed toward Summer Solstice. Cumani continued to perform the regular full moon ceremony with Drok's assistance, the only event which took Drok away from supervising the temple's reconstruction. More and more slaves were needed as the day drew closer. Drok was in a state of agitation making sure all his plans would come about perfectly. He doubled the number of temple guards, enlisting many of the young men who attended his speeches. Two of the new guards came from the metal worker's shop, two brothers. Pobal was an eager recruit, right in line with Drok's philosophy. The younger brother, Pem, intrigued Drok. Pem was a thoughtful young man who reminded Drok of Loka.

Pem felt obliged to continue helping Jorin in the metal shop, sleeping there and helping run the business. He didn't join the group of young men who set up a sleeping camp at the back of the pyramid, but Pobal joined the growing ranks of young men convinced, even eager to see human sacrifices as a way to appease the gods.

Jorin grew to respect and appreciate this younger son of his deceased friend. Pem had an intelligence about him and an innate sense of adaptability to any situation. Soothing an irate customer, or often cajoling a browsing customer into spending more, he was a great asset for Jorin, who felt confident in leaving the operation of the shop with Pem so he could go make the jewelry. Working with his hands was Jorin's first love, while working with people was harder for him. He didn't share the same affection for Pobal, who was louder, less thoughtful, and slightly dull in learning tasks.

Pem did, however, wish to attend the Summer Solstice ceremony, as did everyone in Tula. Pem and Pobal were assigned torch lighting along the stairs of the pyramid. Pobal was especially excited to wear the uniform of a temple guard. The feathered helmet, loincloth and quiver of spears slung across his shoulders and down his back made him feel powerful. Pem appreciated the sandals given to him for the ceremony. He had never had any kind of shoes before, and liked the feel of his foot against the leather rather than the hard-packed dirt and stones.

Below the pyramid, a crowd began to form long before the official ceremony, drinking pulque, pushing together in groups, trying to carve out a small space to stand where they could see the platform far above.

The sound of the crowd below roared like the wind as Drok dressed in the antechamber. Cumani and Loka came to help him prepare for the ceremony.

"How is this Solstice ceremony different from others?" Cumani asked.

"There is much in common with the regular full moon ceremonies, with the sacrifices to Tezcatlipoca," Drok replied.

"Sacrifices? Will there be more than one?" Loka asked.

"Oh, yes," replied Drok. "Tezcatlipoca requires much in return for what we ask of him. Didn't you see that there are three Chacmool statues on the platform?"

Cumani and Loka exchanged glances. The statues weren't easily visible from the ground level. Loka walked to the doorway but remained concealed from the view of the burgeoning crowd below. From this vantage point, he could see the three statues.

"You will perform all of the sacrifices yourself?" asked Cumani.

"I am the priest in charge of this temple," Drok said forcefully. "I have temple guards to light the torches and bring me the sacrificial victims. There is a temple boy to bring me the obsidian blades. What more do I need?"

Cumani shook his head. He had never been able to perform the sacrificial ceremony. Always, Drok had done it for him. He often wondered if his vision was truly from the gods. After all this sacrifice, their city was as dry as before.

This Summer Solstice had the added power of also being the full moon. Drok threw back his head and took a deep breath, puffing out his chest, as he waited for the exact moment to step onto the platform when the crescent of the fading sun sank below the jungle horizon just as the full moon orb started to rise on the opposite side of the plaza.

The crowd roared as Drok stepped to the edge of the platform. In unison, his two torch lighters stepped out behind him to send their fire down to the relay teams of guards standing stoically along the flanks of the pyramid. Each guard lit the torch and returned to his position as the next guard took up the passing of the light. Soon the pyramid stood in flickering brightness, even more imposing than in the daylight. When Drok saw the bottom torch burst into flame, the ceremony commenced.

The people by now were accustomed to the terrified shrieks of the victims, the drama of the slashing, the still beating heart ripped from the slave's chest and offered as a sacrifice. The crowd was not ready for Drok's next move, however. Slowly Drok turned the sharp bifacial obsidian knife toward the heart of the final victim, he slowly chopped it out, and brought it, still beating, to his lips. The crowd watched in fascinated horror as Drok bit into it. Blood dripped down his chin and onto his body before the shocked spectators.

Then he raised the organ, shouting to the crowd, "I eat this in honor of Tezcatlipoca to show I'm not afraid. I'm not afraid of my enemies, I'm not afraid of drought, I'm not afraid of hunger, because Tezcatlipoca will provide. I will even eat my enemies," Drok said with a crazed look in his eyes.

He bit it again before throwing the heart down the pyramid stairs. As it careened toward the bottom, young men surged to grab and bite into it. The crowd roared.

Cumani tried to take in what had just happened before his eyes. How far would Drok go?

Watching from the chamber off the platform, a shaken Cumani turned to Loka. "Will the citizens of Tula now begin eyeing each other as their next meal?" Cumani asked Loka. "I started this trend of bloodshed. And now, it appears there is no end to it. How much more violence will be so easily allowed?"

"It depends. If you are a young man, imagining yourself standing on the platform being idolized like Drok, and you're hungry, this rite probably seems god-sent. If you are older and have weathered tough times before and know that things will eventually improve, you would see the danger in these acts," Loka said.

"We've got to stop this, now." Cumani said.

"How? He already has quite a following. Look at how many young men wear the same earring that Drok designed," Loka pointed out.

Cumani turned to look squarely at Loka. "Do you ever recall a time like this before?"

"No," Loka said. "But, never before have I seen the city in such trouble. The river has never been this low. Never have so many people been living in Tula. And, we've never before had this many years in a row of failed crops. Our people are hungry, angry, and scared—a bad combination."

"What do you advise?" Cumani asked.

Loka thought. "I'm not sure there is anything you can do at the moment. You've given Drok freedom to revitalize the worship of Tezcatlipoca, and Drok continues to be your assistant during the regular ceremonies to Tlaloc for rain. You would have to cast him out of the city in order for him to lose his influence now."

XV

"How long will it take?" Kaiya asked.

"Huh?" Moochkla grunted. He had busied himself working on his plants, and had forgotten Kaiya's presence. "For what?"

"For me to learn about all of this," she said, pursing her lips at the profusion of plant parts.

Moochkla chuckled. "Years of practice, Kaiya. I was taught by the healer before me when I was just a few years older than you. You will learn many herbal medicines, too. And Kaiya, I am still learning after all these years. You can never know them all. You will always experiment. But the important thing is that you will know more than others in the clan so you can help your people."

"What is it that people come for the most?" Kaiya asked.

Moochkla grunted and turned to face Kaiya. "Most of the time, it is for small things. Something is wrong with the skin, perhaps. We live and work where our skin is always being cut, scraped, stuck by something, or exposed to the sun. Our skin is the most important part of our body, because it keeps everything we need safely on the inside, and keeps the sickness on the outside. That's why if there's a cut in the skin, it's necessary to find a way to keep the evil spirits out."

"But what about the big things?" Kaiya asked.

"Sometimes it's so big that a ceremony needs to be performed. Sometimes it's the person's time to return to the Great Spirit so there's nothing I can do. Like your parents. Your father was dead a long time before anyone from the clan found him. Your mother died when I was on my way to help her. It was their time to go."

Kaiya thought about all the people in her clan, and how fragile and precious their lives were. It's amazing any of her people were healthy at all. Accidents and sickness occurred all the time. Some people recovered, but others had lingering effects. She vowed to increase her efforts to learn everything she could. There was so much more than just understanding the plants and their uses. Moochkla was a healer and a shaman, healing bodies and spirits. She doubted she could ever be as powerful as Moochkla.

Kaiya headed down to the creek to refresh herself after a dusty morning pulling plants. Walking with her elegant, flowing stride, she passed by Obaho and smiled gently at him. He breathed a sigh, followed by a lumbering effort to rise. He shook himself, took a few faltering steps for balance and then shuffled off into the forest to relieve himself. In the time it had taken him to rise and return, Kaiya was already back from reviving herself in the creek. Obaho blocked her path. Daintily Kaiya stepped around him. Obaho managed to pivot in time to catch Kaiya's eyes. She saw his love for her pouring out. Inwardly she groaned, but something else in his eyes caught her attention. Two people stood there, one in front of the other. An object flew toward the first person, and that person fell. Obaho blinked, and the image disappeared.

"Do you need any special herbs today, chickweed or sage?" Obaho began, in an attempt to engage and keep her close to him.

She shook her head from side to side, smiled at him, and laid her hand on his arm as she whisked by, her long hair swaying. The place where her fingers had softly curled over the top of his arm retained the memory of her touch. He sighed again.

Kaiya shook her head as she walked home. It was hard to be annoyed with Obaho, as he was so simple-minded. But other young men in the clan also gave her that same kind of look only without Obaho's sweet innocence. She was too involved with her studies to waste time on them. "Just leave me alone!" she shouted into the wind.

Arriving home, Moochkla greeted her in the doorway. "Kaiya, come by the fire." She seated herself, grateful for a moment of rest.

"We are going on a journey. I am very concerned for the welfare of our clan. I want to get advice from other healers I have known through the years. Perhaps they have answers I don't. It will also give you an opportunity to work with others. I have taught you much, and have more to teach you, but sometimes learning others' knowledge and methods can help you grow wiser as a healer."

Kaiya cocked her head to one side and looked straight into Moochkla's eyes. She saw three people wrapped up against the cold, walking into a hard wind. "Who else is coming with us?" she asked.

Moochkla chuckled. "I think I liked it better when you were little and thought I knew everything about everybody." Kaiya smiled at the memory.

"I want to ask Bertok if he would like to come with us. He seems sad these days, and the change of scene would be good for him. Besides, we will eat better if he is with us."

"Can I go ask him?" Kaiya begged.

"Yes. In fact, have him come here."

Kaiya moved swiftly in search of her uncle. A little boy had just seen him heading toward the creek on the steep side. Kaiya made her way slowly down the path. This section of the canyon was so narrow and steep that she needed to side-step part of the way.

She reached the creek bottom and lolled in the creek, watching the dance of dragonflies, butterflies and ripples of water. A yellow butterfly brushed her forehead as it drifted past. Looking in both directions, she heard a faint humming off to the right. Picking her way along the rocky banks, she made her way toward the sound. Coming closer, she saw Bertok on the far side of the creek, engrossed in a picture he was drawing on the canyon rock wall. Counting on the sound of the creek to drown out her footfalls, she made her way along her side of the creek to directly opposite Bertok, with his back still toward her. She sat quietly on a rock where she could watch him work. He had drawn the figure of a Kokopelli, heavy pack on his back, flute in outstretched hands. As the picture unfolded, another Kokopelli faced the first one. Their flutes touched.

Bertok stood back to admire his work. Kaiya hooted softly. Bertok spun around, at first angry, then relieved to see it was Kaiya. "That's beautiful," she said.

Bertok sighed deeply. "Thanks. I had to acknowledge how I feel about Sess in some way."

Kaiya nodded, and rose to cross the creek and give her uncle a hug. He had told her about his feelings. She didn't completely understand why her special uncle had such strong feelings for another man, but she knew it felt real to him and it bothered him.

"I have exciting news! Moochkla is going on a journey, and he wants you and me to accompany him."

Bertok's eyes opened wide. "Both of us? Where are we going?"

"Moochkla wants to visit other healers and talk with them about the troubles of our clan. Maybe he can get help or at least advice."

Bertok looked once more at his new rock drawing, then turned his back and started down the creek. Kaiya followed along behind him.

"When would we go?"

"Moochkla said to come by and talk with him about it."

"Was this your idea, Kaiya?"

"Honest, I didn't mention it, but I think it's a great idea to get to spend time with you. Moochkla said we would eat better if you were with us."

Smiling broadly at Kaiya, Bertok headed toward Moochkla and Kaiya's home. He felt his spirits rise as he could see himself traveling, meeting other artists, and seeing new places to make his heart sing again. He would go.

XVI

This couldn't be what the gods were demanding, thought Pem as he walked away from the ceremony in shock. He recalled the first full moon ceremony he had witnessed with its gruesome sacrifices but nothing had prepared him for what he saw tonight. It was especially horrifying for him because he had been a torch lighter on the top step of the pyramid. Even when he closed his eyes now, he could still see the shiny beating hearts, hear the terrified slaves' last gasps for breath, and see the sickening cannibalism close up. He needed to be alone to think.

At his side, Pobal gushed on and on about Drok. "Wasn't that a powerful ceremony? Did you see Drok bite into that heart and send it spinning down the steps of the pyramid? Drok is the only one who can reach the gods for us now. He will save the city," Pobal babbled.

Finally, Pem couldn't even pretend to listen anymore. He bid his brother goodnight, turning toward the metal shop. His brother stopped in surprise, shrugged his shoulders, and turned back toward the sleep camp behind the pyramid, where other young men would talk through the night about what they had witnessed.

Walking through the packed streets, Pem listened to the passing conversations. Shreds of torn sentences drifted in the air. "Drok went too far....." "The gods don't want this...." "Does Drok think he's a god?" "Did you see him just...." They cast furtive glances around to see if anyone else was listening, maybe even spying. Most people were moving swiftly, pulling their children along, anxious to be off the streets and in their own homes.

Excited shouting came from the throng which hung around at the base of the pyramid, clearly taken in, overpowered by what had just occurred. Tula was a city divided on its opinion of the ceremony.

Arriving at the store, Pem let himself in. Lighting a small torch light, he made his way to his pallet. He jumped back when he saw a tall man in a long white robe at the far end of the stall.

"What do you want?" Pem demanded sharply. The man stepped briefly into the light so Pem could see his face. Pem had seen this man before from a distance. He was the man from the temple with the white skin and pink rimmed eyes who was a powerful adviser to the head priest.

"I am Loka, and you are Pem," the man said by way of introduction. "I saw you tonight lighting torches at the pyramid. Yet you don't wear one of these earrings," said Loka, gesturing to the many partially finished pieces of jewelry lying on the work table.

"I did take part in the torch lighting tonight, but I won't be taking part in any more ceremonies," said Pem.

"Why is that?" Loka pressed.

Pem looked carefully at Loka. This man held powerful sway over the inner workings of the temple, and he was just a boy from the country. He selected his words carefully. "What did you think of the ceremony?" Pem asked.

"I'd like to know your thoughts about it," Loka said quietly.

"Why?" asked Pem.

"I'm thinking that you don't approve of what you saw tonight. You are probably one of the few young men who feels that way. You could help the temple. You are in a position to let the temple know who supports Drok and who doesn't. You see who comes in here to buy these earrings. You know their names."

"So, you want me to gather information and then tell you what I know," Pem said.

"Something like that," Loka said.

"Look, I only got involved at all because my older brother is so taken with Drok. I promised my mother I would watch out for Pobal. But I see now that we are going separate ways. I can't abide this violence. I can't believe this is really what the gods want us to do." Pem took a sharp inhalation of breath, realizing he may have gone too far.

Loka walked around the store, stopping to finger pieces of jewelry as if he were a customer contemplating a purchase. Small puffs of dust rose from his sandals as he stepped around the table. He stopped when he stood directly in front of Pem.

"Drok is becoming uncontrollable. There may be a time when he goes too far. If that happens, he could be banished from the city by the temple council. Some will want to follow Drok. Many are swayed by what he is doing and would continue to take his orders, even follow him out of the city. We need to have a way to know what he's doing, even if he's gone and taken an army with him."

The light from the lone torch flickered as the men shifted in the small space.

Pem digested these thoughts before he spoke. "So, you're asking me to be a spy for the temple."

"I know that you are devoted to your brother. If he left with Drok, would you go with him in order to look out for him?"

"Yes, I probably would. But it would be hard for me, because this violence is wrong."

Loka said quietly, "I know it is, Pem. I've been watching you for some time. And, Jorin is a friend of mine. He's talked with me about both you boys. That's why I wanted to know your thoughts. You could watch out for your brother and be of service to the city of Tula by letting us know Drok's plans."

"How would I be able to get word to you?" Pem asked.

"There is a temple boy who is highly trusted. He would take whatever information you obtain back to us. Then he would try to catch up with you again. He could go back and forth, depending on how far away Drok plans to travel."

"So, you have this very well planned. What if I say no?" Pem asked.

"You want a way to help your mother. We would make sure your mother has all she needs to live comfortably and raise your younger brothers and sisters. Jorin told us what a difficult time it has been for your family since your father was killed. Think of this as a way to help your family."

Pem thought through all this, realizing that the support of the temple could help, but also could hurt his mother and younger siblings. The arm of the temple had a long reach. Soldiers could bring supplies, but they could also take away what meager foodstuffs his mother had hidden away. He thought about his father, wondering what he would have done if presented with such a difficult choice. He realized what his father would have done—whatever it took to protect the family. Could he do any less?

"When might Drok be banished?" Pem asked.

"The temple council is waiting until harvest time before making any decisions. Even though the crops are thin this year, help will still be needed. All young men will be used to help with the harvest. If there is still reason after that time to think that Drok is a danger to the city, then he will be banished. In two moons time, we will know."

Pem asked, "Why me?"

"Jorin is a reliable source. If he says you would be good for this work, I believe him. I will contact you again in the future. Say nothing of this conversation to anyone."

With that, Loka slipped back into the shadowed streets, a ghostly outline against the adobe walls, moonlight on the path before him.

XVII

Kaiya stood at the doorway to test the air. It slapped her with a hard north wind and bone-chilling cold. Inhaling sharply, she shivered and stepped out into the swirling flakes coming down furiously. She watched for a moment as the pattern in the snow changed from falling straight down to a vertical slant to a tiny whirlwind blizzard. She wished she had gathered wood earlier as now it was piling up rapidly.

Stepping away from the house, she noticed how the northwest side of the trees had snow smacked against their bark like the wind had slapped her face. She wondered if the trees liked that cold, wet blanket. She stood still to watch the snow clump in the needles and decorate the branches. Chilled, she hurried off toward the stack of wood and retrieved as much as she could carry. Why, on that pleasant fall day, had she stacked the wood so far from the house? She knew not to stack it right next to the house, in case of fire, but this journey seemed much longer on a blustery day than in the sweet days of autumn.

She watched two young elk frolicking in the snow, and a bull elk waiting out the storm under a snow laden tree. Arriving back at the doorway, she stomped to shake the snow off before pushing aside the deerskin. Neatly stacking the wood near the fire, she prodded the embers and added some kindling, crouched, and warmed her hands over the small blaze. The firelight flickered over her face; she felt wonderful.

Sighing, she rose to return for another load when the deerskin was suddenly thrust aside. Startled, Kaiya jumped back against the wall.

It was Obaho, loaded down with twice as much wood as Kaiya could possibly carry. "Obaho, you scared me!" Kaiya said.

His eyes widened and his face sagged.

"I am sorry," he said. "I never want to scare you. I only want to help. My mother likes it when I bring her wood."

"Oh, Obaho, I am very, very grateful that you brought some. I never could have carried that much in one load. See this pile? This is a load I just brought in, the most I could carry at one time."

"I know. I watched you."

Kaiya stared at him for a moment.

"Obaho, do you follow me in the forest sometimes?" Kaiya asked.

Obaho looked down at his feet for a long time. "Yes," he finally said. "Is that a bad thing?"

Kaiya sighed. "No, Obaho, it's not a bad thing. But there's no reason for you to be creeping around watching me. If you need something, just ask me."

Obaho took a deep breath. "I want you to be my wife," he mumbled.

"What?" Kaiya shouted.

Obaho looked up, shaken by her outburst. "Does that mean yes?" he asked.

"No!" Lowering her voice, she continued. "I mean, no, Obaho, I can't be your wife or anyone else's. I am meant to be a healer, and I can't be with any man for a very long time, until I have completed all of my training."

"Oh," Obaho said. "I can wait."

With that he dropped the wood on the floor by the door and shuffled back out into the storm. Kaiya slumped to the floor, holding her face in her hands, groaning. Pushing herself off the floor, she stepped to the doorway, tying the deerskin closed. Turning, she tripped over some of the logs Obaho had just deposited. Catching herself with her hands, she sprawled over the wood, both laughing and crying. She finally roused herself and stacked the wood near the fire.

Shaking her head, she vowed to herself to be more observant when she was alone in the forest. Obaho was harmless, but if he was sneaking around watching her without her knowledge, it would be possible for others to also do so.

She was grateful that springtime would take her away from here on the journey with Moochkla and Bertok. She felt too many men of the clan pressing in on her. As a visitor in other villages, she hoped to just be Kaiya the apprentice healer, not Kaiya that everyone knew was unmarried.

Outside the wind moaned like a wounded elk.

XVIII

Cumani called the temple council together after Drok's full moon ceremony. An undercurrent of tension had existed in the temple since Summer Solstice, with some younger priests excited about the introduction of consuming the flesh of the sacrifice and other officials not. But this Harvest Moon ceremony had alienated many.

The conch shell called the long procession of priests to file into the chamber in the pyramid. The walls were dark grey, the benches lining the wall made of limestone, cool to the touch.

Cumani began, "Please, your attention." Cumani waited for the talking to cease. "We are here to determine the fate of the young priest named Drok. I allowed him to restore the worship of Tezcatlipoca, and permitted the renovation of that temple. And yes, I am the one who received the message from the gods that sacrifices were needed to bring back the rains. Drok was my assistant in those ceremonies, and he included it in his ceremonies. I am responsible for some of his actions, but he took events much further than my vision. I never advocated multiple sacrifices, and I certainly never thought about eating the victims. What we all saw two nights ago violated our religion."

The room was silent as everyone present recalled that horrific sight. Not only had Drok performed the ceremony of sacrifices, but he then flayed the skin off a victim and threw the skin over his shoulders like a cape, dancing wildly along the edge of the platform, skin from the victim's arms knotted under his neck to hold the garment while he danced. This time the crowd below the temple remained silent, too shocked by what they were witnessing.

Cumani continued, "Drok has many supporters. As soon as the harvest is in, we need to make a decision whether to ban him from Tula. Some men will follow him. I have a feeling that he may have lost some followers by doing—what did he call it? The Xipe Totec ritual?"

Many heads nodded solemnly in agreement. One older priest slowly stood and flattened the back of his hand against his shoulder, a request to speak. Cumani nodded curtly in his direction.

"I say we cast our votes now, and not wait for the end of the harvest." The old priest slowly returned to a sitting position on the bench with his back against the stone wall of the temple chamber.

Many heads around the room nodded in agreement. Cumani glanced at Loka, who stood in a corner shadowed in darkness. Loka dipped his head slightly forward in consent.

Walking to the platform at one end of the chamber, Cumani climbed up and turned toward the priests. "This is a serious vote," Cumani said. "Never in my lifetime has a priest been cast out. Long, long ago in the past it was done, but never before have our people had to endure conditions of such drought and famine for so long. At first I thought Drok was trying to help. Now I'm not sure."

There was an uncomfortable silence, and much shuffling and shifting, as most priests thought of the close relationship that existed between Cumani and Drok. Many held the position that things would not have progressed this far if Cumani had been more strict with Drok from the beginning.

"If you believe that our city would benefit from the removal of Drok the priest, stand forward now," Cumani said.

There was a pause as all in the chamber collectively held their breath. Some looked pinched from the stress of this weighty decision. Others had a defiant set to their chins as they waited to see how others would vote.

Standing slowly, the old priest hobbled forward. He stood alone. Then, one by one, every priest in the chamber stood to join him. Cumani's heart sank as he realized Drok had no support among the council. He had hoped that something could be done to change the direction that Drok was heading and still keep him working in the temple. But now he could see it was not to be. He looked at the corner where Loka had stood and saw that it was empty. Loka had vanished upon witnessing the result of the vote.

"It is decided," Cumani said. "Drok will be banished from Tula. He will leave here in two days hence." With that, Cumani left the chamber, hunched over, defeated, his staff members scurrying along behind.

Loka walked the streets in the early evening, looking for Drok. He stepped quickly along the adobe walls, glancing each way every time he came to a cross street. Finally, he found him in the plaza with a group of young men, going over plans for his next ceremony. Looming over the circle, Loka's presence cut off the voices one by one until only Drok was speaking. Glancing up, Drok's eyes opened wide to see Loka standing there.

"I need to speak with you," Loka said quietly.

Drok nodded and strode away from the group to the corner of the street. Loka's long strides enabled him to arrive at the corner at the same time as Drok.

"What do you want?" Drok demanded, an edge of irritation to his voice. He leaned his back against the adobe wall with a cocky air, arms folded across his chest.

Loka stood as if at attention in front of him. "I am here to inform you what the temple council decided."

"About what?"

"About your future here."

Drok's heart pounded. He had felt uneasy and worried ever since the Xipe Totec ritual. After the Summer Solstice ceremony, he had gone out into the jungle, alone, to commune with the gods.

Swallowing the sacred peyote, he first had to endure the nausea and vomiting. After that, he had a vision about a ritual called Xipe Totec. This was a departure from the usual ceremonial practices, but it seemed clear to him that it was what the gods wanted him to do. Excited, he performed it at the Harvest Full moon ceremony. Used to the rousing cheers from the crowd, he was stunned by the silence from below the temple. What had gone wrong? He felt sure that this was what the gods had told him to do. He had felt surges of power as he performed the ceremony, further convincing him that he was acting with the gods on his side. But since the Xipe Totec ritual, there was an undercurrent of discontent in the city, and Drok felt it was directed towards him.

"What do you mean?" Drok was finally able to ask Loka.

"It was decided that you have gone too far. The Toltec religion was not meant to be this bloodthirsty. You have taken us in a direction that the temple doesn't want to go. The council has decided to banish you from Tula."

"Banish? What do you mean, banish? I am a priest here! Where else would I go? Things are hard enough here! I am trying to help save the city, and should be appreciated for that, not cast out!" Drok shouted.

"Drok, I have served you as I have served many priests over the years. I am doing you a favor by letting you know this before you are officially informed. I'm giving you a chance to think things through, make plans, get supplies, and maybe talk some of your followers into going with you."

Glaring at Loka, Drok spat out, "You could better serve me by changing the minds of the council."

Without all his priestly garb or an audience to impress, Drok's scarred face crumpled into the face of the young man that he was. He paced back and forth between Loka and the corner, waving his hands and ranting. Loka let him burn off some of the anger, then reached out to grasp Drok's shoulder. Drok turned in a fury and shrugged Loka's hand away.

Loka spoke low and vehemently. "I have helped you all along the way, and I was willing to offer more help. But not now. You are on your own."

Watching Loka's back disappear down the street, Drok suddenly felt a lurch in his stomach. Loka had always been there, quiet but with good advice. Who would be his advocate now? What would become of him?

At dawn two days later, Drok stood on the platform of the pyramid for the last time. He had only his personal possessions and a small pack with a blanket, weapons and some meager foodstuffs. His dangling earring sparkled in the rising sun. He bid farewell to the city of Tula in a solemn, low voice, so unlike his ceremonial priestly persona. Instead of disappearing into the antechamber at the top of the pyramid, he marched down the front steps into the crowd below. The crowd parted, creating a wide swath for him. Alongside, soldiers from the temple marched, forming a barrier to make sure Drok could not turn back towards the temple.

A tired looking woman tried to thrust a bundle of food into his arms. He started to push her away, but upon a closer look, realized it was his mother. He took the bundle, but rebuffed her attempts to embrace him. Behind him he heard her start to wail. He walked faster, realizing his own eyes were tearing up. Keeping his head high, he wove his way through the streets, hurrying to leave the city as quickly as possible. Lost in his own thoughts, he reached the edge of the city and turned around for one last look, satisfied to see a large group of young men following closely behind him. His devoted supporters had formed an army to accompany him. As he exited the city walls, the group stayed with him. Drok picked up his pace, lifted his head high, and let out a howl. It was answered by his ragtag army of followers. Drok's grin further distorted his disfigured face. He had won a small victory over the temple.

Loka stood in a partially closed doorway, watching the procession leave Tula. He looked through the faces of the young men, many with dangling earrings, as they passed his doorway. He saw Pobal, and not far behind was Pem. Stepping forward, Loka motioned with his hand until he caught Pem's eye. Both men nodded at each other, a look of understanding passing between them.

Betatakin

XIX

It was snowing lightly as Kaiya, Moochkla and Bertok left their canyon. Grey, heavy winter clouds, scudding across the treetops, obscured their view of the mountain. They slipped away just before dawn, having made their preparations and said their goodbyes the night before. An almost full moon, Morning Star in the dawn sky and an elk heralded the beginning of their journey. Moochkla assured them that they would be dropping quickly into warmer country.

Moochkla set a pace that surprised Kaiya. It wasn't a run, but it was a brisk walk, an easy enough pace for Kaiya, whose favorite method of movement was running. Bertok kept up effortlessly with his long, loping hunter's stride. Their quick breaths blew little clouds ahead of them into the frosty air. The closer they got to the mountain, the weather improved, until they were able to see Sacred Snow Mountain High Place. Kaiya had seen it all her life from her home. Clouds boiled over the top, inhaled by crevasses, then emerging on the other side.

"It's as if the mountain is breathing," Kaiya declared with wonder.

"Oh, yes," Moochkla responded. "Sacred Snow Mountain High Place is very much alive. It's where the Rainmaker lives, along with the Twins, Thunder and Lightning."

Kaiya shivered, remembering the violent storms she'd witnessed in the summers. The sounds had scared Tal when he was a kitten.

"See that red hill over there? It has been said that people saw fire and rocks thrown out of its top. Burning ashes filled the skies, and the winds blew it as far away as Homolovi. People say the hill belched and spewed for days. It must have been a fearsome spectacle," Moochkla mused.

They walked silently for a while, each imagining the unnatural glowing skies, their own breaths quickening.

"The one good thing people said was that ash was everywhere. Usually they had very little ash, just from their fires, to mix with their soil. The crops were very plentiful for years afterward. The extra food enabled people to be healthier, and women were able to have more children. Then, more crops had to be planted to feed the larger population. The ash dissipated with time, and the soil became depleted. Then the crops failed. People began to starve because there were just too many of them to feed. A least, they did not have the worries that we do about water. There was more rain and snow back then. We don't know why," Moochkla sighed. "Maybe we have displeased the Great Spirit somehow now."

The sky remained a sullen grey as they moved swiftly along. They would be spending their first night at Wupatki. There were many clan members there, so they knew they would be welcome.

Just before sunset, the clouds faded away. Their long day of walking and talking had brought them from the pinyon and juniper forest lands to the wide swath of grasslands. Looking backwards, Kaiya saw the moonlight cast over the snow-covered peaks of Sacred Snow Mountain High Place. With all the open space around her, the mountain seemed to loom larger. Ahead they could just make out the great stone houses of Wupatki. Kaiya was amazed at how these houses seemed to grow out of the open plain. She was so accustomed to being surrounded by trees or canyon walls that all this open space made it seem like she was in a different world.

Kaiya realized that Moochkla's house, although much smaller, looked like these great stone houses. Several levels high, log ladders were used to get from one level to another. Kaiya was familiar with ladders as there were hard to reach granaries at home which needed ladders, too.

As they approached the dwellings, the familiar chant welcoming the full moon could be heard rising into the chilly air. As they joined in the chorus, their footfalls matched the thumping of the big drum. They were invited to stay at the home of the master healer, an old friend of Moochkla's. The men spoke in low tones of the troubles among their people. Bertok went off to look for some fellow artisans.

Moochkla nodded his head in sympathy and understanding as Toor described the problems of his people. Waterholes that should still have winter snow melt were dry. Animals normally in the vicinity were nowhere to be found. Crops that should already be shoots of green were barely started because of the dry, dry soil. Kaiya listened for a while, and then wandered back outside to gaze at the moonlight on the mountain. The evening chill eventually drove most people inside. Reluctantly, Kaiya too turned to head back in. The men had finished their serious talk and were visiting as preparations were made for the three guests to stretch out their sleeping furs for the night.

The morning dawned cold and clear. Kaiya could see her breath as she dashed outside to relieve herself. She stood transfixed at the sight of Sacred Snow Mountain High Place, so familiar, yet so different from this viewpoint. Kaiya knew they had to leave early, so darted back inside to pack up her belongings. She carefully rolled up in her sleeping furs the extra tunic and sandals. These were made especially for her for this trip by the loving hands of Jumac. Kaiya wrapped everything in her carrying sling, which went over her head and one shoulder, then down her back, leaving her hands free for balance. Moochkla thanked his friend Toor heartily for the kind hospitality, as well as the extra deer jerky for the trail. The three of them fell back into their easy rhythm of trotting and talking.

"There is a good place to cross the river up here," Moochkla said. "After that, the river turns toward the place of the setting sun and falls way down to the bottom of a big canyon. Then it goes until it meets the Mother Canyon, Kuktota."

Kaiya was disappointed she would not get to see the Mother

Canyon on this trip. She had heard so much about the tremendous depth, the wide expanse, and the magnificent colors. As if sensing her discontent, Moochkla insisted, "Ah, but Kaiya, you WILL get to see Her someday, of that I am sure."

There was, in fact, plenty of water in the river. Kaiya had heard of the huge waterfall which ran every spring due to the snow melt from far away mountains. She was sad they weren't going to be traveling that way this time to see this waterfall. They stopped to refill their water bladders and drink from the river. It didn't even come up to her knees and was moving sluggishly. But Kaiya could tell by the big banks and the wide, deep cut channel that there were times when this river ran fast.

They camped near the river that night. The soft swish of the water lulled Kaiya to sleep.

Days passed with their steady rhythm of walking and talking. Moochkla always knew where to find water and the best places to camp. His knowledge of plants helped them supplement Bertok's finds from the hunt. Although Moochkla seemed perfectly at ease at home in their canyon, he seemed to relish this life on the trail as well. Some of the tension and unease he had been carrying sloughed off with the long days of walking and the constantly changing scenery. Bertok enjoyed disappearing for a while, returning to brandish a rabbit or prairie dog to provide their evening meal.

They entered a land of abrupt cliffs with high, flat lands on top. They headed down a trail and swung suddenly to the right, where Kaiya was surprised to find they were at the front of an overhanging cave that was also a dwelling. Betatakin was a beautiful cliff house, nestled so cleverly into the recesses of a canyon wall that only the locals could find it.

Moochkla again sought out an old healer friend and was welcomed into his rooms. Kaiya was immediately joined by two young girls. Giggling, they each took Kaiya's hands and guided her back down to the base of the dwelling. There were words in each language similar enough to make themselves understood. The girls tripped over each others' sentences in their eagerness to question

Kaiya.

"How far have you come?" demanded the younger of the two.

"Who is the younger man?" asked the older, blushing slightly.

"Why are you traveling with these two men?" asked the first one.

Kaiya pantomimed the trip thus far, finding common words to help her tell the story. But—how to explain why Moochkla had brought her on this trip? She, herself, did not completely understand that.

The next day she was sad to leave this place, as it felt more like home than the wide open spaces they had crossed.

The next days were long and harder than the beginning days. There were steep ridges to climb. Sometimes they would surprise a herd of pronghorn antelope grazing. Always there seemed to be interesting rock spires and highlands along the way. Juniper trees would appear on the horizon, tiny specks in the distance, gradually become larger, and then shrink to minuteness behind them. They crossed a big river, the biggest and swiftest Kaiya had ever seen. They actually had to swim part of the way with their packs held high on their heads. Because of the great force of the river, they ended up quite a ways downstream from where they had entered. Sitting on the other side in the sun, they caught their breath and dried their clothes. Laughing, they were exhilarated by their swim, and in knowing that they weren't very far from the place where they could stay and rest for a few days—Hovenweep.

Kaiya was used to how people lived at her place, all packed together in the cliffs. The great houses at Wupatki with the wide, open sky all around had at first frightened, and then intrigued her. But nothing had prepared her for Hovenweep. This remote outpost attracted the artists and builders of the time. Great towers rose from the desert terrain as if sculpted by nature. Each building included scenery within its line of sight, a distant mountain peak here, a ridgeline there. The design always had an eye toward beauty and originality, some curving, some rectangular, some square. The buildings were constructed to play with the laws of balance. Some seemed to teeter on precarious boulders, others hidden down in canyons, or across great fissures in the rocks. Bertok, with his artist's eyes, admired the unique architecture all around him. Kaiya liked the familiar feel of the T-shaped doorways. Some buildings were like a maze with curved round walls, built with precision and care.

Moochkla led them to the home of the healer. While the two men talked, Kaiya stood outside listening to the sound of the wind whistling around the rock walls. She gazed off in the distance at the snowcapped peaks. The mountains picked up the slanted rays of the setting sun and glowed a shimmering pink. She could only tear herself away to go inside after all that vibrant color faded. Ducking through the doorway, she found the two old friends deep in conversation.

"What do you hear among your people?" asked Clee, the healer of Hovenweep.

"They are scared," replied Moochkla. "There has never been a time of so little rain in the long memory of our people. The Spirits seemed to have deserted us. We perform the kiva ceremony with the same devotion, presenting our offerings of corn meal, carefully ground by the clan's virgins for purity. No results. The animals are scarce, driven farther away from us in their own search for water. Springs which have always flowed freely now are mere dribbles. Clouds form in the sky but never bring us moisture. Even the winter snows are light and infrequent. We can feel the agony of the land crying out for water. The forests are dying because the bark beetles are eating the sap from the outside in. The only thing left for us to eat is corn, and not much of that. Corn was never meant to be the only thing for us to eat. Our bean and squash crops shrivel and die, crying out for moisture. Our people become desperate and leave their homes and villages looking for water and land which will support crops. Along the way they may encounter others who are desperate and looking for a place where they might survive. Some have met up with travelers from the South. That is what I fear most," Moochkla said with unaccustomed anger.

There was a long pause as Clee thought through all these points Moochkla had raised. Kaiya pondered, also. Why have the rains and snows stayed away? Just in her short lifetime she watched the moisture dry up and the land become parched. Could her people have anything to do with these massive changes in climate?

"What of these people from the South? What say they?" Clee queried.

"They are an evil, hurtful group," spat Moochkla. Kaiya's head jerked up in alarm. She had never heard her healer speak so heatedly in all her years of working and staying with him.

"What is it they do that infuriates you so, my gentle friend?" Clee prodded.

"They advocate violence. Not for a sacred purpose, like the killing of a deer to feed the tribe, or the killing of a bear which is about to attack a child. No, in their religion they kill people to appease their gods," finished Moochkla.

Kaiya watched Clee's face for his response. He was clearly shocked. He swallowed hard, and then in a low voice quietly asked, "How do they do this? Have you seen this done?"

"No, I have not seen this done for myself. But I have heard many different Kokopellis tell of these things being done in the land of the South. At first it was done sparingly and only for certain situations. But there was one man of their high priesthood who became increasingly enchanted with all the blood-letting. He created more and more reasons to call for these sacrifices. Many young men idolized him. He continually called for sacrifices, and even consumed part of the victim in front of the stunned crowds. Frightened, the other priests called a council and forced him to leave their city. But he had gained many admirers, other young men restless and anxious. This is the group which is headed north to spread their message of sacrifice to our people, and try to gain supporters."

Moochkla paused and took a deep breath. "His name is Drok and he will be at Chaco Canyon for Summer Solstice."

XX

All Drok could think to do was walk north along the river. Nothing had prepared him for the vastness of land beyond Tula, but the immediate problem of keeping his army together and under his control kept him occupied. Some small settlements were scattered to the north, but he had never been to any of them. Having spent his entire life in the confines of the walls of Tula, with only occasional forays around the perimeter and down to the river, he hadn't realized there was so much land beyond. What could he do to show his army that he was their leader and had everything under control? Nothing had prepared him for this role, but conserving food and keeping his group near the river was the best course of action for now.

When they stopped to camp for the night, he would take stock of exactly who was part of his army, and what resources he had. He would rekindle the fires of the men's wildness with some of the tricks he'd learned from his temple rites. One need was for scouts, those known to be fleet of foot. How about Ako? He would make a good scout, Drok mused, since he'd won so many races in Tula against the village of Tezontepec. And Bako was famous for catching rabbits when they eluded everyone else. Who was that man who handled his spear so well and drew the admiration of many? The rest of the troops would surge forward raiding villages. He would rile them up the way he had at the temple. Putting as much distance as possible now between his army and Tula was as important as providing food and water. He was certain an army of temple soldiers would be sent to kill him. He saw the eyes of the temple elite on him as he left, tensions taut in the air. He shuddered, recalling the palpable hatred shooting from many priests' eyes. The rustling of their robes as he passed by reminded him of the flapping wings of vultures. They were afraid of him. Most would have preferred him on the altar instead of letting him go.

Calling a halt to the march, he was grateful also to call a halt to his thinking. As the sun was slinking along the edge of the mountains, he wanted enough light to take a good look at his group. He noted Jamax from the temple, the loutish Pobal and his quiet brother Pem, among others. Drok gave a rousing speech of celebration.

"We are free, free of the old priests, free of the old laws of the temple. We, this army, now are a law unto ourselves. If we couldn't bring the rains to Tula, then we will march to a place where the rains exist. No longer welcome in our home city, we will find us a new home."

This brought shouts and cheers from his men. They would head north, eager to follow him.

Arriving early in the morning at Tezontepec, the men swarmed through the village. The frightened citizenry scattered, screaming, before the advancing army. Drok, his frustration and anger increased by the hard days of walking, grabbed the first young woman who ran by him. She fought, kicking wildly, her long, thick, black braid swung behind her like a rope. Twisting her arm behind her back, he yanked her other arm toward him, picked her up and threw her on the rock wall surrounding the well in the town center. She spat toward his face and kicked, trying to toss him off. He dragged her tunic over her face. Thrusting his loincloth aside, jaguar belt clattering to the ground, he entered her. His army howled and plundered the village.

Grabbing some baskets of cornmeal and a blanket, Pem retreated from the village into a small copse of trees where he could observe. He understood the need for supplies, but he couldn't stomach the violence. He turned away in disgust as Drok raped a second woman, always hiding the face. Where was his brother? He spied Pobal laden with bowls of beans and an armload of corn. Pobal approached Drok, who had finally pushed himself off his sobbing victim. Drok twisted to face Pobal and roughly knocked the pottery out of his hand, spilling valuable food. He indicated where Pobal was to put the food by jerking a finger toward the center of the village and stalked off.

Pobal couldn't believe Drok had thrown down the pottery. He stooped to finger the broken shards, beautiful in a crimson color with white bird designs, similar to their own. Pem saw Pobal shake his head, rise, and follow Drok back to the troops. Why did this evil man have such a hold over his brother? And why, Pem thought ruefully, had he promised his mother he would watch over his brother?

The plunder became routine, the days of marching endless. Drok continued to enthrall his men with rousing speeches. "Everyone of you will have a new home, and you will be rulers of fertile lands in a place of plentiful rain. No more being outcasts, we will be the elite, we will tell the city what to do!"

Between pilfered food and meager game, the army had enough to survive on and stay strong to continue marching north. Sitting by the fire in the evenings, Pobal loved to sit by Drok, to hear him speak and cheer him on loudly. Pem preferred to camp by himself, within sight of the main body of troops but with some space in between.

One night Pem lay awake, watching the slow sweep of stars across the blackened sky. He heard a soft rustling, and a footfall close to him. Reaching for his obsidian knife, he clutched it tightly to his side, his heart pounding. Someone crawled toward his blankets. He sat up abruptly, surprised when a strong arm shoved him back to the ground. A temple bracelet gleamed in the starlight right above Pem's nose.

"Pem," a soft voice said. "It is Jeetba, from the temple. Be still. Loka sent me."

Pem thought hard—who was Jeetba? Loka had told him a temple boy would find him, but Loka never mentioned the boy's name. Then he remembered. Jeetba was Jamax's younger brother, an odd boy, a loner, able to melt into crowds. He spent most of his time alone in the jungle, only resurfacing occasionally to gather supplies, then he would disappear again. It was said his tracking skills were unrivaled. The temple used him to find people who owed money. Tracking an army leaving this swath of destruction in its path would be a simple enough task for someone with the skills of Jeetba.

"It is good you camp a ways off from the main group. Continue to do this so it will be easy for me to find you."

Jeetba removed his arm from Pem's chest so he could sit up again. Quietly the two exchanged information.

Pem said, "Drok plans to continue north. He talks to the Kokopellis he meets along the way. He treats them well, so from them he has learned that to the northwest lies a great canyon too hard to cross. He will stay east of that, following a series of small rivers. Eventually there will be a meeting of two great rivers. Drok will follow the one that goes north. He has heard of a large gathering for Summer Solstice at a place where the people of the North meet. He wants to observe their strength and see if he should join forces with them or try to take over their cities. Now tell me, what is going on in Tula?"

Jeetba, in exchange, said, "There are still bad feelings in the city. People are suspicious of the temple. Soldiers have stepped up patrols within the city. The people are afraid to talk at all, because some people were taken away for talking bad about the priests. Those people never returned to their homes. Even with many of the violent young men gone with Drok, the temple continues its ceremonies of sacrifice. Still, the skies there remain blue and cloudless. The people and the land still cry out for rain. I will come again when I can." Jeetba crawled backwards away from the camp and became part of the black night.

Pem lay awake thinking until a soft light ruffled the clouds in the eastern sky. Why do I stay? Because I love my mother and want to honor my promise to her?

By now he realized he didn't even care about his brother anymore. Pobal had just changed too much. His brother was enthralled with his worship of Drok. Pem was afraid of the influence of the temple, slightly in fear of Loka and what it could all mean for his family.

Should he continue on with this gang of outlaws? For how long and how far? Something was drawing him north with this army, he could feel it, something personal. He couldn't identify it, except that its pull was strong, something he couldn't name. For now, he would stay.

XXI

Entering at dusk, Kaiya just couldn't get a feel for the size of this settlement. She felt it was big—bigger than any place they had visited along their way. This was a spirit center; her body tingled at the power and presence of the Creator. The feeling was in the red dirt, the stately cottonwood and pine trees, and the surrounding hills nearby. Even the yuccas stood straight and tall, sentinels to all who entered this holy space. The people they passed on the broad trail leading to this place were subdued, heads bowed, no eye contact made. These were the keepers of the Great Kiva, the holders of sacred power for all of their world.

Moochkla spoke quietly to the guardians of the Great Kiva. A ceremony was just beginning, and Moochkla wanted Kaiya and Bertok to experience the energy of this place. One of the guardians disappeared down a ladder, returning shortly just far enough for his head to show and his hand to beckon toward Moochkla.

"Good to have friends underground," muttered Bertok. Moochkla shot him a dark look and shook his head. This place was sacred.

Descending one rung at a time, Kaiya smelled sage and breathed deeply, appreciating the familiar aroma. Hearing soft chanting, she tried to place the tune, but could not. When her foot touched the dirt at the bottom, she released her hands and turned around and gasped at what she saw before her. It was an enormous room, the biggest circle she had ever seen. Huge pine logs held up the ceiling, which had smaller logs and twigs criss-crossing the roof expanse.

Around the wall of the circle were benches filled with people of all ages from many different clans. Kaiya saw hair braided with feathers, beautiful, tightly woven blankets wrapped around one or sometimes two persons. One elderly woman had brightly colored turquoise beads strung around her neck and wrist.

In the center of this cavernous room was a fire pit, which was filled with a fire fed often by several children. A man of Moochkla's age with long, grey hair walked around the exterior of the circle, smudging the participants with a sage wand. The three travelers crowded together to sit in a small, unoccupied section of bench. Torch lights were strategically placed along the walls, flickering brightly, each with an attendant close by. The ladder opening banged closed, causing Kaiya to jump. There was sudden darkness as the torches were extinguished, the only light the glowing fire.

The chanting had stopped with the bang. A drummer began a loud heartbeat rhythm, pulsing, insistent. The chamber echoed with deep, low notes of the bass drum, until Kaiya could feel it entering her own body's rhythms. She closed her eyes and swayed with the crowd, the chanting beginning again. Sitting in this warm room between the two men she trusted completely allowed her to sink deep into the roots of her being. She felt One with the Creator, with all of Creation. She knew her place in the world among the plants, the animals, the rivers, the canyons and the mountains. The crowd ceased chanting, but the music carried on, sung by one man and one woman, timeless twining of their voices, low and high, plaintive and wailing. Kaiya felt her Spirit rise up to the rafters of this Great Kiva, separate from her body, yet still attached by a cord of life. All the lost love from her dead parents flowed back into her, starting at the tip of her head and swirling down to her toes. She felt complete, whole and loved. Slowly, she felt Moochkla and Bertok moving on either side of her and realized the chanting and drumming had stopped, although it still hummed inside of her. The torch lights along the walls had been relit, and people were talking quietly, greeting friends with hugs. People moved slowly, as if waking from a dream. Some shuffled up the ladder and disappeared into the night. Kaiya felt ethereal hands gently pull her Spirit along the cord of life back into her body. She came back to her place on the bench in the Kiva.

"Kaiya, are you all right?" asked Moochkla, concern on his face. "I never had a chance to tell you much about this place because it was so windy while we were walking to get here. And, when we arrived and I realized a ceremony was about to take place, I felt it was more important to get you inside. This is one of our most sacred sites. The power of Spirit is strong here."

"I know, I could feel it," Kaiya said slowly. "I could look down from up there," she said, gesturing up to the ceiling with her bottom lip, "and see what was going on down here. It felt very strange, floating in the air as if I were floating on the water in the creek."

Moochkla regarded her thoughtfully. He had never had an out-of-body experience, but had heard other healers talk about this. "Did you get any messages from Spirit?" he asked.

"Not a message, exactly, but feelings. Feelings of love and of belonging to everything."

"Well, that is certainly true, Kaiya. We are one with all on Earth, which is why we all suffer now, because we are out of balance. Koyanisqatsi. I hope our Summer Solstice ceremony can restore balance, bring back the rains, make the crops grow, and bring back our food animals. And," he added, "help us get along with others."

The three travelers were given their own room, on the third level, requiring two ladder climbs. Several hundred people lived in this place, as well as the many people who came for spiritual rites. Other than the Great Kiva, there were many more small kivas, where different ceremonies were performed, ceremonies to heal the sick, clear troubled minds, give thanks or help make weighty decisions. But during these days of drought and hardship, many came to find answers to hard questions, questions with no answers.

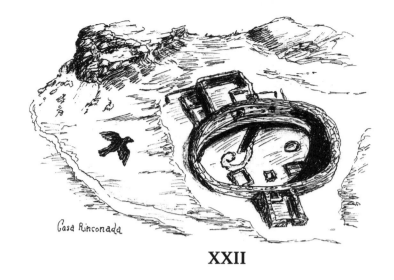

Casa Rinconada

XXII

As Moochkla, Bertok and Kaiya approached Chaco Canyon, Kaiya felt the power of the place rise around her, pressing against her body. The towering canyon walls seemed to be part of the city, enlarging rather than dwarfing the huge buildings. Some structures were five levels tall, surrounded by multiple kivas. Seen from their approach, the city looked like a fortress, with a long, straight wall guarding the openings, then curving around behind the buildings in an enormous half circle.

As they arrived in the outlying village, a whirlwind spirit gathered up a piece of cloth, swirling it higher and higher. It looked alive, dipping from side to side, finally coming to rest on the side of a cliff high above. Cries of dismay arose from the group whose cloth had been snatched. A nimble boy scaled the cliff and retrieved the cloth. He wrapped it around his body to allow his hands to be free for the treacherous descent. Kaiya shuddered, remembering from her own experiences in her canyon how much easier it was to charge up a steep slope than to come back down. She felt the restless wind contained many spirits, adding to the tension she felt in this place.

In all their travels, Kaiya had never seen this many people gathered in one place. Dazzled by the staggering variety of clothing, hairstyles and jewelry displayed by the crowd, she wished she could just sit down in the midst of all the commotion and take it all in. There went a man carrying a load of animal skins she had never seen, tawny with black splotches. A young woman carried a basket of shells. Kaiya had seen shells from Kokopelli, but these were as big as her head, curling inward, with the insides as pink as a dog's tongue. People walked by with hair gathered in a bunch knot on top, then spilling down their backs. Some women had braided their hair, then looped the braids back up and pinned them on top of their heads, creating huge ear circles.

But Moochkla picked up his brisk pace and was fairly dragging them through the crowd. He twisted and turned his way through the throng, finally ducking into a doorway leading to a small chamber. A man looked up, startled by their sudden appearance, his face immediately breaking into a grin as he recognized who had entered.

"Moochkla!" he exclaimed, striding forward to embrace the old healer.

He was a short, stocky man with dark skin. His nose was his most arresting feature, long, with a curved tip and bulbous nostrils. He definitely was not one of Kaiya's people and looked nothing like anyone she had ever seen before. As he chatted excitedly with Moochkla, Kaiya heard a cadence which had overlays of another language. Moochkla squatted listening to the animated man, nodding and occasionally offering a word or two. Kaiya wanted to slip back out onto the streets and watch the intriguing people. Finally Moochkla put up his hand to the man to stop the outpouring, and motioned Kaiya to come to him. The man greeted Kaiya by bowing low.

"Rowdu, this is Kaiya, my adopted daughter and apprentice to all I know. Kaiya, this is Rowdu. This is Bertok, uncle to Kaiya, great hunter and artist of our clan. Rowdu is from Tula, a city far to the south."

Kaiya bowed her head in acknowledgement. Rowdu glanced back to Moochkla.

"May I speak freely in front of them?" Rowdu asked.

"Oh, yes," Moochkla responded. "Kaiya and Bertok have traveled with me throughout many villages. They have heard much of what I have."

"I am an artist," Rowdu began, turning toward Kaiya and Bertok. "I look at a piece of stone, see what is hidden in it, and work away until I free the trapped image."

"As a young man, most of what I was told to carve were shapes, columns and sometimes animals. It was fun, and I felt proud of my work. But as time went on, I wondered what had become of the gods I had known as a youth. The artwork the priests required became ugly, bloody as they called for more and more sacrifices. I found other places to be on the days when the sacrifices took place. But one day, I was told to watch a ceremony so I could recreate a frieze of a priest ripping out the heart of the human victim. I went as I was told, but was so repulsed by what I saw that I packed the few belongings I had and prepared to leave."

"Leaving behind the man I loved was my sacrifice, but it wasn't safe for both of us to leave. So I slipped away. I headed north, and after a very long and hard journey, arrived at Moochkla's beautiful canyon, where I was met by his friendly and accepting people. I helped repair and build some of the dwellings there and gradually came to trust Moochkla and told him my whole story. Then I traveled with him here. They always need good stoneworkers here, and it was a much bigger place. I stayed, found another man to love and became respected for my work."

Rowdu continued, "But I never could forget about Tula. I started paying the Kokopellis for information and swore them to secrecy. Gradually I found out that Tula was torn apart by conflict. I was told about a young and vicious man who had twisted the minds of many who followed his belief in human sacrifice. Finally the priests threw him out. I have heard that he was heading north with an army. If he hears about the Solstice gathering here, he might come this way."

Rowdu had spoken all of this in a rush, hardly taking a breath. He now sat back on his heels and looked expectantly at Moochkla, Bertok and Kaiya.

Bertok was clearly agitated. "You love other men?" he managed to croak out.

Just then, a handsome man walked through the door and draped his arm across Rowdu's shoulders, and planted a kiss on Rowdu's head, before continuing into the inner chamber.

Bertok gaped in astonishment. "I thought I was the only one who had feelings like this. I thought there was something wrong with me."

Rowdu threw back his head and gave a hearty laugh. "There's nothing wrong with you that being with another man can't cure."

Moochkla patted Bertok's back. "See? There are other reasons I wanted you to come with us besides your hunting skills and charming company. You needed to see that although you may be the only one in our clan who feels this way, you are not the only one in the world who feels this way."

Bertok's eyes filled with tears.

Moochkla returned his attention to Rowdu, nodded, squatted on his heels, and spoke his mind.

"All that you say I have heard from other Kokopellis. We have no warriors here, nor do we have any throughout the Land of the People. Men and some women within each clan are skilled hunters, and sometimes defend their clan from intruders like the Toltecs. But we have no forces to repel a large army."

Rowdu responded, "I think it would be wise to gather up all strong men and women to keep watch over the city. If each had a weapon, and they learned to work together as a team to watch from all directions, at least we would be warned if the Toltecs were spotted. A few people with weapons could give the illusion that the city is prepared and ready to defend itself."

"Could you help to lead and train such a force?" Moochkla asked.

"If the shamans will it, I will do it", Rowdu said.

"Good. I will speak with them," Moochkla said. "Come with me, Kaiya and Bertok."

The three of them reentered the busy streets. There seemed to be even more people, dogs and flocks of turkeys than before. To a girl who on some days heard only the wind in the trees, this din was a new experience, incredible to Kaiya's ears. Voices everywhere shouted, laughed, scolded, chattered. Everyone seemed to be in a hurry, darting and bobbing in between people who had stopped to talk. The flow of people moved around clumps of talking friends like water flows around boulders in a stream. Children ran, lunged and weaved through the crowd.

Suddenly it all seemed too close, too ponderous. Kaiya wanted to be free of the tumult, high on a tableland looking down on all this. She felt assaulted by the unfamiliar smells of people and foods trapped between the buildings on the streets. Leaning against the wall while her heart pounded, she tried to catch her breath. Moochkla sensed her distress and turned back toward her.

"Where we are going is much quieter," he said. "It is a little ways out of the city up that hill." Moochkla pointed to the south of the main area, to a slight rise in the land and a small row of buildings. She nodded and peeled herself off the wall to follow Moochkla. Bertok said he would meet them back at Rowdu's later in the evening.

A short while later Kaiya and Moochkla were on top of the small hill. Kaiya looked back to the city which didn't seem as chaotic from this vantage point as when she was in its midst. They trudged almost to the top of the hill to a long series of small chambers.

"This is where the shamans live. They spend most of their time in the kivas so their homes are very small."

Moochkla led them down the long row and singled out one chamber to enter. The change from lightness to dark tricked Kaiya's eyes upon entering, and she thought the chamber was empty. Then she realized they were not alone. A woman sat cross-legged at the back of the chamber, her eyes closed, her face serene.

XXIII

How long ago had they left Tula, Drok wondered. He could just barely remember what it had been like to live in a city, let alone his former life as a high priest of the Toltec empire. Their lives on this march had turned into a dismal, predictable pattern. Food was always in short supply, water always hard to find, desperation and hardship their constant companions. Even Drok had wearied of the rape and carnage.

Then, several villages had banded together and come after them, inflicting the sting of slaughter upon the unsuspecting Toltecs. Taken by total surprise, nearly half of Drok's army had been killed, wounded or captured. The rest fled into some nearby foothills, stumbled upon a small spring, and holed up for a while, allowing the injured time to heal. Taking stock of their situation, Drok realized he had nothing left to offer these men. Not even leadership, he thought. He was used to the support of a city. He looked like a man beaten by the elements and time, much older than his age. His facial scars had become part of the weathered leather of his face.

Secure in their small ravine surrounded by high cliffs on the two wide sides, Drok posted guards at each narrow end to guarantee control of the precious water supply in this arid region. Next he sent out hunters; then he also left the safety of their hideaway. He was pretty sure they were close to a Kokopelli route and wanted to see if any were passing by.

He was lucky. After traversing a wide open space of harsh sunlight and little shade, he encountered a riparian area, lush with cattails and reeds along its banks, overhung with leafy willow limbs. Shedding his tattered loincloth, he slid into the cool wetness and startled two ducks, which shot out of the water with a flurry of beating wings and loud quacks. This, in turn, brought a shout and an explosion of splashes and sputters off to his right. Drok lunged toward the shore, and turned to see another naked man standing among the reeds. Lifting his hands palms up, he showed the stranger there was nothing to fear from him.

Grinning, the man sloshed back to shore and retrieved his loincloth. Drok did the same, then waited to see if the man would be willing to talk.

The man walked to a nearby cottonwood tree, reached around the base, and produced an enormous traveling pack. Now it was Drok's turn to grin, realizing he had indeed happened upon a traveling Kokopelli.

"Greetings," Drok said in his native tongue.

"Greetings," the man returned in the same language. "My name is Sess."

"You speak Toltec!" Drok exclaimed.

"Some. I have traveled there before, but not for a long time. Are you from there?"

Drok hesitated, fearful of how much he should reveal to this man who traveled widely and spoke with many people.

"I lived there long ago, when I was a boy. Now I travel north with a small band of men, looking for a place to settle where there is water and land to grow crops. Then we can send for our women and children." Drok lied.

Sess scrutinized this man. He was scrawny and weather beaten. He had a feeling this man was younger than he looked. The unkempt hair and lack of clothes seemed at odds with his story. He decided to play along for now.

"Up farther to the northeast is a place where the two great rivers meet. There are settlements on both sides of the big river, but if you stayed on this side of the smaller river, there would be places for you and your men to settle. How far away are your families?"

"Oh, not far," said Drok. Quickly trying to change the subject, he added, "Also, I have heard of a great gathering of people of the North for Summer Solstice. Do you know anything about that?

"Oh, yes! People come from all over to attend. I can show you how to get there."

The two men walked over to the sandy bank where Sess grabbed a stick and drew a map in the damp sand, which Drok committed to memory.

"Following the big river, you will come to another large river heading off to the northwest. Follow this, even when it turns smaller. Eventually you will come to the roads which lead you there."

The Kokopelli used the stick to show roads radiating out from the canyon, starting off narrow on this side, but getting wider and wider closer to the canyon.

"You can't miss it," he said. "And, I won't either. Most of us Kokopellis try to be there. Great trading opportunities." Sess grinned, and prepared to shoulder his pack. Drok stopped him with a hand on Sess's arm.

"These people, are they warriors?" Drok queried.

Sess turned his head, busying himself with fastening the straps of his pack as he thought about his answer. He was pretty sure he knew who this man was. The scarred face, approximate age and that haunted look would fit the Toltec priest who was cast out from Tula.

He had left with a sizable army, but from the look of things, had fallen on hard times. Sess decided to feign ignorance.

"They are a heavily fortified people, but welcoming to all who come for the Summer Solstice. There will be many, many people there, too many for one army to overtake. If you and your men approach lightly armed and in friendship, you will be welcomed and given food, water and shelter. You could talk with leaders of clans from all over, see if any of them need strong young men in their villages. Be sure to enter the city all cleaned up, though. They hold great stock in appearances."

With that, Sess waved a friendly goodbye and headed off on his route. Drok watched him go, realizing that his dreams of entering a city with a conquering army were shattered. I've become a beggar, he thought. What am I going to do now? I don't even know if we could raid anymore, maybe only by stealthy thievery. And, I'm a failure at living off the land.

Not for the first time, he wished that Loka was nearby to talk things over. But, that life was gone. He only wished he knew what lay ahead.

XXIV

Moochkla slid off his pack and let it land noiselessly on the ground against the wall, motioning for Kaiya to do the same. He leaned against his pack and rested. Kaiya followed his lead, sitting in the cool dark of the small shelter for a long time. Kaiya's eyelids fluttered against her cheeks. The long trek had caught up with her. She sleepily wondered what they were waiting for.

A woman's voice floated into Kaiya's consciousness, chanting coming from the back of the chamber. Kaiya's eyes snapped open to see that the singer was younger than Moochkla, but with that same quiet power. Her voice was sweet and clear, singing chants Kaiya thought she had heard before somewhere. Where, she wondered. The woman's eyes were still closed as her voice rose and fell with the cadence of the song. She held one long note, then spoke.

"Moochkla," she said, her eyes still closed. "Who do you bring to meet me?"

"She is the daughter of my heart, Kaiya, born to Saratong and Borhea. She is my apprentice."

"Come closer, my child," the woman said. Kaiya moved toward the back of the chamber and squatted before the woman. The woman's gnarled hand grazed her hair, then her cheek and chin. She said nothing but began again with the sweet chant. Kaiya's eyes closed as she reveled in the soft caress, like a mother's.

"I never knew your father, but I remember your mother as a little girl at my fire. You are much like her, but you have an older soul, and you can see the future in the eyes of others. It is a rare gift, and I know Moochkla has trained you well."

Kaiya realized with a start that the woman was blind. Her eyes showed a cloudy whiteness covering the place where the pupils should be. Kaiya knew there was no cure for this kind of blindness.

"Who are you?" whispered Kaiya.

"I am Kairee," she answered. Your mother named you partially after me. I am the sister of your grandmother, your mother's mother. That makes me your great aunt."

Kaiya reeled from this information. She thought she was alone in the world, none of her relatives left alive. She whirled around to Moochkla.

"Why didn't you tell me I had a great aunt?" She demanded.

"I didn't want to raise your hopes. I thought that if she was still among us, it would be a pleasant surprise for you. If she had returned to Spirit, there was no reason for you to know she had lived here."

Kaiya was breathing shallow, fast breaths. She stared at Moochkla a long time, struggling to gain her composure. Finally she knelt by Kairee.

"I am so happy to be with you, Great Aunt. We have so much to say to each other."

Kairee held out her arms, and Kaiya collapsed in her lap, sobbing. Moochkla eased out the door and left the two women. Kairee rocked the younger woman and chanted. When the sobs subsided, Kaiya sat up, bursting with questions.

"Did you ever live in our canyon?"

"Yes, when I was much, much younger I lived with your grandmother there. We had both lost our mates, and your grandmother was trying to raise Saratong alone. I helped out as much as I could, but the cloud blindness was getting worse and worse. I noticed as the Great Spirit closed off my sight, She opened my mind. I knew my own feelings, and could sense the feelings and thoughts of others. I realized I was becoming a seer."

She chuckled and shook her head. "No one believed me at first. No one except Moochkla. He came to rely on my second sight to help him with healing and to help the well-being of the clan. Our clan had no seer for a long, long time. Once people knew I had this gift, it was amazing how much more kind and thoughtful the clan members became towards one another. I was good for the clan." Again the low chuckle filled the shelter.

"Then a message came through a Kokopelli that the head seer here had died. I was summoned by the head shaman to come and help with the ceremonies. I didn't want to leave my familiar and comfortable home, but to live and work at this most magnificent place in all of our world sounded like a calling to me from the Great Spirit. So we took off, Moochkla on one side of me and Saratong, your grandmother, not your mother, on my other side. It was a long, hard walk for me, and for Moochkla and Saratong, too. Every step was a mystery, never knowing what my feet would find under me. My ankles were worn out from balancing on rocks and sliding down or stepping up unexpectedly."

Kaiya knew her grandmother had the same name as her mother. She vaguely remembered hearing where her own name had come from, but now to be sitting with the woman who shared a part of her name and her past moved her deeply.

"I tire easily, child, so go now, and we will talk more later."

Kaiya reluctantly rose to her feet, kissed her great aunt, and went back out into the fading sunlight. Moochkla was waiting for her just beyond the ridge.

Together in silence they watched the purple shadows throw themselves before the great red buttes across the canyon, then slowly creep up the crimson walls until they fell over the top. As the light faded slowly from the sky, Kaiya saw a whirlwind form where the boy had climbed to retrieve the cloth scrap. The sound it created slid down Kaiya's back and clawed at her nerves.

XXV

Twenty men.

It was all that was left of the great army which had marched away from Tula. Hardened by all they had done, and by the strong sun, these men looked weather-beaten and menacing. In the beginning, they followed Drok north because they believed in his message and power. After their first surge of triumph came the realization they had traded one miserable life for another. Now they followed him because they couldn't turn back. A swath of devastation of their own making lay behind them. They dared not show their faces in those villages again, and knew they could not return to Tula. They trudged ahead, each wondering what would become of them.

Pem was still a part of the troop, but had taken a stand against Drok. One night as they hid in the side canyon soon after the time the villagers retaliated, Pem stood by Drok near the fire.

"Drok, I tell you now that I will continue with you for my brother's sake. I do think your plan is a good one to head north to this Summer Solstice gathering, and see what those people are like. However, we are too close now to be attacking villages. When we arrive, they would have learned about us and what we'd been doing. They probably would kill us outright. So, I will travel with you, I will help with the hunting, but I will no longer attack villages."

Drok stared at Pem for a long while. He felt shaky, unsure of his abilities, unsure even of his goals. He wished for a second in command he could trust, someone who could help him make the tough decisions and plans. He looked around the fire circle, the men lounging nearby. They all seemed to be holding their breath, waiting to hear how Drok would respond.

Drok spoke softly, and from his heart. "My men, we have been through much together. We left Tula over one hundred strong. Some have died along the way, some deserted, and others were so injured they had to be left behind. This was not my vision when we left. We are now in a harsh, vast land that we don't know. We are too few to conquer new lands. I am ready to join with new people, and start a different life. Perhaps at this Summer Solstice, we can find work and get food and shelter. I am exhausted from running. We can recover and think of a new plan."

The men glanced at one another in astonishment. They had never heard Drok speak like this. No dramatic posturing, no ranting about their future as conquerors, but saying what many of them had already been thinking. They were all out of energy.

"Pem, I hear what you say, and you are probably right. We have done enough raiding. But, the prospects of hunting are very slim. This land is so much drier, drier even than Tula. The Kokopelli showed me the route, but we must leave the river to find the roads which guide us there. We should all hunt now, stockpiling as much food and water as we can carry. We will hunt for the next few days, and then resume our path northward. Anyone have other thoughts?"

The men around the fire were silent, shocked that Drok had asked their opinion. A few shook their heads no.

Pobal stood forward and declared, "Drok, I will follow you." Many nodded in agreement.

Drok breathed a sigh of relief. He still had some support, after all.

"To enter this city, the Kokopelli said we should present a good appearance. So, we need to clean the clothes we have and maybe make some new ones from the skins we get from our hunt. Let's look the best we can when we enter this new city."

XXVI

Several days had passed since the Toltecs had entered this new city. Curious to explore, they wandered and observed the massive amount of people assembling for the Summer Solstice.

"Stop!" Drok commanded.

"Why?" Pobal asked.

"There she is again!" Drok said.

"Who are you talking about?" Pobal asked.

"Over there, next to that old man," Drok said impatiently. "The other day in the marketplace, we bumped into each other. She and I turned at the same instant, and when she looked into my eyes, something happened. I felt my heart lurch and my stomach churn. She looked into my eyes for a really long time. As she turned away, I felt a sensation I can't explain. Like something passed between us. Then, she melted into the crowd. I was so shocked I couldn't react fast enough to follow her. And then I felt grief, like I had lost something valuable. I must find her."

Pobal cast a glance at Drok to see if he was serious. He was.

"Well, what do you want me to do about it?" Pobal asked.

"I want you to follow her and find out who she is. Then, find out where she goes, what she does, so that I can be in the same place."

"All right, I'll see what I can do." Pobal walked away, making sure he was far enough away from Drok before he shook his head and laughed. He didn't know who that woman was, but she certainly was not one of the peasant girls whom Drok dominated to get what he wanted.

The marketplace bustled with shoppers as Moochkla and Kaiya

approached.

"Over here is what we need," the old man called out.

"Oh, look at all these herbs! This one is almost as grey as our squirrels back home. Oh, look at this one! I've never seen anything like this before. Do you know what they are? We should learn about their uses and get as many as we can carry to bring back home with us," the young woman chattered excitedly.

"And, where is home?" the stranger asked, sidling up beside the old man and young woman. His face was disfigured, but that wasn't what caused Kaiya to recoil. It was from remembering the other day when she looked into his eyes after their accidental encounter. What she had seen swirled again through her head; images of blood, bludgeoning, a child kicked, violent attacks, chaos, a woman sobbing, something thrown. Destruction. This man had taken part in much destruction.

Moochkla had moved away from Kaiya to squat down near Drok so he could feel the texture of some herbs tied together in a bundle. He answered Drok's question, unaware of Kaiya's distress.

"Oh, we live many days travel to the west, by the big mountain before the Mother Canyon."

Kaiya reached over to clutch Moochkla's arm.

"So, you are here for the Summer Solstice ceremony?" asked Drok.

"Yes, we are," the old man said, moving protectively closer now to Kaiya, realizing something was amiss. "You appear to be from the South."

"Yes, I am. This is my first time here. Can you tell me where the best place is to watch the ceremonies?"

"We will stand over there," gestured the old man with his bottom lip.

"Have you been here before?" the stranger spoke directly to the young woman.

Kaiya turned away, picked up bundles of plants, pretending not to hear the question. Drok walked around to Kaiya's other side, making eye contact. To Kaiya's relief, the horrifying images she remembered did not reappear.

"I'm sorry, I'm busy choosing herbs. I can't concentrate and talk with you. I don't have time for idle chatter right now."

Drok was taken aback, but remained frozen in place staring at Kaiya. "I just want to get to know you," he said sullenly.

"Why? We have nothing in common. I am a healer, and you are a destroyer," she replied fiercely. "Just leave me alone."

"What have I done? What do you mean, I'm a destroyer?" demanded Drok angrily.

Moochkla stepped in between them, gently putting his hand against Drok's chest. "I think it would be best if you did as she asked," Moochkla said softly.

"And who are you, old man?" Drok snarled the words.

"My name is Moochkla. I am healer for my clan. Kaiya is my apprentice. It is important for her to learn her craft and she is busy now. She has no time for strangers."

Drok pushed Moochkla's hand away and glared at him. Then he turned back to Kaiya.

"I will see you later," he growled. It sounded like a threat.

XXVII

For the gathering, the plaza was transformed to a raucous market. People lingered and visited. They pushed forward to touch the softened deer hides and stroke the smooth, slightly oily beaver pelts. A baby reached up above his mother's head to grab a hanging gourd rattle.

Several days after their encounter with Drok, Kaiya and Moochkla pressed through the crowds, allowing scent to lead them to the herb center. Stopping, Kaiya breathed deeply, head back, eyes closed. The mixture of wild plants created a heady intoxicant for Kaiya's well-trained nose, causing her to almost swoon with delight. Clutching Moochkla's arm for balance, she inhaled long again. Mint predominated. Opening her eyes, she saw bushy arms of mint lying in heaps by her feet. Although she loved the aroma, it was a common plant at home, not worth carrying back. She picked up an unfamiliar sprig.

"What's this for?" she asked, waving the branch at a woman kneeling on a blanket. The woman's long hair was lined with strands of grey, occasional black streaks peeking out. A wind swirled down from the cliff walls, threatening to disperse the neat piles. Leaning forward, the old woman placed rocks on some of her piles of herbs in baskets before answering.

"That one has a strong flavor, good for stews. Dry it, store it, and it will last a long time. It helps us get through the winters while there are few green things to eat. It helps prevent the loosening of teeth. It comes from the South and the people there use it in many of their meals."

Kaiya liked its smell, pungent and strong, the leaf like a small hand with three feathery fingers.

"Here are the seeds," said the old woman. "I know you are a young healer." The woman lifted her leathery cheeks into a smile, handing Kaiya a small handful of seeds. Opening her pouch wide, Kaiya tucked them away carefully, smiling gratefully at the woman. Pinching off a leaf of mint, she sniffed, then popped it in her mouth.

Across the broad plaza, Drok watched her stroll around the circular walls of a large kiva. Kaiya stopped to admire the rockwork. How did they get the rocks to fit so perfectly, she wondered. She thought about the structures in her own canyon, the clunky rockwork, chinked with adobe and mortar, with only function in mind. No artistry. She traced her fingers along the stone wall; no place could even a baby finger slide between the rocks. Feeling a presence nearby, she looked behind her to see Drok standing by a ladder.

She shuddered and hurried across the plaza, heading for a familiar chamber. Drok moved swiftly to intercept her. "Hello," he said haltingly in her language.

Avoiding his eyes, she mumbled her reply. Anything but his eyes. What she had seen unfold on their first encounter was too powerful. The violence, the inhuman behavior, the indifference toward the pain of others, all went against every fiber of her being as a healer.

"I want to be with you," he said. "Will you come to my camp?"

His words in her language were awkward, but his meaning clear. Inching along the face of the building, she felt the smooth sun-warmed masonry pressing into her back as she tried to get to an open doorway just beyond her reach. Again, Drok moved to obstruct her way. Frustrated, she flounced back against the wall, crossed her arms over her chest, and glared at him.

She spat at him, "Stop stalking me like I'm an animal!" As the words left her mouth, a violent explosion of squawks and beating wings launched through the open chamber directly at Drok. He jumped back as a scarlet macaw came at him with claws and beak. Drok put up his arms and tried to ward off the angry bird. He cowered on the ground, covering his head with his arms. Finally, he heard a loud whistle, and felt the bird lift and fly away. Crouched there, catching his breath, he raised his head slightly to see where the creature had gone. To his astonishment, it had not gone far. It perched on Kaiya's shoulder, cooing, rubbing the side of its head against her cheek, and tugging gently on strands of her hair. She smiled smugly, reaching up to pet the bird's feathers.

"What, what, what was that all about?" he sputtered.

"This is Bato. When he was a very young bird, Kokopelli brought him up from the South. He was supposed to live here in this canyon, but had been injured by a hawk. Kokopelli knew how much I love animals, so he left this bird with me while he healed. We came to love each other very much, this sweet bird and I. He sensed that you were trying to hurt me and came to my rescue."

Drok picked himself up and dusted off his loincloth. "I wasn't trying to hurt you, I just want to be with you."

"Well, I'm not interested in being with anybody but Moochkla. I am training to be a healer, and all of my time is devoted to that. So please, for your own safety, leave me alone. I am well protected."

"I suppose you have one of those grizzly bears I've heard so much about trained as well," Drok retorted.

Kaiya smiled and laughed. "Oh, you'd be surprised." She entered the open chamber door with Bato still perched on her shoulder, and snapped down the blanket behind her.

Bertok walked through the busy city, not seeing much before him. He thought of Rowdu and his lover, how ordinary it seemed to them, two men who loved each other. All his life, since he was old enough to understand, he had only been attracted to men. Women were friends, nothing more. But he had been the only one in their small clan to feel that way. When he confided in his brother Borhea, Borhea sympathized, but encouraged his brother to try with a woman. His few attempts were humiliating. With his brother gone, he confided in Moochkla who also sympathized, but didn't suggest another woman. Instead he spent time with Bertok, becoming his trusted friend. When Kaiya was old enough to understand, Bertok was able to talk with her. Kaiya said she loved him just as he was. She once told him she didn't care if he was in love with Tal.

That memory brought a smile to his face as he walked through the city center. He noticed the group of Toltecs, one slightly apart from the others. They really did look different from his people. He found a place to sit where he could observe them, planning eventually to draw them. He picked up a twig and drew in the dirt for practice; lines, circles, the sketch of a head, then a body. Absorbed in his work, he slowly became aware of someone standing close to him. Glancing upwards, he saw one of the Toltec men looking at his work in the dirt.

"Very much like them," he said haltingly in Bertok's language.

Bertok laughed, erased the drawing with his foot, and began again. This time he drew the man standing next to him, blunt cut hair with a headband tying back the bangs and sides, loincloth covering his middle, wiry legs, bare feet. It really did look like him.

Pointing to the portrait in the dirt, then the man, he waited for a reply. The man squinted at the artwork, then threw back his head and laughed.

"Pem. I am Pem," he said.

Then Bertok pointed to himself and said "Bertok."

Bertok stood and extended his hand in greeting. Pem grasped his outstretched hand.

"I'm going hunting," Bertok said. Would you like to come along?"

"Let me get my things," said Pem. He walked back over to the group of Toltecs, talked with one of the men, picked up a small bundle, then returned to Bertok.

"Just letting my brother know where I'm going. Let's go."

XXVIII

She had to get away. She needed to be alone.

Kaiya walked toward the tableland to the north of the city. She so missed the quiet life in her canyon, the whoosh of the wind as it swept through the tall pines, the croaking ravens and the pounding of deer hooves on the dry pine needles. She also needed to get away from the constant threat of running into Drok; and so she began her climb up the steep cliff. The exertion of climbing felt good; lungs heaved, hands and feet searched for footholds and firmly fixed boulders. Reaching a small ledge, she paused momentarily to catch her breath. She could see most of the city from this vantage point. Smoke rose from fires in kivas and homes. Skinny ladders led people from one level to another. Crowds, turkeys and dogs congregated in the plazas. The sounds of laughter and barking dogs wafted up to her. She noticed a figure walking away from the city, looking very small from her high perch.

Resuming her climb, Kaiya zigged and zagged, finding the easiest route toward the top. She pulled herself over the final ocher boulder, and found herself on flat land. She sat admiring the city's architecture from this bird's eye view. Just amazing to see this big city spread out beneath her, so unlike her own small village tucked down in her canyon.

A small noise below made her jump. Flattening herself against the boulder, she peered over to see what caused the rocks to move. She saw someone climbing up the same route she had just traveled. It couldn't be. She pulled herself back, heart pounding. She risked another peek to be sure. Drok. Coming after her.

Standing swiftly, she tore away from the cliff face. But—where to go from here? Were there other ways down? If only she had chosen a more hidden route. Too late. Glancing behind her, she saw he had reached the top. She dashed away from him, but heard his footfalls swiftly approaching. Defiantly, she turned to face him.

"Finally," he panted, still catching his breath from the climb. "I have you. And we are alone."

"You don't have me now, and you never will," Kaiya retorted.

"I don't see any attacking macaws, old men or your uncle anywhere." Drok's disfigured grin slashed his menacing face.

"Where I come from, if a person says go away and leave me alone, the other person accepts and honors that."

"Where I come from," sneered Drok, "I give a command, and people follow it." He moved to stand right in front of Kaiya.

"Well, then go home," Kaiya said. "No one will listen to you here."

"You will listen to what I say!" yelled Drok. He grabbed her shoulder and tore her tunic as she whirled out of his grasp.

"Don't touch me! Leave me alone!" she shouted.

Drok dropped his hand and staggered backwards as if he had been struck. His mouth gaped, eyes huge. Unable to speak, he raised his arm to point at a boulder behind and above Kaiya. She heard a hiss, then a snarl. Whirling around, she saw a large animal crouched on the rock. The animal sprang into the air and landed by her. It was Tal. He remained at her side, hissing and growling, tail whipping the air. Although she hadn't petted him in ages, she reached for his head and stroked the side of his cheek as if she had just seen him yesterday. Tal turned toward her, and scraped his raspy tongue across the back of her hand. She raised her head to look at Drok. He stood still, stunned by the scene before him.

"No," he whispered hoarsely. "That can't be possible." He spoke in Toltec, but it needed no translation. Who was this woman? How did she have the power to control animals? And, how could he possess her and her powers? He stepped backwards, then turned and fled.

Kaiya collapsed in a heap. Tal circled her, sniffing. Satisfied that she was unharmed, he let out a small mewing sound, just like when he was a kitten. Then he bounded away, gone in three giant leaps.

The sky turned pink and slowly faded to grey before Kaiya was able to rouse herself and return to the city.

Drok raced down the cliff as fast as the steepness allowed, stabbed by fury and fear. How could that woman continue to get the best of him? He had never met anyone with such power. He thought back to his brutish father, the priestly elegance of Cumani, and Loka's solid power. None of them had the powers he felt from Kaiya. He wanted her for sex, and he wanted her for her powers. His breathing and heart slowed to normal when he reached flat ground, and he was able to think more clearly. Positioning himself in the shade of the city wall, he pondered what to do. He was used to dominating crowds, filling people with emotion, leading the multitudes. There would be an audience during the Summer Solstice ceremony. He could regain his former glory then.

Casa Rinconada

XXIX

The sun seemed to hang in the sky during this time, rising in the same place for a week. Ancient astronomers had long watched the movements of the Earth, determining over time exactly where the sun would strike first on this longest day of the year. But the drama of the sun striking those niches in the wall was the moment the people waited for to see harmony in their world; night follows day, spring follows winter. The shamans had prepared the statues for this spectacle; one male, one female, showing the balance reflected in the faces of the watching crowd.

In the pitch black, people made their way toward the Great Kiva. The best view was with their backs to the east, facing west. The multitude stood silent, waiting. First came the trill of flutes. Kokopellis appeared on the western side near the curved wall of the kiva, urging the sun to rise with their music. Drummers joined in, followed by chanting singers. A glow appeared in the east, pale and airy. It grew into a slightly pink softness, then flashed into orange. With increasing light, more musicians joined in. A rounded sliver of the top of the sun appeared, its heat instantly felt. The full heart of the sun shone brightly as it pulled itself from the grasp of the horizon. A square window alignment filled with the light, sun's rays shooting into a niche on the opposite wall, landing on the statue of the sun god. Slowly the sun's amazing alignment filled this niche perfectly, then moved to the next niche where the rain goddess statue awaited the glow. The musicians were now joined by a host of voices, for all watching were joined by the power of this moment.

Dancers emerged from the ladder of the kiva to greet and celebrate this longest day. The dancers adorned with the spirits of animals welcomed and blessed the sun as giver of life. The splendor of their dress represented their world in its beautiful entirety. Feathers of birds, antlers of deer and pronghorn, bighorn sheep skulls with their curved horns, skins of cougars, bears, coyotes and wolves danced on the roof of the Great Kiva. People in the crowd swayed with the music and stamped their feet with the dancers, singing and chanting, building a sound for the celebration of life.

Next came the dancers calling for rain. No feathers, skins or skulls here. Instead, black painted faces and white spikes of fur stuck out from their heads representing storm clouds. Each arm and leg was decorated with zigzag lines of lightning. Shells tied around each ankle rattled as they moved to the music's driving beat. The tempo picked up, the chant more insistent, calling for rain. The dancers leapt from the rooftop into the crowds, commanding the people to join in. Voices of thousands of people roared through the plaza, echoing off the cliffs.

Surely the Great Spirit would hear, would answer.

Kaiya closed her eyes, swaying with the crowd, feeling the power of the music course through her blood. Dancers pounded the ground around her. She felt their heat as they passed, heard their breathing. Memories flooded through her of home: herbal bundles dangling from the ceiling, Tal sleeping in the corner, the celebration of making pottery, all connected to the Great Spirit, the turning of the season to summer.

And in mid-summer, the rains must come for them to be able to survive.

As the morning continued to heat up, the music and dancing gradually came to an end. The crowd began to disperse. Suddenly a commotion erupted from the top of the Great Kiva, from where the dancers had emerged. A man had jumped up there. It was one of the Toltec men.

Drok had saved some pieces of regalia from his life as a Toltec priest. The arm cuff gleamed, the belt caught a beam of sunshine, shooting it back into the crowd. The unique earring dangled, touching the scars of his face. His loincloth was tattered, but he had somehow found an animal skin, and thrown it around his shoulders as if it was a Toltec robe. Invoking Tezcatlipoca, he implored his Toltec god to intercede on behalf of these people.

The crowd hushed, looking up at the roof. This was not part of the Solstice Ceremony. Drok told the assembled crowd that the rains would come only if they were willing to provide sacrifice. He regaled them with the Toltec tales of how first plants, then animals, then human virgins had been offered up to the gods. But the gods weren't satisfied. They had demanded more sacrifice. Human sacrifice. Shocked murmurs shot through the crowd.

"There are some among you who have great powers. We should put our powers together to bring the rains. Kaiya, where are you? You who has power over animals. Join with me and together we can save these people and this land."

Angry mutterings floated through the crowd. Many people knew of the beautiful young healer, her uncle and the well-respected old healer. People made way as Kaiya, Moochkla, Bertok and Pem pushed through the crowd. Kaiya stepped back, putting her hand to her mouth when she saw who it was who had called out to her.

"No," she whispered.

Kaiya strode angrily forward to the wall of the Great Kiva below Drok, and turned to address the crowd.

"This man," she said, pointing up to Drok on the roof, "is the priest cast out from Tula for being too vicious. He wasn't satisfied to follow the teachings of the head priest. Instead he added more gore to the ceremonies by eating the heart of the victims on the altar."

At this, a horrified gasp rose from the swelling crowd, people coming back towards the Great Kiva as they realized something more was happening.

Kaiya continued, "He hasn't changed since leaving his city. He has killed and raped many along the way in his journey. I have heard this told by many." She gave a brief glance toward Pem before going on.

"The Goddess has given me the ability to see events sometimes when I look into people's eyes. When I first encountered Drok in the marketplace, I was stunned by the destruction I saw in his eyes. This man is a destroyer."

Many in the crowd nodded their heads. The rumors of the abilities of this young healer had spread through the city's streets.

"I state now that I never want this man near me. Please aid me in this," Kaiya said emphatically.

With that, she stalked off. The crowd watched her go, then as one turned back to look at Drok, still on the roof. The faces in the crowd clouded over, became unfriendly faces. Drok shuddered, remembering his final walk through the city of Tula. This felt worse. None of these people had ever been under his sway. He jumped from the roof, disgusted, and stalked away in the opposite direction from Kaiya, shaking with fury. His face was contorted with evil.

XXX

"I've never seen Drok act this way before," said Pem. "But of course, he's never had a lasting relationship with any woman. For him, it's always been about possession."

Bertok and Pem had come to Rowdu's that evening to say goodbye. Moochkla had finally convinced Kaiya that it would be in their best interest to leave under the cover of darkness.

"I think that we've seen and heard enough about him to know that he will stop at nothing to get what he wants," Moochkla said. "Also, Kaiya saw some disturbing images when she looked in his eyes."

"I worry about you both," Bertok said. "We could hike with you part of the way if you want."

"No it's all right," Moochkla said. "We'll be fine. I'll have to do some of Kaiya's training on our walk home. I've been gone a long time, and need to get back to our clan. I miss our canyon."

"So do I," Kaiya said. "I never realized what a perfect life I had there. I was born to live in that place. I can't wait to get back."

"There are many beautiful places in the world," Moochkla quietly reminded her. "We have just seen many such places."

"I know," Kaiya said softly. "I am grateful to you for taking me with you. I have seen more new things than I did my entire life in our canyon, and I have a lifetime of memories to relive and think about."

"And, I too, am very grateful you made me come with you. It has changed my life. Pem has changed my life," Bertok said.

Pem smiled shyly, not understanding all of the conversation, but comprehending that Bertok's warm tone was directed towards him. A look of understanding passed between the two men.

"What will the two of you do now?" Moochkla asked.

"I'm taking Pem to see some of the buildings we saw on our journey. He's fascinated by the buildings here and wants to see the other stonework I've told him about. We'll see if we can find a place where we want to stay for a while," Bertok said.

"I will send messages to you through a Kokopelli," Kaiya said. Moving into her uncle's arms, she quietly said, "I'll miss you so much." A tear descended to her chin, and Bertok playfully licked it off. They both laughed, and held each other tighter. "I am so glad you found happiness," Kaiya whispered.

"You've always been my staunchest supporter, Kaiya."

Kaiya and Moochkla shouldered their packs and entered the warm and starry night.

Their long trek home was uneventful. Lingering at nearby Homolovi, they visited with relatives and rested before the last section of their journey. From there, they could see Sacred Snow Mountain High Place, shimmering ahead of them, beckoning. The mountain dominated the horizon, showing them their way home. They had come almost full circle on their sweeping journey.

Back home life eventually settled into a routine for Kaiya, once the novelty of sharing their stories from the trail had circulated through the clan. Several people had died in their absence, and the clan's situation was unrelieved as the drought stubbornly held on.

Kaiya was relieved to be free from the threatening presence of Drok. She reveled in hiking in her familiar forest, collecting herbs and firewood. She pinched herbs and sniffed them, then gathered the leaves for tea. She stood entranced by the crisp blue sky as a backdrop against the green pines. She realized how much she had missed trees on the journey. She waited until dusk changed the sky into swaths of violet in the west. A thumbnail sliver of a moon smiled down on her from just above the treetops. The moon, the trees, so commonplace, she thought. But I never realized how much I hold them dear.

A line of elk strolled by her, unafraid of this human being rooted in place like the trees.

Sess the Kokopelli strode quickly into the village. His pack was much lighter than usual, much to the disappointment of the people who saw he was carrying little to trade. Instead of his usual social self, he seemed upset, and demanded to know where Moochkla was. He didn't have far to look as Moochkla was right on the rim, talking with some children about the fading cliffrose plants. Sess swooped down on the group and scattered the children with promises of stories later.

"Catch your breath," said Moochkla. "You look like you ran all the way here."

"I practically did," Sess said. "We need somewhere to talk."

Moochkla looked around and saw no one nearby except Kaiya.

"We need to be away from her ears," Sess said.

"All right, let's go for a walk." Moochkla grinned. Sess groaned at the suggestion.

"All right then, let's just walk far enough until we are alone, and then you can find a good log to sit on and rest," Moochkla smiled.

When Sess was settled, he launched into his story. "After you and Kaiya left, Drok caused an uproar. He turned the place inside out looking for her. When he realized she was gone, he was furious. He ranted and heaved rocks, shouting what he was going to do to her when he found her. "How dare she shun me publicly," he screamed. He was beside himself. I took off. I'd had enough of the big city and needed to get back on the trail. I moved quickly, because I had a light pack. But when I neared Homolovi, in the distance I saw Drok and four of his men heading that way. Moochkla, he's stalking Kaiya. It will take him a while, but he will eventually find his way here. You've got to hide her somehow."

Moochkla rocked back on his heels. "Somehow, all along, I knew Drok would come after her. As soon as we got home, Kaiya spent many days alone in the forest, possibly just to give some space between us. But also, I knew she needed time to think over all the information I'd pounded into her, as well as what she had learned and seen on our trip. I've seen her just stand and stare at the deer or the forest, as if they seem changed to her somehow now." Moochkla stood, shaking his head. "And now, I have to ask her to make the biggest sacrifice of all and leave this place of her heart that she loves so deeply."

"Kaiya, you must prepare yourself to go now," Moochkla said sharply.

Kaiya huddled beside the fire, arms around her knees, rocking herself. Tears streamed down her checks.

"Moochkla, why is this happening to me? What have I done? I just want to stay here!" Sobs erupted, shoulders heaved.

Moochkla knelt before Kaiya on the dirt floor and gently grasped her shoulder. He took her chin in his hand, and lifted her face close to his.

"Look into my eyes," he commanded. "You must leave this place."

Through her tears she stared into his steady gaze. There, she saw the Toltec warriors. There was a fight. Someone fell. She realized she had observed this scene before, but in whose eyes? No time to recall. Events shifted. She was running, being pursued. Suddenly there was water everywhere. More running. Swimming across a big river. Panting, a hard climb. Pain. Terrible pain. Death. Was it hers? Blackness. Peace. Calm. Someone's face close to hers, a face filled with love. For her. The image in Moochkla's eyes shattered then faded. Kaiya fell backwards, stunned by all that had been revealed.

"Kaiya, Kaiya, come back, wake up!" Moochkla called.

She sat up, slowly returning to her world. "I see now," she said dully. "I have to go."

Moochkla and Kaiya held each other close, and both of them cried.

XXXI

Drok's fury, as fierce as the fiery sun, pushed him to move faster. Each day he pounded the dirt angrily, sending up puffs of sand with each footfall. He was accompanied by only four men: Pobal, Ako, Bako and Tova, all that was left of that Toltec army which followed him out of Tula. No matter. These men were warriors, and didn't complain about long days marching over rough terrain. Faster pace now, less stopping. He had a mission. Find Kaiya. All felt renewed from their time at the Summer Solstice. Their bodies were hardened from the privations this new life had thrust upon them.

Tracking was difficult in this rocky land. Sometimes they would catch a glimpse of a footprint and head in that direction. The old man had said they lived west, near a big mountain and canyon. So west they went, through endless fields of grass. There were low bushes, bristling with thorns, scratching the bare legs until blood oozed. Cactus plants poked menacingly at bare feet. Pronghorn startled up from hillocks and bounded away, frustratingly out of range of their spears. Rabbits were plentiful, so they didn't go hungry. But water was scarce.

Finally, far in the distance they could see trees, and knew water must be close by. Tova smelled it first. They ran into the river and fell face first, drinking their fill. Then Ako heard a dog barking, and realized there was a settlement nearby.

They approached the village in the shape of an arrow, with Drok at the point. Coming out from the village was a group of men wielding spears, stone blades, and rocks. Halting his group, Drok called out, using words he had learned at the Summer Solstice. One man answered back, "Go away!"

"I am looking for someone, a young woman healer," Drok yelled, and thinking to himself, a beautiful woman with fierce powers. "Is she here?"

"No. Get back."

"Do you know the way to the canyon where she lives?" yelled Drok.

Again, "No, we know nothing of any such woman."

Drok started walking closer to the men. Weapons clattered as the men stepped forward threateningly.

"Come on," Drok said to his men. "No use staying here."

They returned to the river to camp, drinking their fill again. Splashing in the water, Drok felt some of his pent up anger slough off. They were getting closer to his target, he thought. Any day now he would have her in his possession.

When the sun cracked open in the morning, it shone fully on a sharply defined mountain in the distance. That's it, thought Drok. "Just keep heading toward that mountain," he called to his men.

Days later, the terrain changed abruptly, rising, filled with small undulating hills. The vegetation changed, too. Grasslands faded away, replaced by scrubby trees and bushes. Tova discovered that under the small pine trees were sometimes oval, brown nuts which he could crack between his teeth, exposing a soft nut. "Mmmmm," he muttered appreciatively. "It tastes bitter, but rich. It'd probably taste better roasted."

The forest began sparsely, but thickened as the land rose.

Temperatures cooled slightly, and it was a relief to have some bigger trees for shade. Ako stopped to sniff the red colored bark, and found it had a smell sweet. Squirrels appeared, and Tova made great sport going after them with his spear. Bako caught a whiff of a campfire, and urged them to proceed cautiously. Other human signs began to appear; trails, snapped off tree limbs, and broken pottery shards, ocher with black lines. The Toltecs pushed closer together, creating a huddle, watching for any sign of people. Voices were heard, far off. Drok called a halt.

"Let's hide now and wait until dark," he said. "Then we can creep up and see the size of this encampment."

As twilight cast long tree shadows, the men crept closer. It was difficult to know where this village was. Voices were louder, but where were the buildings? This was nothing like the Summer Solstice gathering place. Bako went forward, and suddenly disappeared.

"Where did he go?" hissed Drok.

Bako's head reemerged. "Over here," he called softly.

The men edged closer toward Bako's voice. Then it became clear. They were on the edge of a canyon, and the village itself was down in the canyon. That's why they'd been hearing voices for a long time, but couldn't see anything. Now they saw campfires, people moving about, children running up and down the canyon walls.

She lives with that old man, thought Drok. But, how to find them? The men quietly inched their way along the rim closer to the big part of the canyon. Below them they could see an enormous island of rock. In places were occasional light torches along the rock wall.

Ako pointed. "Look. Many of the dwellings are around that huge rock, and also across from it. There are black holes that must be caves."

As they continued, they saw a main trail heading down toward the village, people carrying baskets full of foodstuffs, and pottery jars filled with water etched with black and white designs. If only he knew exactly where Kaiya lived, he'd grab her and take her. Drok let his mind go wild thinking of how he would have her, how badly he had wanted her at the Summer Solstice place, and how she had refused, even scorned him there for all to see. His eyes narrowed as he felt himself harden. His breathing grew ragged. He must have her.

"Drok, come this way," whispered Pobal. There is another part of the canyon over there. There are fewer people on that side. Maybe we can find someone alone and make them tell us where she lives."

They swung wide through the forest to avoid crossing the main trail. Cutting back toward the canyon, they saw another trail that led out of the canyon into the forest beyond. Although by now it was past sunset, the light of the almost full moon helped keep them on the path.

Ahead they could just make out a single rectangular dwelling in a clearing. Smoke drifted lazily from a hole in the roof. Someone must be home. A figure emerged from the doorway, grabbed something, and turned back inside. The light had been dim, but Drok's sharp eyes picked out the slightly hunched shoulders, the long grey braid down the back, and the worn tunic. Moochkla, the old man. Kaiya lived here.

Drok crept forward, dodging behind trees as he edged closer and closer. He paused, and melted into a giant pine tree as Moochkla reemerged. Drok was close enough to hear him talking to someone. Drok rushed in closer, and Moochkla spied his movement.

"Who's there?" Moochkla called.

In answer, Drok hurled his spear. At the precise moment it winged its way through the air, another person stepped out of the dwelling in front of Moochkla. The spear made contact, and the person made a sickening grunt and fell to the ground. Drok had missed his target and hit someone else. He ran forward, to make sure it wasn't Kaiya. Moochkla raised his eyes from the body in front of him and glared.

"Where is she?" demanded Drok.

Moochkla continued to stare at Drok with a furious face. "You have just killed an innocent man," he said.

"I have killed many. It's not Kaiya. Where is she, old man?"

Moochkla bent over the still body of Obaho. There was nothing he could do to save him. Blood poured out of the wound, and his breath was shallow. There was only a rapid, faint beating of his heart.

"She is gone," Moochkla said. "And you won't find her."

Drok stepped closer. "Tell me where she's gone."

In response, Moochkla threw back his head and began the death wail. Others down the canyon heard his howl, and responded in kind. People hurried on the path toward Moochkla's voice. Drok heard their footfalls and realized he'd better get out now.

"I'll find her, old man," he said with a sneer. He dashed off into the forest ahead of the first arrivals.

Moochkla stopped his chant. "I fear you will," he said.

XXXII

Usually, Kaiya noticed the beauty of her surroundings as she ran. But this time her pounding heart and labored breathing were not a result of her physical effort, but from the shock of Kokopelli's news. She was stunned that Drok's anger drove him to track her down. But she didn't doubt Kokopelli, as he had always been her friend. So northbound she ran, stopping only to catch her breath, sip her water from the bladder pouch, or take a bite of dried berries, looking back over her shoulder each time she stopped. She never saw anyone, but she felt exposed. She kept on the move.

Moochkla had warned her to stay away from the known settlements. "Leading the warriors there would only cause trouble for those villagers," he said. She longed to stop at those familiar places where she could pour out her troubles to sympathetic clanspeople. But she couldn't. Moochkla had gone over with her the routes to water. "But don't camp near it," he warned. "They will be looking for water, too."

She continued to run. She found a ledge with a small cave near the river, and tucked herself into it. With Moochkla's loving voice in her head, she fell asleep for a short while.

Restarting her hike along this river, Kaiya knew it would lead to the big river in the heart of Kuktotoa, the Mother Canyon. "Watch out for quicksand in the small river," Moochkla warned her. But the drought left only damp patches, no quicksand. The red clay in the riverbed was brittle, curling upwards, like pottery someone had forgotten to finish. Further along, cottonwood trees provided shade from the hot sun. Feeling too vulnerable on the ground, she climbed a few branches upwards, and rested in the crook of the tree. Wind whispered through the leaves, soothing Kaiya's frayed nerves.

She awoke with a start as her balance shifted and she felt only air beneath her. The sun's slanting rays told her it was getting late. Unwinding from her perch, she almost stepped on a snake as she jumped from the tree. It was a harmless one, more surprised than she, anxious to get out of the way of her tramping feet. It was the first living thing she had seen in several days.

Moochkla had told her about the narrows. "Watch for deer trails," he told her. "Follow them up above the places where it's too steep to stay along the river." It made the going longer, but it saved her from being trapped in any of the pools where there might still be quicksand. Rising above the river bed, she took shelter from the sun under a ledge. She felt safe in her little perch with the many birds swooping past her to chase insects.

Her reverie was shattered by the sound of distant voices. Looking way up to the rim, she was shocked to see silhouetted figures. How many? Five. "There will be five men," Kokopelli had told her. She watched the figures search for a way down the cliff face. They would find deer and bighorn sheep trails too, just as she had. She must go, hurry to safety on the north side of the Mother Canyon. Any joy she had felt at finally getting to see Kuktotoa vanished as she realized the danger.

Drok would soon be upon her.

XXXIII

Kaiya ran as fast as she could after she realized how closely she was being followed. Finally pausing to gasp for breath and collect her thoughts, Kaiya scanned the canyon. The way was strewn with boulders and ledges in between the splashing waters of the river. There was only one way through this canyon and that was to follow the river bottom. Anyone else passing this way would have to do the same. Leaping from stone to rock to hide her tracks, sometimes tugging herself up and over boulders then splashing down into pools, she ignored the scrapes and cuts which tore her legs.

Eventually she had to stop and get out of the blinding sun. A shaded ledge sheltered her as she gobbled some nuts and surveyed her surroundings. This part of the canyon held steep straight cliffs, red rocks etched with black streaks of desert varnish showing the way water had coursed down the walls. Only a few ledges were in sight. Behind her a bank of clouds built to the east. Blue skies were still overhead and she couldn't remember any rumblings of thunder. Her pounding fear had blotted out the sights and sounds around her.

Kaiya's breathing eventually returned to normal as she gathered her thoughts. She was sure she could stay ahead of the Toltec warriors. But the problem was it was obvious which way she was heading. She was leading them right into the heart of a quiet farming community unprepared to defend themselves.

Once she got out of the blue green waters and entered the Great Mother Canyon, she would have to be diligent in hiding her tracks. That way she could at least arrive at Unkar with enough time to give the people there warning to hide or flee.

Kaiya brushed herself off and clambered down from the ledge back into the riverbed. Overhead toward the east, grey clouds sank heavily into the canyon. Out of the corner of her eye she caught one streak of lightning touch both cloud and ground. She stopped to listen, but no rumble of thunder. Good. Too far away to be a danger for her here.

Then, without warning, those distant clouds crashed together and unleashed a monstrous deluge through sun scorched pathways to lower ground. The narrow canyon in which Kaiya ran was that path.

The only path.

Kaiya heard a rumble behind her. She whirled around and was stunned at the sight coming toward her. It was like a wall built by her people. But it was rolling toward her, waves undulating and spewing spray up high, tossing along boulders, branches and whole trees. She turned to run away, but the red, debris-filled wall of water caught her at breast level and carried her along like a twig.

The choppy water pushed her down to the river bottom and impaled her left leg into the stony bed. Then just as fast, she was propelled up and out of the water, gasping for air, only to find herself being hurtled along with crashing boulders and branches in the roiling water. Kaiya knew she would die if she couldn't get out of this.

Fighting against the raging current was futile. It kept her in the middle of the river. She positioned herself so that her head was upstream leaving her feet free to push away from the debris. The only thing she could do was ride this wild current until somehow she could get closer to the banks.

All the running and leaping had already exhausted her. Now, the suck of the current pulled her head below the water, then sent her up sputtering for air. Her head cracked into a boulder. There was spinning, spinning.... and darkness.

Then, face down, she clenched her fists around some matted grasses. She must be near the shore. She coughed and choked, retching up dirty water. Suddenly she was being pulled roughly by her tunic over a boulder that was still somehow planted firmly in the banks. Too worn out to even protest, she felt herself being yanked and dragged onto a ledge. She heard a snarl, and twisted her head. It was Tal standing above her, his mouth pulled back in a grimace. His fur was matted and glistening wet, bits of grass and tree bark clinging to his tawny sides. He hissed first, then softly called, licked Kaiya's face and was gone.

Kaiya had no idea how long she lay there face down on that ledge, too battered to move. She must have slept, because she woke to shadows of night starting to creep over the canyon. She pushed herself to a sitting position, and turned to look at the river below. No more rolling rocks.

Shaky and sore, with cuts, bumps and bruises all over her body, she grabbed a nearby stick to help her up. Then, using the stick, she measured the depth of the creek. It had subsided to knee level. The scene before her was one of devastation; logs now jammed between boulders, shredded pieces of bark floating by. Rocks tumbled in the still strong current, clicking and grinding together, fracturing into pieces. All vegetation was stripped bare away from what used to be the river bank; now just a tattered edge of crumbling dirt and rocks. This violent marauder had rolled right over the sparkling blue green waters and left chaos in its wake.

XXXIV

Kaiya paused, bent over with sobs and shaking, hands on her knees. When her sobs were spent, she rose and continued on. Tal had disappeared as magically as he had bounded into her crisis. She stumbled along beside the river, still a churning muddy red-brown slurry mixed with chunks of torn branches. A fawn floated by, its carcass bloated and its eyes wide open with terror. Kaiya shuddered, her own fear revived by what she saw reflected in the dead fawn's eyes. She scurried along faster, sometimes climbing up onto rock ledges to skirt places where the flood had ripped out the river bank. She had to stay out of the river for now, away from the inexorable crush of the current against her body. She watched a ground squirrel, caught in the suck of the current, far out of its element, frantically trying to swim to shore, seeing in its eyes her own confusion she had felt while caught in the flood. One last pleading look at her, then it disappeared over the swirl of a small waterfall and was gone.

The river channel widened, and she could see where it joined the Great Mother Canyon. She crossed the river, remembering what Moochkla had told her about the healer guardian who lived at the confluence of the two great waterways. "His name is Tapeats,"

Moochkla had said. "He's an old friend of mine. We grew up at each other's fires. He lives in a house just like ours, only smaller. Look for it on the left side."

She arrived at the dwelling just before dark. She saw a small fire glowing from within. She approached shouting, "I am Kaiya! Are you there, Tapeats?" A man's wizened head popped out of the doorway, mouth dropping open in surprise.

"You are Kaiya, Moochkla's apprentice? Come in then, come in." He stopped his welcoming and squinted hard against the oncoming dark. "What has happened to you?" Tapeats demanded.

Kaiya stopped in the doorway and glanced down to observe her appearance. Muddy red-brown clods clung in bits and pieces to her soaked deerskin tunic. Her hair was entangled with leaves and twigs. Finally she noticed that the front and sides of each leg had been scratched open by repeated bashings against the floor of the riverbed and the dragging of the current, rocks and pebbles grinding into her flesh. She sagged against the lintel and would have fallen but Tapeats grabbed her, helping her to the floor. He hummed and chanted under his breath as he gave Kaiya something to drink. She suspected it had something medicinal in it as she felt herself relax. Or perhaps it was the relief of safety and a familiar-looking house filled with herbs and a kindly face. She eased back on the clean dirt floor and smiled with contentment.

Tapeats bustled about, preparing poultices for her many wounds and applying them deftly. She felt as though she was out of her body watching him from the herb-hung ceiling as he worked on her many scrapes. Trying to comb through her tangled hair was beyond him, and she heard him sigh and give up. She smiled again, and didn't feel anything else until the downward whistling scales of a canyon wren announced the first light of dawn.

Kaiya opened her eyes and her body's soreness overwhelmed her, pain flooding over her with the effort just to sit up. Standing took a long time, her legs like a wobbly toddler's as she tried to get them to move. She hobbled from the house to find Tapeats. He was down at the mouth of the small river, fishing. She knew she couldn't walk that far just yet, so lowered herself down haltingly to await his return.

The day was perfect, nothing to indicate yesterday's mayhem. Deep blue skies overhead belied the monster storm clouds of the day before. Trembling all over again just thinking of her experience, she knew she had nearly died. Her thoughts then turned to the other death threat, that of the Toltecs. She had no time to lose. Getting to her feet was agonizing but necessary. She had to prepare her body to move on to Unkar.

After a time, Tapeats returned with several lines of fish.

"What are those fish?" Kaiya asked.

"They are bony, but good; chub," Tapeats replied. "I will cook them for us, and then you will tell me your story."

He skillfully filleted the fish with his cutting stone. He had hafted his stone onto a yucca stalk, and secured it with yucca fiber. That way he had a handle, and didn't have to risk cutting his hand with the stone. His small fire had been going all night, so he just added more wood for cooking and soon the smell of frying fish filled the air. Kaiya salivated. It had been a long time since she had eaten anything more than nuts and dried berries.

Over this good meal, Kaiya recounted to Tapeats all the events leading up to her flight.

"And the really scary thing is that I don't want to lead them to the farming community at Unkar. How can I get there without putting the village in danger?" Kaiya asked.

"There really is only one way to get there safely, and the Toltecs may not know that," Tapeats replied. "You must go up one rock layer above the river. There a trail winds in and around through the ravines. You will see it descend down the cliff to the holy salt caves, but you stay on the ledges above the river. It is quite a winding trail that will frustrate you as it goes back and forth and back and forth across that rock layer. You will get to a place where the great walls of the Mother Canyon fall away into the distance and the banks of the river flatten out. Watch for a place where the river is the lowest and you should be able to cross easily by walking or swimming. You may have to wait a while for the river to go down after yesterday's flood."

"No, I can't wait," Kaiya said. "I have to get there before the soldiers do. It's not even safe for you to be here. You need to find someplace to hide until you know they've gone by. They would think nothing about torturing you or making you lead them to Unkar."

"I have many places to hide. Don't you worry about me. But, I am worried about you. You are so stiff and sore. Let me put more salve on your scrapes and then you can try walking. I'll walk along with you to explain the rest of the directions." Tapeats briskly rubbed more salve into Kaiya's wounds, flexing her limbs to work it in better. She winced as he pulled her to her feet and led her around in front of his house.

"Once you get across the river, you climb up the cliffs, over the ridge in the back of that canyon because it's too steep right along the river. Once again, you'll have to go back and forth and back and forth across that rock layer. Eventually you'll be able to see the village at Unkar and the trails leading down to it. I'll be able to come with you for the first part of this trek, because it leads to some safe places for me to hide. First I'll make my house look like no one has been here for a while and then we'll go. You need to bend more to make yourself ready for this long hike. I'll give you food to take with you, and you go now to fill the water bladder down at the river."

Kaiya stepped down to the banks of the river, stopping to look at a rock layer she hadn't seen before. The rocks were actually green, with purple-ish stripes running through horizontally. She thought at first that something was growing on the rocks to make them that color, but then she realized the colors came from the rocks themselves. She wished she could study then more, but she heard Tapeats yelling her name. Locating him, she saw that he vigorously pointed back upstream. Way in the distance she noticed tiny figures moving in their direction. Panic closed her throat, and she moved as fast as she could back towards Tapeat's home.

"They are coming!" he said. "I have everything we need, and my house looks abandoned. Let's go!"

He took off at a dead run, with Kaiya stumbling awkwardly behind. She felt some warmth emanating from the salve, and it worked down into her aching muscles and helped them to move. Soon she was able to trot along, not at her usual swift pace, but at least good enough to keep Tapeats within her sight.

XXXV

Far, far below in the depths of the gorge, Drok watched a tiny figure skitter along the riverbanks.

"Pobal! That's her, down there! Get the others and help me find a way down," Drok yelled.

The men scattered along the cliff's edge, searching for a way down without plummeting over impassable rock layers. Bighorn sheep came this way, as evident by their scat. Deer also passed this way. Ako yelled and pointed down below them, motioning to a deer on its way down the cliff face. Bako hurried in that direction, but yelped as he slipped over the edge, grabbing a tree root to break his fall. Tova, luckily nearby, laid himself over a huge boulder, and reached down so Bako could grab his wrist. The two men grunted and pulled, and Bako, kicking his legs, slid up and away from the precipice.

"Less hurry, I guess, if we want to make it down there alive," Pobal said. Drok shot him a dirty look, and continued to thrash his way down the cliff side.

The river enticed, wet and shimmering, calling the hot, dry Toltecs farther down into the depths. The sun beat ferociously against the mostly shadeless wall of rock and dirt. Rocks gathered the heat and beat it back against the men as they picked their way down the ankle-twisting steepness. It took all day to make their way to the water. Clouds arrived, big and dark, right as they staggered through the last searing expanse before the river. The men flung themselves into the water, reveling in the luscious wetness, but disappointed to find it tasted bad. They drank sparingly, afraid it might make them sick. What had looked like sparkling jewels from above turned out to be water full of heavy sediment and minerals.

They rested in the water, lingering longer than Drok wanted. But he, too, was exhausted from their efforts in getting down there. The cloud cover was such a relief from the fierce sun that it was hard to start hiking again. The clouds sunk lower, turned from grey to black, and hurled jagged spears of lightning.

Tova jerked his head up as he heard a tremendous noise from upstream. "What's that?" he exclaimed.

Those were the last words he ever spoke. Around the corner came a violent surge of roiling water. Tova, Ako and Bako had been floating in the river and were swept away. Drok had been near the shoreline, getting ready to resume their hike. He scrambled away from the flood and found temporary refuge on a high ledge. Pobal was also swept along on the wave, but managed to pull his way to shore downstream from Drok. He found safety on top of a large, flat boulder. The two men waved frantically, assured at least each of them had survived. They watched as the flood tore out entire embankments, uprooted trees and created a maelstrom of churning water. The roar reminded Drok of the sound from atop the pyramids of Tula, the sound of angry crowds.

Sunset came and went, and still the water raged. When there was just a shred of light left, Drok cautiously made his way off his ledge and down to the shore. Boulders still rumbled past, logs crashed together, making his journey to Pobal difficult. Pobal kept shouting, guiding Drok with the sound of his voice. The two men were reunited in the blackness, waiting out the night on Pobal's boulder.

The faintest of morning light allowed them to see that the water level had lowered, although debris still swirled through the muddy red water. They splashed their way through the river, dodging around logs, branches, even dead animals. All they could do was continue downstream, hoping to come across the other Toltecs.

Finding Kaiya had generated a lot of trouble for them. But, Drok thought, the more elusive that woman was, the more it made him want her. His nights were filled with feverish dreams of her, being inside her, thrusting deeper and deeper. His daydreams while they tramped along were always of her, those flashing eyes, swaying hips and long, thick hair swishing as she walked, her powerful essence consuming him.

Pobal, slightly ahead of Drok, shouted back to him. He had found one of the men. Tova lay broken and battered, neck at an odd angle, stuck between two boulders, face down in the creek.

"He probably died instantly. Look at how the side of his head is bashed in," said Pobal.

Drok looked away, disturbed. "I hope we find the others alive."

At least now they could revive themselves in the water when the sun became unbearable. Eventually they could see that this river flowed into another bigger canyon.

"That must be what they call the Mother Canyon," Drok said. "We should go to the left when we reach the place where the two rivers join."

Where the two streams mingled, the muddy red water from the river's flash flood swirled into the bigger waters, creating a whirlpool emitting a sucking sound. The vortex appeared as a big hole, boring its way down to the center of the earth. Drok and Pobal looked at each other, and back to the hole. Was the whole river like this, Drok wondered?

"How are we ever going to get across this bigger river?" asked Pobal.

"Let's cross over this smaller river and climb that cliff. Maybe we can see farther downriver from up higher."

The men waded across the smaller river, and saw a small dwelling which looked abandoned. Drok turned to walk away, but noticed a small piece of torn deerskin on the floor of the doorway. Retrieving it, he held it to his nose. Kaiya. He could smell her. She had been here. He turned around in a circle, trying to find her tracks. Further away from the house he found a small footprint, a woman's track. His disfigured face contorted into a grin.

"This way!" he called out to Pobal.

A faint track was evident, pulling away from the dwelling and heading up the cliff. Because the flash flood made the ground damp, it was easy to follow the tracks. There seemed to be two people, with Kaiya's steps small, not the usual long strides Drok had seen her take before. Maybe she had also been caught in the flash flood and was injured. Good, Drok thought. That will make it easier to catch her.

Meanwhile, Pobal and Drok labored along the cliff, sometimes skirting the edges of a large ravine. What should have been just a short hike became a long trek to avoid going all the way down to the bottom of the ravine and then all the way back up. Both men were already tired from lack of sleep and the exertions of the day before.

At a high point along the cliff face, a promontory afforded a clear view downriver. Far, far in the distance, two tiny figures bobbed along the edge of the cliff. Drok stopped and hunkered down to watch the people until they disappeared over the cliff face. Only one person emerged at the bottom of the cliff. Was it Kaiya? Whoever it was struck out across the big river, was swept along by the current, but finally came out on the opposite shore.

He memorized the place where the crossing had occurred. Night was falling, and he was exhausted. He knew now where he would go in the morning.

XXXVI

It was such a pleasure to have Tapeats to talk with after the many long days alone. He was a wealth of knowledge, talking the whole way about how to cross the river and get to the village at Unkar. Kaiya wished he could come the whole way with her, but he needed to climb the cliffs to a hiding place which the Toltecs would never find. The open wounds on her leg still ached with every step, and she was woozy from her flood experience the day before. But the urgency of staying ahead of the Toltecs pushed her through the pain.

Still roiling from the extra flow that had come down yesterday, the two rivers swirled together in the bottom of Mother Canyon. Tapeats had assured her there was a cobblebar near the right bank of the river which would allow her to get out of the current and make it to shore. They had stood for a while along river left watching the current. If she could just get across part way, she might be able to get her feet under her and scramble to shore. The roar of the river made her uneasy, reminding her of the trauma from the day before. But this water was constant, not a sudden flood. Kaiya had hugged Tapeats tightly before they went their separate ways. Waving to him, she plunged in.

Kaiya stroked her way through the strong current. Unlike yesterday, it was easy to keep her head above water, being splashed occasionally as she pulled as hard as she could to the opposite shore. The water was pushing her much farther downstream than she wanted to go. Thrashing and kicking, she fought to get to where it looked like shallow water. She felt her feet kick bottom, and scrambled upright, panting as she used her hands to push herself out of the water.

Checking to be sure no one was following, she found a nook of shade to rest in and dry out. The next part of the hike would be a steep climb up the cliffs and back into a canyon to avoid river side cliffs. Like the hike she and Tapeats had taken together, this one wove back and forth to avoid dropping down lower. She figured she should at least get up to the tableland before stopping for a brief rest.

The sun shot over the canyon walls and shook Kaiya from a deep sleep. She wondered drowsily why it seemed so hot since she had been dreaming she was curled inside her dwelling with Moochkla. Cracking one eye open, she scrambled to her feet as reality crashed into her consciousness. She had slept through the entire night. Horrified that she had wasted so much time, she knew she must hurry to make up for that. Glancing anxiously around and seeing no one, she pushed her stiff and sore body into a slow trot. If she could just get to Unkar, there would be help for her in the village.

The increasing heat made her wounds ache and muddled her thoughts. Why was she here struggling so hard? Then, the full terror of the Toltecs would wash over her and speed up her pace. A scraggly tree appeared, and she sat in its scant shade, panting, sipping her water and wiping away the sweat. Too restless to relax, she resumed her hot trek toward Unkar.

About to give up and find a place to camp for the night, Kaiya heard a faint sound in the distance that sounded like voices shouting. Just as it became too dark to hike safely, she looked down to see campfires. It was exactly what she needed to urge her forward. Half sliding, half jumping down the cliff face in her haste, she landed hard on her ankle and cried out in pain. This alerted some nearby children, who surged forward accompanied by furiously barking dogs. Curious villagers came closer. Kaiya noticed through her exhaustion that although they were strangers to her, they somehow seemed familiar. She knew she was safe now, among friends. She had made it.

XXXVII

The women of the clan flocked around Kaiya, then whisked her off to a nearby wikiup, a shelter made from logs and brush, where they could work on her many wounds. Kaiya never had felt so grateful to be surrounded by women. They clucked and sympathized, rubbed salve into sore places and used a stiff grass brush to comb out all the tangles from her tortured hair, smoothing it into a long, tidy plait secured with yucca twine. Freshly cooked fish and corn meal cakes were brought, cool water served, and a pallet prepared for her bed. When she was settled, a man came in to talk with her.

His commanding presence and startlingly familiar face made Kaiya sit upright abruptly, shocked by his appearance. He could have been Moochkla.

"You are from the canyon of many caves?" the man asked.

Kaiya nodded her head yes, unable to speak.

"Is Moochkla still the healer for that clan?"

"Yes," Kaiya said, finally retrieving her voice. "I am Kaiya, Moochkla's apprentice. What is your name?"

The man squatted down on his heels beside Kaiya's pallet in a motion so much like Moochkla that it made a catch in Kaiya's throat. If only this man were Moochkla, she could throw herself into his arms and sob out the fear, pain and tumult she'd been through since leaving her canyon home.

"Souva is my name. And how is Moochkla's wife?" the man asked.

Kaiya realized Moochkla had never talked to her about his wife.

"She died when I was a baby. I never knew her," Kaiya responded.

The man rose abruptly to his feet and left the shelter.

Kaiya didn't know what to make of this sudden departure, but the exertion of the day drew her to lie back down. She must have dozed, but awoke with a start when she realized she was not alone. The Moochkla look-alike had returned and was staring down at her.

"Tell me your story," he demanded.

Kaiya struggled to sit up and shake the sleepiness from her head. She started to tell about being caught in the flash flood, but the man waved his hand to stop her.

"No, I want you to start at the beginning. How did you come to be Moochkla's apprentice?"

Kaiya's eyes opened in astonishment. This man wanted her whole life story. She told of the death of her parents, her apprenticeship to Moochkla, the suffering of their clan, and her journey with Moochkla and Bertok to talk with other leaders and healers about how to help their people. She soon realized this man was genuinely interested in every detail.

"Tell me about the different places you visited on your journey," Souva interrupted. The night wore on as different members of the clan gathered quietly around the shelter to listen to her story. More food and drink appeared. She warmed to her story, realizing what an incredible life she had experienced. Her stories of Tal brought gasps of disbelief from the villagers. Murmured whispers rippled through the crowd as she told of her ability to see events in other's eyes. More people quietly arrived, sitting near the shelter. Finally Kaiya described her swim across the river and her arrival at their village.

"These Toltec warriors will arrive here soon. Is there anywhere for us to hide?" Kaiya asked.

The leader stared at her as if in a trance from her story. Finally he roused himself. "There will be time tomorrow to create a plan for us. As for you, you must go north. Once you climb out of the canyon, you will be able to hide in the forest. But it will be a long, hard hike. So rest now, while it is still night. You will start early tomorrow." With that he turned away from her and left the shelter.

Kaiya's heart sank. More running? She was so exhausted and sore, and now more hiking? She thought about what Souva had said. Had he said climb out of the canyon? To the top? How could that be? She recalled the sheer canyon walls rising up from the river, towering above her. Far above in the hazy distance, she did remember seeing trees. Was that the forest he was talking about? Overwhelmed by the thought of all that hiking, she fell into a troubled, restless sleep.

A gentle hand on her shoulder shook her, becoming more insistent. "Kaiya, you must wake up. The sun is coming."

One of the friendly women from last night roused her. Kaiya could barely open her eyes. When she finally could pry one eyelid open, it was still dark.

"Look to the east," the woman said. Kaiya's one eye followed the woman's hand to the slits between the branches of the shelter. A soft suggestion of light hovered over the canyon walls. Kaiya groaned and struggled to a sitting position. The woman handed her water.

"It has herbs in it to make you strong," the woman said with a smile.

Kaiya did feel better after the drink. She packed up and went outside. Souva waited there to give her final directions on how to get to the north rim of the canyon.

"What about the Toltecs?" Kaiya asked with a frown of concern.

"I will deal with them. You need to get yourself to safety. Go now."

Kaiya started down the path where he had pointed. Stopping part way, she turned back. Souva still stood and watched her.

"Thank you, Souva," Kaiya called back.

He waved at her until she was out of sight. Then he sat down and wept.

XXXVIII

Drok and Pobal made it across the river without mishap, but knowing where to go from there was puzzling. High canyon walls lined each side of the river. When the men finally found a break in the sheer walls, it was a miserable, hot climb to the tableland above. Like their hike the day before, they had to weave back and forth, following the edges of steep ravines to avoid the climb all the way down to the bottom and back up the other side. The sun was unrelenting, making them wish for that cloud cover before the flood. Heat bugs kept up their indefatigable screeching, increasing the feel of the heat. Sometimes walking parallel to the river, other times away from it, they made their way toward the big drainage they could see coming in from the northwest.

Over a rise, they caught a glimpse of smoke rising straight up into the sky. Upon reaching a viewpoint, they were surprised by the sight of a small village down below.

"Kaiya must have been heading there," Drok said.

Pobal had been scanning the cliffs above his head, watching a bird soar and then return to its cave. His eyes detected another movement that was not the thunderbird.

"Look up there," Pobal called out. "Is that a person?"

Drok followed the direction of Pobal's gaze. Rising above the tableland to the northwest, movement could be detected, the halting walk of someone moving slowly. Drok watched for a moment, and thought it could be Kaiya, somehow wounded, probably from the flood. He calculated a route, and told Pobal of his plan.

"I'll follow her, while you go into the village as a distraction," Drok said. "Then no one will follow after me. Wait here to give me a head start."

The sun was still out, but skimmed the top of the northern wall by the time Pobal entered the village. He was immediately surrounded by six men of the clan. Grabbing his arms and shoulders, he was pushed into a wikiup. Someone ducked through the door and turned to face Pobal, who breathed sharply at the sight, shocked by the man's face. He looked just like the old healer who protected Kaiya. Pobal wondered how that could be, as they had left Moochkla behind at the village in the canyon.

The leader tried to question Pobal, who hadn't been very good at catching on to their language while he was at the Summer Solstice ceremony. Pobal tried to think of the word for "brother" to find out if this man was Moochkla's brother. The leader became more and more irritated as Pobal failed to understand any of the questions. Unable to explain himself, Pobal was placed under guard. He pantomimed the need for water, and the guard asked a child to bring some. Pobal quickly drained the gourd cup and asked for more. The child brought three scoops full before Pobal finally felt satisfied. He laid down on the warm dirt floor and fell asleep.

While Pobal distracted the villagers, Drok struck out across the rugged terrain, trying to match his path with that of the figure struggling on the cliffs above him. Uninjured in the flood and being just within reach of possibly catching Kaiya made his pace quicken. The person was clearly visible against the red cliff face, easy to keep track of inching along. Drok ran where he could, hopping over obstacles and pulling himself over boulders. Soon he was close enough that he was positive it was Kaiya. That pushed him forward even faster.

Kaiya was hurting. Her wounds from the flood ached with every step. Her shoulders pulled back from the weight of her pack, which the village women had kindly filled with food for her, but now it seemed an unwelcome burden. She was hot, tired and discouraged, dismayed by how far away the top of the cliffs seemed. Knowing she couldn't possibly make it to the top today, she started looking around for a suitable place to camp. There wasn't any hurry, anyway —it would be several days before the Toltecs found the village at Unkar.

She paused beneath an overhanging ledge for a sip of water and a gnaw on some deer jerky. Leaning back against the wall, she dozed on and off before falling into a deep sleep. Waking sometime later, she did feel better. As she got up, though, she groaned at her sore legs. She began to plot the easiest way up this next section of cliff. Suddenly, she froze. Below the cliff, out in the big drainage where she began her trek early this morning, someone moved. She crouched low, watching the person. Her heart began to pound. It couldn't be, but it was. Drok.

At once the painful aches were replaced with terror. With all of her being she summoned reserves she didn't even know she possessed. She felt her legs spring into action as she pounded up the next section. She ducked and weaved, trying to stay in the shadows and niches of the canyon walls. In her fear, she took bigger risks— tiptoeing along ledges, hopping over dangling boulders and shoving herself into spaces with few hand or footholds.

Drok, meanwhile, was on fire. Bolting up sheer cliff faces, he leaped across open spaces, and charged straight up steep inclines. Occasionally, he caught glimpses of Kaiya high above. She must have seen him, too, as her pace increased. But he had the advantage of seeing the whole scene from down below, and how he could shortcut some of the space between them.

Drenched in sweat, panting, and exhausted, Kaiya pushed on. She wouldn't let him catch her.

The sun crept up the slope, sliding over the north rim of the canyon. Shadows deepened at the base of the cliff as the sun pushed westward. Glancing below, Kaiya realized it was too dark to keep track of Drok anymore. She sharpened her ears, and held her breath to listen carefully, but any sounds that might have drifted up to her were drowned out by the pounding of her heart. She kept on.

Drok now paralleled an unsuspecting Kaiya. He kept hidden, only moving along side of her when she was focused on hand and footholds. Watching where she went made it easy for him to stay alongside, out of sight and steadily moving closer toward her.

He was within spear-throwing range of her now. He cocked his spear on his atlatl, and sized up the situation. If he could throw it close enough to trip her, or at least startle her, it would give him just enough time to close the distance between them. He had to wait until the ground between them would allow for his quick jump right to her.

She had to stop to catch her breath. It had been quite some time since she last spotted Drok, so she felt sure that he was far below her. She leaned against a rock, gasping for breath. She was so much higher up the canyon wall now that the drainage below looked like a string of leather. She smiled, realizing she really would make it to the top before it was completely dark. Fleeing Drok had goaded her into hiking uphill faster than she thought she could. The part of the cliff she was on still had some beams of sunlight. Shadows were falling, so she shouldered her pack and turned to start uphill. A cold chill filled her as she looked southward to see Drok advancing toward her along the same trajectory where she stood.

He raised his arm. Too late, she saw a spear being flung in her direction. She raised her arms above her head for balance and jumped down to a ledge below. The spear caught her in the belly. She shrieked as she fell, felt the searing pain, and landed on her back. Wrenching the spear from her flesh, she crawled into a small cave whimpering in pain. Blood oozed from the wound. She grabbed her traveling pouch from her pack and pressed it against the gash to staunch the flow. Panting, she clutched the spear and crouched in the back of the cave. Her only hope was to remain absolutely still. And when he came close enough looking for her, plunge the spear into him.

Drok couldn't see exactly where Kaiya had jumped because the shadows were deepening. But he heard the scream and knew his spear had made contact. She couldn't have gone far. He had only wanted to startle her, not hit her. He sat back and sniffed the air. A faint smell of fresh blood reached him on the slight breeze. He followed the thread of the scent.

Kaiya held her breath as long as she could and willed her heart to calm down enough so she could listen. Stones rattled, the soft sounds of bare feet moving in dirt came closer to her. She moved slightly towards the edge of the cave. She could see him now, but she remained hidden. He edged toward her hiding place, slightly above her position. She waited, watching his every move. When he was almost directly above her, she gathered all of her strength and courage, and launched herself upwards, thrusting the spear into his groin. He screamed, reeled about, and reached for her.

Suddenly a flurry of fur and claws leapt between Kaiya and Drok. Tal. The cat had Drok's back pinned on the ground, shredding his flesh with the sharp back claws of one foot. Kaiya yelled and pulled at Tal's neck, just as Tal's powerful jaws sunk deep into Drok's side. Tal turned in a fury, facing Kaiya. The two stared at each other, Tal's mouth dripping with Drok's blood just inches from Kaiya's nose. Their eyes locked. In Tal's eyes, Kaiya saw death, Drok's death. Then another scene played across Tal's eyes. Kaiya was sick, very sick, but a man cared for her. Then she was well, happy and a man walked beside her. But, who was this? Not anyone she knew. The vision in Tal's eyes faded, and Kaiya snapped back to her horrifying present, an extremely agitated cougar inches from her nose, and a dying man moaning on a rock above.

"Tal," she said in a soothing tone, "Good boy. Thank you. You protected me. It's all right now, he can't hurt me anymore. You saved me from him once before, and you pulled me from the waters of the flood. You have more than paid me back for rescuing you when you were a tiny kitten. I'll always love you."

The cougar arched his back, dug his claws into Drok one more time, and lunged toward Kaiya. But his movement toward her was to drag his raspy tongue across her face. He sat in front of her, lifted one paw and placed it on her shoulder. He gave a small mewing sound, then rose and brushed against Kaiya as he walked away. Kaiya watched him go, bounding across the steep slope, tail outstretched for balance. Then she turned her attention back to Drok.

He was moaning, grasping his crotch and trying to stem the flow of blood. Kaiya moved toward him, keenly feeling the tear in her own belly with every movement. She glanced at her own wound, seeing that it still was oozing. Pulling the pouch tightly over her wound, she knelt down by Drok's head. He was trying to say something.

"I didn't mean to hurt you with the spear," he gasped.

"Well, what were you trying to do with the spear?" she asked irritably.

"I was just trying to startle you, keep you off balance until I could get to you."

"Oh, and then what were you planning to do?"

"Kaiya, I want you."

"What you want me for you can get from any woman. And you have. From what I saw in your eyes, you have raped and maimed countless women."

"But with you it's different. I feel different. You do something to me no other woman has done before." Drok had to stop talking, as he convulsed and coughed violently. Blood spewed from his mouth, dripping onto his lips and chin.

"Kaiya, you're a healer. Help me."

Kaiya looked at his wounds. Her own damage from the spear was severe. There was no staunching that flow. Tal's tearing with his claws had shredded Drok's legs, which bled profusely. But the big wound in his side which Tal had torn open with his jaws was the killer.

"Drok, there is nothing I can do for you. You've lost too much blood, and your wounds are too deep. I don't think you're going to make it."

There was silence. Then, a question. "Kaiya, will you hold me?"

Kaiya moved closer, evaluating. She reached over to touch his hand. He moved to grab hers, but there was little strength in his touch. She scooted closer. He raised his head, and she slid her knee under it. His head fell back, and his lips distorted into a smile. His breath became shallow, his eyes struggling to stay focused on Kaiya's face, his speech barely above a whisper.

"When I was little, the only person who was kind to me was my mother." He paused, catching his breath after the exertion of talking. "But she had no power. My father," Drok coughed violently. "My father had all the power. And he used it on me. In a drunken rage, he threw a pot of hot oil right into my face. The other kids made fun of my face. So I got tough—tougher and meaner than my father and fearful enough so the other kids would leave me alone. I looked for any way I could to be in command."

"I always wanted to be a soldier," he gasped. "It was luck that brought me to the temple that day. There I gained more power than I ever dreamed possible." His breath was labored now. Kaiya placed her finger over his lips.

"No, I have to tell you this," Drok panted, waving her hand away. "When I was thrown out of Tula, I was lost. I was no leader of men without the spectacle of the temple to back me. We just traveled north without a real plan. Until I met you. I wanted you for myself. I wanted your body, and I wanted your powers. You are very powerful, Kaiya. The most powerful woman I've ever met. And, the sexiest." He grinned again, but the movement cost him. He began a violent spasm of coughing.

When he caught his breath, his voice was considerably weaker. "You were so different, Kaiya. I realize now that it was because I fell in love with you. But I couldn't have you. It made me insane. And, look where it led me—to death. Today." He grabbed her hand with all the strength he had left.

"Love. It's what I wanted my whole life. I hope you find it, Kaiya. Think of me when you do."

Drok's eyelids fluttered. Breaths came infrequently, shallow, then the rush of air ceased.

Kaiya sat for a long time. Darkness fell. She felt her own wound; wet, painful, open. Slipping her knee out from under Drok's head, she rose unsteadily and gathered her things. Without glancing back at the still form of Drok, she leaned over her wound and labored up the last portion of the canyon's wall. Finally reaching the top, she curled up beneath the trunk of a large pine tree and collapsed, bent over her pouch, sobbing herself to sleep.

XXXIX

The sunlight filtering down through the pine needles settled softly on Kayko's bare chest, startling him with its sudden warmth. The sun had moved so much that it already had entered his shady refuge. Had I dozed, he wondered? He felt around for the piece of obsidian he had been working on, finding it in the dirt by his knee where he must have dropped it when he fell asleep. Grinning at his own laziness, he realized he had been lulled by the warmth and peacefulness of a late summer's afternoon. His loyal dog Chee lay panting in the shade nearby.

He arose and started his rounds, clicking two small stones in his hand and whistling to discourage any animals from invading the rows of corn, beans and squash. In his other hand was his seeing stick, which he swept back and forth across the way in front of him to locate any obstacles. He paused as a flurry of beating wings left the garden, Chee barking and chasing after them. Chickadees, he thought. He could picture them in his mind's eye although he'd never seen them, but his father's descriptions had given him a strong image.

Kayko's world was of sound and touch. Somehow because of the difficulty of his birth, during which his mother had died, his sight had been damaged, but that didn't stop him from enjoying his life. A much loved member of the clan, he was admired for his perseverance and gentle sense of humor. He volunteered for this lonely job of protecting the crops in the highland because he wanted to be of use to his clan, and he loved the sounds, so different from those down by the river. The wind through the trees, the birds and the animals were his companions, as well as his faithful dog. Chee was Kayko's third dog, and by far the smartest one. He seemed to intuit Kayko's need for help, and continuously circled him, never far away.

When he wasn't tending the crops, Kayko worked on creating the clan's arrowhead supply. When he had a fair stockpile, he enjoyed carving animal shapes out of wood, fantasy shapes, since he'd never seen any. Tails, funny-shaped ears and enormous eyes appeared in the wood under his nimble fingers and obsidian blade.

He left the open glade and strolled toward the rim. Air currents shifted around him as he neared the edge, and his seeing stick stopped him before the drop off. Seated on his favorite rock, with its familiar shape and roundness, he listened to the distant sound of the river grinding its way through the canyon. He suddenly felt very alone, and hoped for a visit from someone of the clan. Chee's nose pushed under his hand. He smiled and ruffled the dog's coarse fur, grateful for the companionship.

A scraping noise caught his attention. Too loud for a squirrel or rabbit, the sound was like a deerskin being pulled over dirt, a deerskin with something heavy on it. He heard it again, a pause, then again. Slowly he got to his feet and inched toward the sound. There was a muffled groan, then a small voice. "Help me." Had he really heard that? Then, silence. Chee started in that direction, growling, fur raised on his back.

Alarmed now, Kayko picked up a hefty rock and then cautiously edged forward with his seeing stick both sweeping the ground and then being raised in the air as a club. He heard breathing, labored and shallow, coming from his right. But no movement. He slowly moved in that direction until his seeing stick touched a lump of something soft, from which came the breathing. Bending down, he felt a soft mane of tangled hair attached to a human head. Feeling further down, he encountered a tunic covering soft breasts. Who was this and what was wrong with her? Continuing down her body, he arrived at her belly, sticky with blood. The wound was vicious, seeping and wide open. Kayko leaned on his knees, shocked by this wounded stranger so close to his home. Chee circled the unconscious form, sniffing and whimpering.

"C'mon, boy, we've got to help this poor girl." Carrying her back to his shelter, he thanked the Great Spirit for all the time he had spent around the fire of Tapeats. His own father had pretty much abandoned him to the women of the clan when he was a baby. Even when Kayko was a young boy, Souva had only paid attention to criticize or discipline him. It was Tapeats who pulled him under his wing and opened up the world of healing to him. Kayko had been a sympathetic assistant, using his gentle demeanor to soothe the terror of a small boy of the clan who might have a gash on his leg. But now he was thrust into the role of sole healer, something he had never done.

Moaning piteously as Kayko carried her back to the shelter, she slipped into unconsciousness and remained so as he examined her wounds. She was badly battered from head to toe, her feet torn with deep cuts, as if she had been walking a long time. There were countless scrapes along her legs and arms, as if she had been dragged. But the serious wound was in her belly, deep and wide, jagged and oozing. Staunching the blood flow was to be first priority. But there also was a fever. She pitched back and forth, moaning and calling out for Moochkla or Bertok. He knew the name Moochkla, but not Bertok. He had to get her calm enough so that he could clean out and suture that gash.

Kayko whistled as he prepared a sleeping draught. His small herb collection was carefully organized, but he checked and rechecked the pouches for the valerian root and passion flower before dropping them into the cooking pot. After the mixture cooled, he knelt beside the thrashing woman and lifted her up. She resisted at first, then greedily swallowed the draught. It took a while, but her tense body finally relaxed, and she fell still on the sleeping furs.

Feeling around the edges of the jagged wound, Kayko gently worked a poultice into the tear, using it to clean out the dried blood and any dirt or pus. Occasionally, the woman let out a small whimper, but she remained still so Kayko could work on her. Every time she emitted a noise, Chee's ears shot up and he studied the woman until she settled back down. Satisfied that the wound was now clean, Kayko used the sharp tip of a yucca as a needle and a slender thread of yucca fiber to close the wound. Time stood still for him as he labored by touch over each stitch into the flesh, feeling as though Tapeats was right beside him the entire time, guiding him through this tricky process. At last every jagged edge was closed, and he sat back, exhausted by his concentration. Not yet finished, he smoothed an infection-preventing healing salve made with sage over the stitches before bandaging it with a clean rabbit skin, tying it around her middle with strips of leather. He washed the other numerous cuts and scrapes on her legs and arms. Some needed bandages and salve, too. He finished up by washing her face and trying to tidy her hair. Finally satisfied, he curled up next to her and fell fast asleep.

Wakened later by a stream of sunlight hitting his face, Kayko rolled over. His unknown patient was breathing deep, full breaths. He touched her arms, then her forehead. Good. The fever had subsided. He touched the bandages, good—still in place. He silently moved out of the house and over to the crops for his rounds. The forest burst with birdsong; nuthatches beeped, chickadees pronounced their names, and raucous jays screeched over their territory. The corn plants rustled in the wind, while the big leaves of the squash flapped in the updrafts coming from the canyon. Chee darted about the garden, chasing squirrels and birds which dared to come near his domain. Kayko was amazed that he had slept all the way through the night, but after the ordeal of finding and tending to this woman, he had needed the rest.

She slept all through that day and into the next. Kayko was hauling water in a pottery jar from the cliff spring back to his shelter when he heard a small voice. Hurrying to the doorway, he heard a rustling sound.

"Don't try to get up," he said. "You were badly injured, and it's going to take a while for your body to heal."

"Who are you?" she asked feebly. "Where am I?"

"You're in the highlands on the north side of the canyon. You're safe here. I live here in the summers to guard the crops. I'm the only one here right now. I am called Kayko. And you?"

"How did I get here? Oh, I am called Kaiya."

"You must have come up from Unkar. You were badly injured. I heard you call out and found you, but you were unconscious. I brought you back here and tried to work on your injuries. It's good your fever broke, so I think you will recover. But it's going to take time, a lot of time."

Chee pushed his nose under Kaiya's hand, begging to be scratched. She stroked his brown fur, but felt exhausted by the effort. She fell back on the soft sleeping furs. Finally she asked, "Are you a healer?"

"Not really," he replied. "But I spent my childhood at the fire of our clan's healer, Tapeats."

"Oh! I know Tapeats. He helped me get here. He is an old friend of Moochkla's."

"How do you know Moochkla?" Kayko asked.

"My mother died when I was just a little girl. She didn't survive giving birth to my new sister. My father had died in a hunting accident earlier that winter, so I didn't have any close family other than my Uncle Bertok. I lived for a while with an older woman of the clan, Jumac. Then Moochkla took me on as his apprentice. Do you know him?"

Kayko shook his head. "No, but I certainly have heard a lot about him in many different ways."

"What do you mean?" asked Kaiya.

"Well, he's a legend for his healing abilities. And, he and Tapeats were close friends growing up. They, and my father were inseparable. Until there was a big fight."

"Wait—is your father Souva?"

"Yes," replied Kayko.

"Are he and Moochkla brothers?"

Kayko nodded.

"What do you mean, until there was the big fight?" asked Kaiya.

"How well do you know Moochkla?" Kayko asked.

"He's been like a father to me. I love him dearly."

"Has he ever talked with you about his wife, Osa?"

"Only that she died when I was too little to remember her, and that he has been very lonely ever since. She used to help him with his healing work. He had been looking for someone in our clan to become the next healer and learn all he knows, and I guess he thought that was me. I loved growing up with him."

"Well, there's certainly more to the story than that," Kayko replied, stretching his long frame into a standing position. "But I think that's enough for now. Let me get you something to drink, and I'd like you to try some broth."

"Wait!" cried Kaiya. "I have more questions!"

But all she saw was Kayko's back, and heard his whistling as he exited the doorway. She heard a sound, like a stick scratching the earth as he walked. But that small conversation had tired her, and she laid back down on the soft furs and promptly fell asleep.

XL

Kaiya drifted in and out of sleep, turning carefully to avoid her wounded belly. Often when she opened her eyes they would land on Kayko seated nearby, greeting her with his friendly smile. He seemed intuitively to know what she needed when she woke, a drink, some food, help going outside to relieve herself. Every movement she made exhausted her. Even sitting up to sip water from a gourd made her fall back onto the furs from the effort. She couldn't believe how weak she was, and was embarrassed by her helplessness.

Kayko gently prodded her with his patient questions, trying to help her remember. She was frustrated by her chaotic mind, so full of gaps in her memories. Sometimes she could think clearly and make sense when she tried to tell him about her life. Other times her thoughts seemed a jumbled mess, hard to sort out and explain. She laid her head in his lap one evening as they talked, a small fire going in the shelter to keep away the slight chill of the evening.

"But, how did you keep going after all that?" he asked her.

"I didn't have time to stop and think. I just knew I had to keep going."

"What did you think would happen if the Toltecs caught you?"

"I didn't know for sure. Drok was so irrational, I couldn't guess what they would do. Beat me? Rape me? Murder me? Whatever he wanted to do, it wasn't going to be pleasant for me."

"Tell me more about your journey here," he encouraged her.

"Well, I ran. I ran until I couldn't breathe, then I stopped and walked until I could breathe again. Then I ran some more."

"How did you escape the heat?" he asked.

"Once I got along the river, at least I could splash myself. It helped to hike wet. There were lots of ledges along the river that I could crawl under for shade."

"But what about that flash flood?" he asked. "How were you able to survive that?"

"Well," she replied. "I couldn't have on my own. Remember when I told you all about Tal? When the force of the water overpowered me, I hit my head on a rock submerged in the stream. Tal pulled me out. I couldn't have done it without him."

"You had so many injuries. How did you keep going?"

"Tapeats gave me some herbs to drink and also some salve for the worst scrapes. The hardest thing was the stiffness. But I found if I walked more, the muscles would move more. So, I kept on going."

"But, what kept you going?"

"Fear is a very strong motivator. So is self-preservation. But mostly, I knew when I reached the rim and got back into the forest where things were familiar, I would be in my world again, the world that I understand and where I belong. I had to get up here, and then I would know what to do to survive. Once I could lose Drok in the forest, then I planned to circle around and eventually make my way home again."

He thought about her with awe, staring toward the fire. She looked at his face in the flickering firelight, and realized his eyes were looking right at her. She smiled at him. No response. Suddenly it all made sense to her. The scratching sounds of his stick as he walked; his deliberate, slow method of moving, the way he cocked his head to listen carefully to an unusual sound. She touched his hand softly, and he immediately turned to where her head lay in his lap.

"How long have you been blind?" she asked quietly.

"All my life," he responded. "Did you just figure it out?"

She nodded yes, and then realizing he couldn't see her, said aloud, "Yes."

"Oh, good," he laughed. I love to see how long I can fool people into thinking I can see."

"Well," she sputtered, "I have been distracted and had a few things on my mind!"

They both laughed, and he gently stroked her face. She continued to hold the other hand, squeezing it, and receiving his light squeeze back. They sat in the fading firelight, each lost in their own thoughts.

"I think I'd better sleep now," Kaiya announced. He helped her move into a comfortable position on the sleeping furs and stirred the remaining embers before slipping out into the darkness.

In the morning, Kayko arrived with some tea and a stick. "I think you should try short walks on your own, so I've made a walking stick for you." He held it out for her inspection. He handed her a stick of a perfect height for her, with smoothed sides, and a carving with the most incredible likeness of Tal at the top. Under Tal was an indentation where her petite hand could grasp the stick.

"Oh, Kayko, it's beautiful!" she cried. "Thank you. You made Tal look so real. It must have taken lots of time for you to do this."

"You described Tal so well that I really could "see" him. And, the only other person around here sleeps a lot, so I have plenty of time to do other things."

She made a harrumphing noise, and snapped a nearby rabbit skin at him, smacking him in the face. As he chuckled, she reached for his hand to pull him closer to her. She planted a delicate kiss on his cheek. He was startled, then grinned broadly. Kaiya blushed, surprised at herself for making such a move, grateful he couldn't see her embarrassment.

"Your exercise starts now," he announced. "I want to see if using the stick can help you get up on your own."

She gritted her teeth as the pain enveloped her, but pushed herself to her knees, using the stick to raise herself to standing. She felt woozy and nearly fell back from the effort, but Kayko was there to steady her.

"All right, let's see how far you can go without help. I'll be right beside you all the way."

They took a slow walk around the rectangular dwelling, Chee bounding alongside of them. The house was substantial, made of carefully placed rocks, built so long ago that no one could remember the builder. So well constructed, it was almost possible to visualize the builder standing there, next rock in hand, analyzing the possible choices of where it might best fit. The rocks were flat pieces of the common white rock in the area, mottled with orange and yellow, and sprinkled with light greenish lichen. Shadows from the towering pine trees dappled the outer walls, emphasizing or eliminating the colors of the rocks at the whim of wind and sunlight. Smoke curled lazily out of the chimney hole. Farther back, the corn stood in straight rows, green soldiers against the hunger of the clan. Closer to the edge of the canyon, the vegetation subtly shifted. Gone were the towering red-barked pines. In their place, scraggly cliff rose bushes bloomed their small whitish-yellow flowers, the soft perfume a welcome scent on the breeze. Junipers clung to the rim, gnarled and twisted from the howling winds blowing up from the canyon's depths. And at last, unfolding before the last step, was the view of the canyon itself. Ridge after ridge arose, rock walls of ocher, foam, yellow and darkness, carved into shapes of spires, pillars and fortresses. When the distance became too far for the eye to focus, it turned into a violet blue haze. On the horizon, Snow Mountain High Place thrust skyward, blackly etched against the twilight. Above the peaks, a thumbnail sliver of the moon. It was in the position of a smile to match the one on Kaiya's face.

All this grandeur, and all she had to do was step outside the house. She described it all in detail to Kayko, who listened with rapt attention. As they turned back to the house, Kaiya noticed a tear streak down Kayko's check.

"Kayko, what's wrong?" she cried.

It took him a while to compose himself. Reaching for her hand, he said, "No one's ever described the canyon to me like you just did. I really can see it now."

She reached her arms around his waist, and leaned against him. He held her gently, afraid of hurting her wounds, but loving her closeness.

XLI

Later at the house, Kayko knelt down beside Kaiya and reached for her hand. She slipped her hand into his. They just sat there, holding each other's fingers and thumbs. She shivered as he swirled his fingertips over hers.

"Are you cold?" Kayko asked.

"No, just the opposite."

Heated by an inner warmth, she felt a sizzling sensation from deep within her. Kayko's closeness made her giddy.

"Kayko." "Kaiya." They had each spoken the other's name out loud simultaneously. They both burst into laughter and squeezed their hands together tighter.

"Go ahead," Kayko offered.

"No, you go first." Kaiya said.

Kayko sighed deeply, gently pulling Kaiya into a sitting position beside him.

"I don't know where to begin," he said. "Kaiya, I have very strong feelings for you. From the moment you arrived here, I felt like I had been waiting for you all of my life. I want to be with you, and I want to be with you like this."

With that, he leaned toward Kaiya's face, brushing the tip of her nose with his lips and then slid down to her mouth. Finding her lips, he starting kissing them tentatively at first, but then drew her closer and twirled his tongue around hers. When they parted, Kaiya's pulse was racing. She was stunned. Did he feel the same way about her that she felt about him?

Kayko pushed Kaiya's tunic up over her head. Letting the garment fall to the ground, he then returned his fingers to Kaiya's neck, sliding his hands downward to cup her breasts. Pushing her gently back down on the mat, he brought his lips to her nipple and teased it with his tongue. Kaiya moaned softly. He grinned and switched over to the other nipple. His lips kissed their way down her belly, stopping to kiss the scabbed over area from the spear wound. She trembled as he stopped at each scar which he knew so well from taking care of her. He arrived at her mound and teased her legs open with his tongue. He lowered his head and began to explore her delicate parts. With her clit being licked and sucked, Kaiya felt a gush of wetness. Kayko moved his fingers around the outside of her, and then entered her with his fingertips. Kaiya's body responded by arching toward his hand, plunging his fingers deeper within her. Kayko kept up a rhythm of licking and plunging as Kaiya writhed with pleasure. She groaned and reached her arms around his neck, pulling that tantalizing tongue back up toward her face. Kayko and Kaiya kissed passionately, merging their fire. Kayko stopped only long enough to remove his loincloth, then lay down on top of Kaiya. She wriggled, pushing her hips in search him, feeling the stab of his erection. He pulled back as she tried to pull him closer.

"No," he whispered. "Let me make love to you."

Panting, Kaiya lay back down on the mat. Kayko was on his knees above her. He moved one knee, then the other so that her legs spread open before him. He lowered himself onto her, just touching his hardness to her open lips. He teased around her opening before inserting himself just a little. Kaiya gasped. It felt so good to her—the smoothness of his skin sliding into her wetness. She arched trying to bring him closer. He pulled slightly back, but Kaiya reached for his buttocks to pull him closer. "Please, now," Kaiya murmured. He pushed himself slowly into her. Kaiya gasped at the same moment when Kayko felt a small resistance. Then he pushed all the way in. Kaiya groaned from deep within her. He connected with the very center of her being, sending sensations up her spine. "Oh, Kayko," she whispered. "I love you."

Kaiya grabbed his buttocks as he thrust into her flesh. She felt herself rising higher and higher as if she were floating. Then sensation overwhelmed her, and she felt herself spasm and twitch with pleasure. Her cries matched the rhythm of Kayko's thrusts as he slowed his tempo. Finally stopping, he continued to hold her tightly. Her shudders subsided as he held her close. He brushed her face with kisses and she kissed him back. He grinned and pushed himself off of her. She saw his hardness still jutting from his body. In the giving over of herself to pure pleasure, she saw that he hadn't really finished yet. She pulled him back towards her. "Are you sure?" he whispered.

"Very sure," Kaiya said.

He raised her buttocks slightly and then reentered her. She felt how her wetness made it easy for him to slide all the way back to that new place of depth within her. She threw her legs over his back and twined her feet together. He was so on the brink that within just a few thrusts he cried out and fell onto her, shuddering. She held him close until he could catch his breath. Then he raised himself slightly so he could kiss her. "I love you," he said quietly. Then he moved his body next to her with his arm across her breasts and ribs. He fell asleep, and Kaiya shortly joined him in their shared dreams.

XLII

As Souva climbed toward the rim, a golden light glowed in the east, soft brushes of pink to the north and west. Soon it would be full sunlight. To avoid the searing heat, he had hiked in partial darkness. Although near autumn, the heat was still pure summer. He strode briskly upwards, determined to arrive by early morning to see his son. He surprised a pair of ravens, picking at something just out of sight of the path. Curious, he swung toward the spot and found a human skeleton. Stooping to examine the remains, he realized it was less than a moon old. Had there been a fight since the last time he visited? Suddenly he was worried. He hurried up the remaining section of trail, arriving breathless at the rim, heading toward his son's summer home.

He stopped abruptly, stunned by what he saw. Slipping behind a tree, he watched Kayko, arm around that young woman Kaiya, kissing her forehead. She laughed, and stood on tiptoe to kiss his mouth. He kissed her again, holding her in a tight embrace.

Souva stomped from behind the tree, announcing his arrival with a sharp "Kayko!"

Kayko spun toward the sound of his father's voice, and dropped his arms from Kaiya. She stepped away, allowing Kayko to walk toward Souva. The two men stopped just out of Kaiya's earshot.

"What is she still doing here?" Souva hissed. "And what do you have to do with her?"

"She has been here recovering from her injuries. We have become very close," Kayko replied.

"Well, I can certainly see that," Souva retorted. "Her injuries weren't that severe. It shouldn't have taken this long to recover."

"You only saw her injuries from being caught in that flash flood. A lot more has happened since the last time you saw her," Kayko said.

"Like what?" Souva demanded.

"She was attacked by that Toltec. He stabbed her with a spear in the belly, a deep, wide wound, and she still has pain from it. I've been taking care of her while she recovers."

"It appears you've been doing more than that."

"You're right. I have. I've been falling in love with her, and she with me." Kayko lifted his head and turned in the direction where he heard Souva's feet shuffling in the dirt several lengths away. Standing still, his chin jutting forward, he faced the direction where he heard his father's movements.

"That woman was supposed to pass through here and be on her way. Why is she still here?"

"She's helping me with my crops and thinking about what she's going to do next. Now that she no longer has to run from those Toltecs, she's in no hurry to go anywhere. But, when she does, I'm going with her." Kayko again looked firmly in Souva's direction.

Souva looked in amazement at his son, this young man whom he had avoided most of his life. Kayko had grown up at the fires of many in the clan, but rarely Souva's. Souva never expected Kayko to be with a woman, but it was obvious what had happened. He wanted to save his son from his own mistake of allowing a woman to cast a spell over him.

He opened his mouth to speak when the young woman let out a screech and hurried toward the rim. Turning towards her, he saw a man approaching, a man he hadn't seen since his youth.

"Moochkla!" Kaiya screamed as she hobbled toward him. "Moochkla!" she sobbed, throwing herself into his arms. He caught her and held her close while she clung to him, wetting his tunic with tears. Raising his eyes above Kaiya's head, he gazed directly at his brother, who returned the gaze with a glare.

At last Kaiya was able to catch her breath and chattered on about all that had happened since she left their canyon. Moochkla draped his arm across her shoulders as they walked back towards the other two men. When they were within several paces, Moochkla disengaged himself from Kaiya, placing a hand on her arm to stop her from talking. She hushed, feeling the tension. Kayko reached out his hand toward her, and she stepped forward to take it.

"Brother," said Moochkla. "We have much to discuss."

"We have nothing to discuss. I said everything I wanted to when you stole Osa from me," Souva snapped.

"Osa came with me of her own free will, Souva. You know that. She made her choice."

"And then you killed her!" Souva shouted.

"She had a sickness in her belly that grew until it killed her. There was nothing I could do," Moochkla said sorrowfully.

"You're supposed to be the greatest of all healers. Moochkla, the famous healer, and you couldn't cure her. Why didn't you heal her?"

Moochkla gazed out over the canyon. Far below them, the river ran ocher-red from the recent rainstorm. Rabbitbrush had burst into yellow. A flock of jays uttered their plaintive cries as they swooped overhead.

When Moochkla turned back to the others, tears streamed down his cheeks. "Don't you think I tried everything I could to save her?" he sobbed. "Do you have any idea how hard it was to stand by helplessly? Watching her die was my agony."

"It must have felt the same way as watching her choose you,"

Souva retorted.

"Well, then—we both suffered a severe loss, brother. We both had her for a short time, and then we each lost her. Now that it's just the two of us left, let's talk about the future of these young people, so that they may find the happiness which eluded us." Moochkla gestured toward Kayko and Kaiya, who were holding each other and listening intently to this heated exchange.

"What is there to say? I left him alone here to do his work, and I come back and he's with this woman who wasn't even supposed to be here this long."

"She was unconscious..." Kayko began.

"No, let me explain," Kaiya interjected. "I have Kayko to thank for saving my life." Turning toward Moochkla, she continued telling him her story.

"And then Drok attacked me with a spear. I jumped down from a ledge, trying to get out of the way of the spear, but instead jumped right into it, tearing a big hole in my belly. I waited until he came closer to my hiding place, then lunged and stabbed him with his own spear. That stopped him, but what really killed him was Tal. Tal appeared suddenly and took a big chunk out of Drok's side. When I looked in Tal's eyes, I saw that same image I saw when I was a child. Now I understand it was Kayko and me, although I didn't know it back then. When Tal left, I knew it would be the last time I would ever see him. He's repaid me for saving him, Moochkla. Drok died in my arms, admitting how wrong he had been. He said he loved me, and couldn't bear it that I didn't love him. He told me to find love, and think of him when I do. I was able to crawl up to the rim where Kayko found me."

"Who's Tal again?" Souva asked uneasily.

"A cougar she rescued when he was just a kitten. Kaiya had watched the cougar family for many weeks while she was gathering herbs. Then the mother and sister died. She realized with the mother gone, the other cub couldn't survive, so she brought the baby home to raise with us. He's rescued her twice before—one other time from

Drok, and then from the flash flood," Moochkla explained.

Souva gave Kaiya a lingering look. A woman who walks with a cougar? An uncomfortable feeling rose from his stomach. Long ago, a seer had predicted there would be a woman who walks with an animal who would be in his son's life.

"And you?" said Moochkla. "How is it that you have a son?"

Souva sighed heavily and squatted down on his heels. Kayko leaned forward, listening intently. He had heard this story many times, from many members of the clan, but never from his father.

"After Osa decided to be with you and I left the clan, I came to look for Tapeats. He welcomed me into the farming community at Unkar. I decided to stay because it was isolated. I was angry and hurt, and just wanted to be alone. But there was a woman, Jahea, who wouldn't leave me alone. She followed me everywhere. I took this job on the rim in the summers so I could finally be alone. But, she followed me up here, too—bringing food or an extra blanket, or some other gift. And she gave herself to me. I didn't want to, but she was insistent, and I was lonely and hurt and..."

Souva looked at the crisp blue sky against the green pines. Small, puffy clouds moved along rapidly, occasionally blotting out the sun before continuing on.

"She had Kayko, and then died," he said bluntly. "I wanted nothing to do with him, or anyone else. Too much pain, too many broken hearts."

"But then, that made both of you suffer," Moochkla said softly.

"I was afraid. Afraid to love another and be hurt again, and afraid of his blindness. I didn't know how to help him. I think it turned out to his advantage, because everyone in the clan loved him and helped him grow. If he'd been with me, he might have turned into an angry, unhappy old man like his father. Instead, he is a kind-hearted and friendly man who is loved by all the clan."

Kaiya glanced up at Kayko to see that his face was contorted, tears dripping from his sightless eyes. Moved by hearing his father's story straight from the heart, he was stunned that his father had been afraid to love him. Kayko always had thought that it was because of his blindness his father had shunned him.

"Do you remember the predictions from Kairee?" Moochkla asked.

"Oh, yes," Souva responded. "She said I would have a son, and he would meet a woman who walked with an animal."

Kaiya and Kayko both looked toward each other. Putting their arms tightly around each other's waists, they leaned into each other.

Souva stood and slowly walked toward his brother. Moochkla hesitated, then walked forward, arms extended. The two brothers stopped and gazed at each other with Moochkla closing the gap, putting his arm around his brother's shoulders. Souva's clenched fists slowly released as his arms raised to embrace Moochkla. Moochkla held him close. Tears were running down both their faces.

XLIII

Deep in the forest, Moochkla and Kaiya faced each other. All sounds were muted by the dense vegetation and the ancient, immense trees all around them. A coyote padded by, coat lush with tawny fur. A nearby grove of aspens showed a tinge of yellow. The wind rustled their leaves, making a tinkling sound, reminding Kaiya of the creek near her canyon home. These small leaves fluttered in the wind rather than roared like pine needles. She wondered how Kayko felt about trees, if he loved one more than the other because of its sound.

"I came because I sensed your agony when the spear ripped your belly. I had a dream where I felt you slipping in and out of consciousness. I had to come find you to make sure you were safe. On the way here, I had a vision of what you must do next. Look into my eyes and see what comes through," Moochkla said, taking Kaiya's hand.

Kaiya felt the warmth of his gnarled, rough skin.

"So many times as I ran I wished you were with me. I was so scared, so lonely. Tapeats was a big help, and the women at Unkar treated me wonderfully. I was shocked when I saw Souva, because he looked so much like you, but he didn't act like you at all. He always seemed angry."

"He always was an angry person. Even as a little boy, another child's teasing could send him into a rage. When we both loved Osa, he just couldn't accept that she chose me. Many times in a clan it happens that a woman chooses between two suitors. But Souva never got over it, so he left. He wasn't mad at you, just mad as part of his personality."

"But now," Moochkla continued, "it is important for you to see what is in my eyes."

Kaiya breathed deeply and closed her eyes, gathering her concentration. She had spent so much of her time lately dealing with her physical condition that her soul felt neglected. When she opened her eyes, Moochkla's steady gaze looked into her own.

At first, it was just his kind eyes. Then images appeared: steep canyon walls, the thundering roar of the river, walking a treacherous trail, a rock tumbling over the ledge. Walking, so much walking. A violent thunderstorm. Then a walk through a short canyon, opening into a peaceful clearing ringed with aspen trees, some rocks surrounding a small pool, caves at the base of the cliffs. Moochkla's voice swirled through her head.

"Little One, burn the image of this place into your mind so you will know when you come to the right place. The rocks will encircle you like the spread of a hawk's wings as it readies for flight. This is where the Great Spirit will speak to you. Build a big fire and dance around it to let the Great Spirit know that you have found your new home."

The images blurred in Moochkla's eyes, upsetting Kaiya's balance. Moochkla grabbed her as she swayed and helped her to the ground.

"What did you see?" he asked her.

She told him about the images. Moochkla nodded as he, too, recalled the scenes from his vision.

"But, how will I know I'm heading in the right direction? It seems like I'm supposed to go down into the canyon, across the river, and up the other side, then head toward the land of the winter sun."

"Yes, that's how it felt to me, too."

"Are you coming with me?"

Moochkla gazed at Kaiya and lovingly reached out to push her hair back from her face.

"I thought you had someone to go with you."

Kaiya smiled, thinking of Kayko. She realized what a dangerous thing she would be asking of him to come on this journey with her.

"Do you think Kayko should come with me?" she asked.

Moochkla listened to the wind begin to pick up the needles in the trees from far, far away, sweeping the roar closer and closer, but only grazing the tops of the trees. Just a slight tickle of air brushed their faces at ground level.

"I can only tell you what your great aunt Kairee predicted years ago. She saw you, Little One, as a great healer. And, she saw you with a man. She saw Kayko as a great healer also, and he was with a woman who walked with a cougar. So to me, it sounds like the two of you were destined to be together. Now we know where it is you should be, and the Great Spirit will help guide you there."

"Kaiya, there's another thing you should know. When I examined your wounds, I saw a dead space in the place where babies live. The wounds from the spear were so extensive that I don't think you will ever be able to have children."

Kaiya rose and walked to the edge of the forest while she pondered this. Although she always enjoyed helping with the babies of the clan, she also saw the tired look in the eyes of the mothers. Her work as a healer would be her life's work, she decided, and that would satisfy her. She must tell Kayko this news and let him think about what this meant for him.

XLIV

Kayko retied the yucca fibers, securing the knot on his pack. Accustomed to the trail from Unkar up to the rim, following it with his feet for so many summers, he knew every turn, every step, every rock along the way. On this vastly different path every step would be a new surprise under his feet. But he would take this journey with Kaiya. Kaiya. She made his heart sing. How had he ever lived without her?

He had carved two new walking sticks, strong enough to support his weight as he tested each step with his sandaled foot. He wove two pair of yucca fiber sandals for each of them, knowing their path would be strewn with sharp rocks. He sewed new water bladders. Turkey and deer jerky would be their mainstay food, plus whatever they could find along the way.

Kaiya had sharpened her hunting skills while traveling with her Uncle Bertok, so she felt comfortable using her deerskin sling and a sharp stone to bring down rabbits or squirrels. Perhaps Chee would occasionally catch something they could add to their cooking pot. Each would carry a bag of corn kernels for grinding to make flour or boil into a stew. Both of them would carry a pottery cooking pot. Sleeping furs and a change of clothes rounded out their packs.

Kaiya had a new traveling pouch after her old one had been soaked with blood during her battle with Drok. Kayko made her a new one from a rabbit skin, fur on the inside. He fitted the straps perfectly over one shoulder so it hung around her middle and she could easily grab items without breaking her stride. Many herbs were also packaged carefully in it, along with food and water.

Souva and Moochkla walked with them to the top of the cliffs to a place where the clan from Unkar had found a way down to the river and across to the opposite side. Toward where the sun sets along the rim they found the big drainage cutting downward.

"We'll leave you here," said Moochkla. "Once you get down below the rim, you'll come to a place where a waterfall gushes out of the canyon wall on the side where the sun rises. From there, follow the creek all the way down to the river. Once you cross, look for a side canyon with a creek to follow up to the wide, level area. There is a small clan who lives along that creek. They tend to keep to themselves, but I hope they will tell you the easiest way out of the canyon."

Kaiya and Moochkla hugged and held each other. "I'll send word through Kokopelli once we're settled. Maybe you could come see us in our new place."

"Maybe, Little One," Moochkla said. "But I feel like the days of all my wanderings might be coming to a close. I think my age is starting to catch up to me."

Souva and Kayko exchanged an awkward embrace, and then the two young people descended into the canyon.

"Good luck, son," Souva called after them. "May the Great Spirit guide your way."

Moochkla and Souva watched them until they were just specks along the animal trail, small puffs of dust rising into the air on the wind.

Kayko slowly worked hard with every step, feeling his way with his sticks and his feet, firmly planting one of each before moving to the next position.

"Watch for that cliff rose branch on the left," Kaiya called.

Chee raced ahead, always circling back to check on Kayko, and Kaiya kept a steady but slow pace out front, calling back to Kayko about protruding roots and drop-offs. Inwardly she sighed, realizing this was going to be a slow, tedious process to insure Kayko's safety.

At last they could hear the gushing sound of water pouring forth from the canyon wall. Chee was beside himself with joy, barking and splashing, then racing to Kayko or Kaiya and shaking vigorously, making Kaiya shriek. They tried to set up camp, but gave up and played in the water with Chee, throwing sticks which he retrieved to return for more. Refreshed, with bellies full of water, all three settled down for the night, the rushing of the waterfall a soothing background for them to float away on their dreams.

Waking with the slight beginnings of daylight, they quickly broke camp to take advantage of the cool of the morning for hiking. Below the spring they picked up the creek, their guide all the way to the big river. Shade was scant as they walked into a wide, open space, but it was relatively flat, making the walking much easier for Kayko. The views of the canyon were spectacular, butte after ridge after sheer cliffs rose as far as the eye could see. Kaiya kept up a constant descriptive chatter so that Kayko could follow her voice down the trail. Chee frequently ran down to the creek to douse, and Kaiya suggested they do the same. It felt deliciously cool to splash water on their hair and bodies, removing the trail dust before shouldering their packs and heading on.

Later, the canyon walls closed in around them, leaving behind the wide area with its distant views. The rock here was dark, shiny pink, and jagged. The creek picked up speed as its course became constricted. Logs shoved up high, boulders ripped from the banks and tossed below showed tempestuous flooding in the past. Kaiya felt uneasy as the walls closed in. If a flood surged through here, she thought, there would be nowhere to escape. This section had canyon walls even higher than where she had been caught before. The walls around them increased the echoing roar of the creek, but above them the skies remained blue with no sign of clouds or booming reports of thunder.

Kaiya breathed a sigh of relief when the creek widened out again.

Ahead they could now see the walls of the canyon rising toward the place of the winter sun. As they followed the creek down to its delta, they heard a throaty roar. They had come all the way back down to the river.

Looking toward the place of the rising sun, Kaiya saw a substantial shelter made out of stones. When they were close, they called out, but received no answer. No one was home, but they decided to stay the night anyway.

"We'll stay and be gone in the morning. I love the sound of the river here," Kayko said.

In the morning they found an easy place to cross the river. Chee treated it as a game, swimming back and forth several times. Once they reached the other side, they encountered a sandy area, hard going for them all. One foot forward meant the other foot slipped back. At last they cleared the sandy stretch, and found the side canyon with the creek in it, just as Moochkla had said they would.

Splashing their way along the creek, keeping wet and cool in the morning air, they turned a corner, and to their dismay saw a waterfall blocking their way.

"We're going to have to climb around this," Kaiya explained to Kayko. It's going to require a lot of hand over hand climbing."

"I'll be fine as long as you tell me if my feet and hands are in a safe place. Let's keep Chee between us so if he gets stuck I can push him up to you."

Kayko with his long legs and arms was able to spider his way up the steep wall easier than she could. Chee only got stuck once, whimpering his fear so that both of them stopped to help him.

"Whew," Kaiya said. "I think that was scarier for me than for you."

"Why's that?" Kayko asked.

"Because I could see how far down we'd fall if we had a misstep, and you could only feel the rocks in front of you."

"That's all I concentrate on—whatever is right in front of me. I can't afford to let my concentration stay in the past or the future. I have to be in the now, or I could get hurt."

Kaiya thought about Kayko's philosophy. It was a good one. When she was a little girl, all she could think about was what her future would be like. When she was being tormented by Drok, all she could think about was her immediate safety. Now, content in her love with Kayko, she was happy to live in the now, but also daydreamed about their future together.

"When you were little, what did you imagine your life would be like?" Kaiya asked Kayko.

"I always felt lonely as a child, because I didn't have any family. I always hoped I would find someone to cherish and build a life together with. But I didn't know if that would be possible because of my eyes."

"I always felt lonely, too," Kaiya replied. "But I don't feel lonely now." She reached for Kayko's waist and drew in close for a hug.

At last they cleared that difficult place and came to a layer of rock with many ledges which threw shade. Grateful to be above the waterfall, and back along the creek, they threw themselves down in the shade. All three of them were worn out from the ascent, and the rushing sound of the creek caused them to nod off.

Awakening in the late afternoon, they started heading up canyon again. Soon Kaiya started reporting signs of the clan that lived here.

"They have corn and squash growing just above the creek banks. It must be easy for them to get water to their crops."

She stopped talking as three men suddenly appeared out of the riparian area by the creek. The men looked unfriendly. Chee stood by Kayko, hair raising on the back of his neck. Kayko grabbed his head and ordered him to stay. Then, stepping forward, he extended his hand upward in greeting.

"I am Kayko, son of Souva of Unkar. I am told you are able to tell us the easiest way to get to the rim from here. We only want passage through here, nothing else from your clan."

The three men conferred among themselves, glancing at Kaiya frequently. One man stepped forward, speaking a language close enough to their own that the meaning was clear. The leader pointed to Kaiya's traveling pouch. "Give us that, and we will show you the way."

"All right," Kaiya responded. "But not what's in it."

Turning her back to the men, she slid her big pack off, and then crammed the contents of her traveling pouch into her pack. Stepping forward, she handed her pouch to the leader.

"Now," she said firmly. "Show us the easiest way to the rim from here."

The leader showed them the route. Kaiya pulled Kayko forward, gesturing for clarification with the leader as Kayko listened intently. Chee wove his way in between and around their legs as if tracing the route with his paws. Finally sure of the directions, the travelers thanked the leader and continued on their way.

XLV

"Why were they so unfriendly? And why did the rest of the clan stay hidden?" Kaiya asked.

Chee also felt uneasy around them and stuck so close to Kayko, he almost tripped him swirling around his feet and walking sticks.

"Can you see them?" Kayko asked.

"No, they've disappeared," Kaiya said. "It's almost as if they were afraid of us."

"What I've heard is that they are possessive of their place here. Different groups have tried to run them out, so they don't trust anybody. But giving them your pouch was a small price to pay for finding the easiest way out of here. I'll make you a new one once we're settled," Kayko said.

Kaiya finally asked the question which had been bothering her. "Is it really all right with you that we won't be able to have any children?"

Kayko slowed his walk and then stopped. "Yes," he said. "I thought about it for a long time after you told me. I always had a hard time when I was young because I couldn't do many of the things the other kids could. So I gravitated toward being with the adults. I never felt that comfortable around youngsters."

Kaiya felt relieved with his answer, grateful for his thoughtful consideration of such a serious issue.

They continued their trudge upwards, stopping now and again to catch their breath and look back. Kaiya described how much higher up in the canyon they were now. "Remember those huge cottonwood trees we passed beneath? Now they look like a small bouquet of flowers. We're making good progress."

Storm clouds billowed over the North Rim, heavy and dark. Kaiya saw a jagged edge of lightning make contact with the ground there. Chee felt it too; he cowered and then jumped against Kayko.

"What's the matter?" Kayko asked.

"I just saw a bolt of lightning strike on the other side. I sure hope that storm's not moving our way."

"Well, we don't have many options. We just have to keep going up. Unless," Kayko said, moving closer to where Kaiya stood and grasping her arm, "you're planning an early camp for some reason."

He gave her a sexy kiss, making her laugh, then drew her in close for a real kiss. As their lips touched, a faint rumble of thunder rolled in the distance.

"Ooooh, that was quite a kiss!" Kaiya said, pulling away. "We'd better keep going. There's nowhere here that would be a good place to shelter from a storm."

Sometimes hiking, sometimes using hand and footholds, they continued their climb. The directions had seemed clear at the time they were given, but the exertion of the hike and Kaiya's nervousness about the storm made her stop frequently to get her bearings.

"Are we lost?" Kayko asked.

"No, I'm pretty sure we're still going the right way. I'm just trying to figure out the easiest possible way for you."

Kayko bristled. "I'm capable of any kind of hiking," he retorted. "Don't try to make it easy on my account. Just pick the fastest way to get us out of here."

A throaty bellow of thunder floated out over the canyon, nearer this time, the sound caught between the buttes separating the North and South Rims, the rumbling slowly fading.

"All right then, I'll try to find the easiest path for Chee. This is hard for me, always trying to figure out where to go next."

Kayko reached to put a walking stick in front of Kaiya, stopping her. "I know, I know how hard this is for you. I wish I could help more. But there is no better guide than you. You took that long journey with Moochkla and Bertok, and you fled across unknown lands to arrive here. I will follow you anywhere, especially knowing I will be in your sleeping furs at night."

Kaiya pushed herself into his arms for a reassuring hug. They were jolted apart by an ear-splitting clap of thunder.

"Let's go!" she shrieked, heart pounding. They took off, Chee wild-eyed and jumpy. Kaiya whirled around to see the canyon disappear behind them in a gauzy curtain of grey.

Kaiya surged upwards, scaling a small cliff in one swift move. She paused, searching the rocks for the next passage. Stepping onto a ledge, she realized Kayko had not followed her up the wall. "Kayko, where are you?" she shouted into the wind. No answer. She let herself back down the cliff, much harder than her ascent. When her feet touched bottom neither Kayko nor Chee were in sight. Yelling their names over and over, she searched wildly about her, finally seeing them way across a drainage.

"No, Kayko, that's the wrong way!" she screamed. The wind ripped the words from her mouth and scattered them uselessly into the torrent. Splatters started coming down in earnest, big fat drops, making puffs of dirt jump up as each hit. She dashed in their direction, but they vanished from her sight.

"No, Kayko, Chee, come back, come back!"

Before her, where she last saw them, a huge ground to cloud bolt of lightning shattered her vision. She screamed and threw herself to the ground in a tight ball, waiting for the storm to pass over her. A brief hailstorm, then she glanced upwards to see a rainbow in the distance. She pushed herself up from the dirt and rushed toward where she had last seen Kayko and Chee, hurrying right past where they crouched, hidden away at the back of a short ledge. Little rivulets of water surged past their hideaway, braiding into a stream below the cave.

"Hey, don't you have sense enough to get out of the rain?" a familiar voice asked.

Kaiya twirled around to see Chee curled into a ball in Kayko's lap, peering out at her from the tiny cave they had found. Chee's tail wagged vigorously, but neither made any move to leave their dry cavern. Kaiya dripped as if she had just emerged from the river.

"Where did you go?" she demanded. "You were right behind me and then you disappeared."

"The thunder was so loud I couldn't hear you. I called out, and that was when the wind picked up and the rain started. Chee barked and went this way, so I figured that's where you were. We had just ducked into this cave when that bolt hit so close that I think it cracked a rock. Are you all right?"

"Only if you come out and hug me," she said. Kayko unfolded his long legs, dumping Chee out of his lap, and grabbed Kaiya. "Ooh, you are muddy!" he laughed.

They stood for a while, watching and listening to the water rush by, the rainbow fade, and the full moon rise behind them. The canyon was awash in light, minute details amazingly clear. Rock ledges on the opposite side of the canyon sharpened, showing their daytime colors. Trees were not just silhouettes, the gambel oaks' scalloped edges were crisp and just a shade greener. Individual pine needles glistened with raindrops. Kaiya traced the shape of the oak leaf on Kayko's arm while describing it all. She guided his hand to show him the wet rock edges, the sharp end of a pine needle, and the coarse brush of the juniper. The moonlight sidled down the cliff, making them part of the glow. Chee's brown fur sparkled with water droplets in the moonlight, a magical dog. They camped in the little cave, peeled off each other's wet clothes and rolled naked onto their sleeping furs.

Stars wheeled overhead, framed by the mandala of jagged canyon walls all around them. Bats zoomed by, greedy for insects after the storm. Kaiya and Kayko held each other close, thrusting, feeling their own cataclysmic shudders, another primal power joining the earth to the clouds.

XLVI

The air felt fresh and clean as the three travelers finished the climb to the South Rim of the canyon. Leaving the desert vegetation behind, the big pine trees with the sweet-smelling reddish bark towered over them once again. Spent from their efforts, they all rested in the shade before moving through the forest to camp among the tall trees.

The next day's hike brought them to the far edge of the big forest and into grasslands where it would be hot for days to come. The Snow Mountain High Place was a soft haziness on the horizon.

After some time of trudging, Kaiya remarked to Kayko, "We are coming to a different kind of mountain, a red, tall butte, flat on the top and sloping down the sides. She put her hands over his to draw the contours in the air of the shape of the upcoming terrain. "Do you know the story of that one?"

"I've heard," he replied, "that some believe it to be the navel of Mother Earth. It certainly is well-protected, as people who have tried to climb it run into many rattlesnakes. It wouldn't be a good place for Chee. He has no sense when it comes to rattlers."

Chee, as if on cue, started leaping and yipping.

"Oh, no," groaned Kayko. "He only makes that sound when he's found a snake!"

Kaiya ran forward to find Chee dancing wildly. "It's only a gopher snake," she called back. "And he's staying pretty far back from it."

"Maybe he's actually learned something. The last time we came upon a snake, he ran toward it. I managed to grab his tail in time to stop him."

They walked well past dark as the coolness invited them onward. They could see the tree line ahead of them and knew they would again be in a shady refuge sometime the next day.

As they walked the next day, the forest enfolded them. The trees were mixed, as if having a hard time trying to decide what kind of forest it should be. Junipers were there, but small and scraggly. Pines were there, the kind that gave nuts. Oak trees were scattered about, a colorful touch to the beginning of autumn. Occasionally the big, reddish pines showed themselves and all three travelers would stop, grateful for the deep shade. A circular grouping of the giant pines made the perfect spot for camping.

Toward dawn a yowling tore the air. Chee bolted upright, and Kayko reacted fast enough to grab him before he took off after the sound. The growls and snarls sounded coyote-like, with the coyote getting the better of the other animal. Kaiya thought it might be a fox, but Kayko wasn't sure. The three of them huddled together as the yelps faded. Something had lost its battle for life.

None of them could sleep after that. Breaking camp early, Kayko finally let Chee run on his own. He barked and yipped, as if trying to reenact the battle of darkness. Kayko tilted his ear up, listening carefully.

"I think he's found something he wants us to see. Let's follow."

"Don't you think he'll just catch up with us? We need to keep going toward the land of the winter sun, and Chee took off the other way."

"No," Kayko insisted. "I think we need to go after him."

Kaiya sighed, shouldered her pack, and headed toward Chee's excited barking. When she got close enough to see him, his ears were perky and his nose pointed at something under a small ledge. Kaiya arrived just in time to see a tiny nose peek out.

"Come hold Chee back so I can see what's in there," Kaiya called.

As soon as Chee and Kayko backed off, a baby fox, no bigger than Kaiya's two hands cupped together, emerged from the small cave. It whined, a cross between a dog's whimper and a cat's meow.

Kaiya surveyed the area, looking for its mama. Chee had wriggled loose from Kayko's grasp and was examining something in the dirt.

The tiny fox retreated, so Kaiya went to recapture Chee. She stopped near him and saw the results of last night's drama. It was the mutilated body of a grey fox, bitten clean through at the neck and chewed on extensively.

In her mind's eye, Kaiya recalled how senseless human violence is perpetrated against its own species. She thought of Drok, and how he had lived and died so violently. She grieved in her heart for all victims of violence.

"Poor thing," Kaiya murmured to the carcass. "You were just trying to defend your babies. I wonder how many you had?"

Kaiya sat off to the side of the ledge, and placed a strip of deer jerky several feet ahead of her. Soon enough, a twitchy nose appeared from the shadow, and eventually an entire head.

"Come on out," Kaiya said softly. "I'll help you."

It took a while, but finally the inquisitive creature couldn't resist the smell of food. It picked up the piece of jerky, working it over between tiny jaws. Kaiya clapped her hand over her mouth to stop the giggles, charmed by this tiny animal. The baby fox came closer to Kaiya, smelling more food in her pack. Kaiya sat still, allowing the baby to sniff her legs, then walk on top of her, resting its paws on Kaiya's chest and staring up into her face. Kaiya's heart melted, and she knew this baby would go with them.

The little fox offered little resistance when Kayko approached cautiously with Chee. Kaiya fashioned a small sling out of a rabbit skin, and slung it over her shoulders, creating a tiny carrying bag for the baby. Kaiya scooped up the fox and placed it in the sling, right next to her breast. The baby nestled there, curled up, its tail over its nose. Chee jumped up to investigate, and licked the baby fox, making Kaiya coo with delight.

"Oh, they're getting along! I was worried that Chee would see it as a threat."

"So, we have a new member of the family now. Tell me about it," Kayko said.

"She's a little female, with the sweetest expression. Her body is grey with tawny markings on her cheeks. There are black and white stripes along her nose, but her ears, legs, and chest are tawny. Most striking is her big bushy grey tail, with a heavy, black stripe running from the base of her haunches to the very tip of her tail. Her eyes are curious and alert. She really is beautiful. Here, let me show you her tail."

Kayko gently stroked the soft tail. "What are you going to call her?" Kayko asked.

"Hmmm. Let me think on that for a while," Kaiya replied.

They walked for a long time in companionable silence, Chee trotting ahead and then circling back to check on Kayko and the new addition. They were back in the forest now with plenty of shade. The light breeze stirred the long pine needles, the occasional pine cone breaking free and clattering to the ground with several noisy bounces.

Kaiya announced, "Heesa. I will call her Heesa. That's the name my mother was thinking of naming her new baby if it was a girl. She'll be the sister I never had."

"Heesa," Kayko repeated. "I like it. It sounds soft and feminine, like you." He reached playfully for Kaiya's buttocks. Kaiya squealed, drawing Heesa's sharp nose out of the rabbit skin. When Kaiya's eyes met the kit's, images wavered, then faded. Kaiya smiled, feeling a closeness to this little being.

"It's all right, Heesa. You'd better get used to that. He's always grabbing me, using his blindness as an excuse that he didn't know what he was grabbing."

Kayko grinned broadly at this accusation, and grabbed further up on Kaiya's body. They stopped to pull each other close for a kiss; tiny Heesa between them, with Chee dancing at their feet.

XLVII

Still no sign. Trudging onward, Kaiya wondered where the landscapes were that she had seen in Moochkla's eyes. Only more of the same dry, scratchy sound of sandals crunching into dirt and rocks. Just more sagebrush and clumps of trees. This journey was starting to take its toll on all of them with the many days of constant walking. Chee had picked up a burr. By the time Kaiya noticed, it was bloody and raw. She cleaned the wound, receiving an appreciative lick for her efforts, but he still favored that foot. Kaiya's ankles felt weak from so many twisting steps.

She turned, looking back at Kayko. He also trudged along, showing with each step that this journey was wearying him. Every move forward was a new mystery to him, feeling with his sticks and feet for tree roots, loose rocks, or other trail obstacles. Chee followed closely behind him, often running ahead, but always circling back to check on Kayko. Kaiya waited for them to catch up to her cool spot in the shade.

After a bite to eat under the pines, Kayko said he needed a short nap. Chee immediately curled up beside him, but Kaiya was too restless to lie down. She walked away and spooked a rabbit. Quick reflexes on her part caused her to pick up a stone and fit it into her sling, always at the ready in the pocket of her tunic. She twirled the sling, let the stone fly, and was grateful to see the rabbit go down. Running toward it, she finished off the struggling rabbit with a big rock. "Thank you, Great Spirit, for this meal and warm fur," she murmured.

Circling back to check on the sleeping Kayko, Kaiya surveyed the landscape before her. The Snow Mountain High Place was very near the place of the rising sun now. This was the point where they must turn in that direction. She bent down and nuzzled Kayko's ear and cheek, getting a low grunting response from Kayko and a wagging tail from Chee. Heesa responded to Kaiya's bent posture by sticking her nose out from the carrying sling, and spotted the dead rabbit in Kaiya's hand. her nose twitched, accompanied by wide eyes.

"Oh, no—you can't have this whole rabbit," Kaiya scolded.

"Why not?" Kayko asked sleepily.

"No, not you," Kaiya stroked Kayko's hair. "I was talking to Heesa. While you were napping, I was out getting dinner."

Kayko stretched out with a groan, then sat up and rose to his feet. "All right, let's go so we can put in some distance before tonight's camp."

They kept on, each lost in their own thoughts. Then Kaiya felt a quickening. An awakening rose within her as familiar images flashed through her mind which matched the landscape before her. Heart beating faster, she ran a few steps forward, then stopped.

"Ahh," breathed Kaiya, putting a restraining hand on Kayko as she took a step back from the scene before them.

"This is it, this is the place!" she cried with excitement.

Before them was the scene in Moochkla's eyes from when they were on the North Rim. She heard Moochkla's words again.

"Little One, burn the image of this place into your mind so you will know when you have come to the right place. The rocks will encircle you like the spread of a hawk's wings as it readies itself for flight. This is where the Great Spirit will speak to you. Build a big fire and dance around it so the Great Spirit will know that you have found your home."

"Oh, Kayko—this is it! I know it. This aspen grove we had to walk by, the narrowing of this canyon, the high cliffs surrounding the pool, it's all here, just like Moochkla showed me. And we're near the Kokopelli trade route. Oh, Kayko, we're finally home." Kaiya rushed into his arms, eyes brimming with tears of joy. Kayko felt relief and wonder at finally finding this place, too. Even little Heesa sensed the celebratory mood, and wriggled out of her sling and jumped down to tussle with Chee.

Everything they needed was right here. Ledges just back from the pool contained caves where they could spend the approaching winter. Downed aspen trees could easily be gathered for firewood, with the longer ones being worked into poles for their wickiup. The forest would provide food, healing plants and game. And from the top of the surrounding high cliffs, the Sacred Snow Mountain High Place could be seen in the distance, just as Kaiya remembered seeing it as a child from her canyon home with Moochkla.

"So, what do we do now?" asked Kayko.

"We must build a fire," Kaiya replied.

And so they did. It took the rest of the day to build one big enough to satisfy Kaiya. As darkness fell, they used their fire starting sticks and a small amount of kindling and pine needles to start the pile burning. As the fire crackled and warmed, Kaiya, Kayko, Chee and Heesa bobbed and weaved around the perimeter, feet hitting the earth in rhythm to the vigorous chant Kayko and Kaiya sang at the top of their voices. Kaiya threw her head back as she danced, the stars twirling with her around the fire. The cliffs above looked like their own smaller version of the Grand Canyon through which they had passed. A moon inched up throwing light beams into their circle of safety.

Kaiya breathed deeply, letting scenes from her life play through her head. All the myriad events and people swirled with her in this dance around the fire. Her parents, memories of them dim but filled with love. Elderly Jumac, who cared for her after her parents were gone. Her great-aunt Kairee, for whom she was named. Beloved Uncle Bertok, now with his lover Pem. Obaho, who had loved her and lost his life by Drok's hand. All those many people she met on her grand journeys who had helped her. And Moochkla, the finest individual she had ever known, who helped her become the healer which she knew was her destiny. She sang her thanks to them all.

For she realized that all of her lifetime of experiences had step by step led her to where she was now—with a man she loved, her sweet animals, her healing knowledge and this beautiful place that was meant to be their home. She stopped, threw her arms up toward the moon and thanked all the Spirit Beings who had brought her to this moment in time.

In response to the Spirits' energy, the fire roared higher. She caught Kayko and held him tight. Nearby an owl hooted. And far, far in the distance, a coyote howled at the moon.

THE END

About the Author

Photo credit Nancy Timper

Nancy Rivest Green was born in Massachusetts. Her family moved to Phoenix, so Nancy finished high school there, and attended the University of Arizona in Tucson. She then entered a 28 year teaching career. Her life changed forever when she discovered the Grand Canyon, living and teaching in Grand Canyon National Park with her ranger husband. She was an award winning Special Education teacher and school librarian. Now retired and living on the edge of the Kaibab National Forest outside of Flagstaff, Nancy continues her love affair with nature. If she's not hiking, running the Colorado River, kayaking, bicycling or traveling, she's reading and spending lots of time on writing.

Three of Nancy's short stories have been published in the "Northern Arizona Authors Association Collected Works, Volume 2." She is currently working on her next book about encounters with animals of the Southwest.

www.nancyrivestgreen.com

ACKNOWLEDGMENTS

Ever since my ranger husband and I lived at Walnut Canyon back in the 1980s, pieces and snippets of this story have floated through my thoughts. Although impossible to thank every single person who helped this story along, there are some who deserve special mention.

A member of my Moon Group gave me permission to use her spirit-name, Kaiya, with the condition that I make her a strong character. Thanks to the raven that helped me name my villain. I knew it had to begin with D, and the raven filled in the rest.

For early editing help, I thank authors Mary Sojourner and David Clement-Davies. Mary taught me that you can't call yourself a writer unless you write every day, and David taught me that writing is all about passion and belief.

Thanks to Tom Martin, who patiently answered my questions about inner canyon places where I had never hiked, but that Kaiya needed to know.

To the Flagstaff Women Writers Group, I can't express enough thanks. To sit in the presence of these amazing writers and authors, week after week, hearing their excellent thoughts creatively put to paper, was simply priceless. I cherish our process—first the prompt, followed by quiet in the room, (except for our furiously working pens and pencils.) Then the call that time's up. Finally, our sharing; always different, sometimes profound, often poignant, or occasionally funny. It's more than just good writing practice; it's therapy, self-awareness, and a deepening of the writer within.

Equally important in my life is the Northern Arizona Authors Association. We come together every three weeks or so, and hear about the progress of each person's current project. A more eclectic group of people, in terms of writing style and content, could hardly be imagined in the same room, but we eagerly listen to the next installment of each person's work. From screenplays, fiction, non-fiction, autobiography, poems and porn, our group has serious writers in every genre. In the fall of 2013, the Association published a collection of our work, which includes short stories, essays and poetry. In this publication, I experienced the first-time thrill of seeing my name AND the word author together on the same page. All the members of this group have encouraged me and appreciated my work. Thanks go out to all of you.

Special thanks to Gary McCarthy, a renowned author of westerns and historical fiction. Gary is a member of NAAA, but, unlike the rest of us, has a lifetime of published books to his credit. I had read his work before joining our authors association, and felt extremely fortunate to associate with a writer of his caliber. Gary has encouraged me, shared his knowledge of the publishing industry, and given me the confidence to forge my way into this amazing world of writing. He called it "my wonderful novel," since he never did like the title.

To Donna Reese, I offer a humble bow and a whole canyon full of heart-felt thanks. When Donna left Flagstaff, it was a great loss to the Flagstaff Women Writers Group. She was looking for some part-time work in her new environs, so I broached the subject of editing. Would she be at all interested in helping me with my first novel? I had always been amazed and sometimes stunned by her writing ability. Since she was a retired high school English teacher, I thought perhaps she could help whip my novel into shape. Donna agreed in the spring of 2011, and we worked together diligently to bring this novel to a readable form. I sent her my original scratchings, and she would send me back papers written all over with her insertions, pithy comments, cross-outs and arrows. My writing always sounded better when I followed her suggestions. This book would not be what it is without Donna's patient ministrations. Thank you, thank you, and thank you again.

The wonderful art work for each chapter heading, and the map end pages, are by artist and writer ValJesse O'Feeney. I so appreciate how it enhances my work. The pictures clearly shine with ValJesse's love of the Southwest and all places wild.

Like Kaiya, I am a motherless only child. The one thing that has helped me endure through time is my circle of girlfriends. I am blessed to have so many who have been there for me over and over again. I've lived in so many beautiful places in Arizona—the North Rim, Sierra Vista, Flagstaff, Prescott and Grand Canyon. I've been fortunate to meet wonderful women in all of these places. I have collected them like glass beads on a string, each a sparkling design all their own. I'm careful to keep them in my life forever like the valuable jewels they are. What would my life be like without their support? I don't ever want to know. Thanks to all of you.

And to Keith, who endured hours of me yelling at the computer when it wouldn't do what I wanted, and for all the hours of my time spent not in this 21st century world with him, but off in the 1100s, shaking the sands of ancient Arizona from my hair. Thank you, sweetheart. You are a treasure beyond this writer's words.

SELECTED BIBLIOGRAPHY FOR FURTHER READING

Anderson, Michael F. 1998 "Living at the Edge: Explorers, Exploiters and Settlers of the Grand Canyon Region" (Grand Canyon: Grand Canyon Association)

Coder, Christopher M., 2000 "An Introduction to Grand Canyon Prehistory" (Grand Canyon: Grand Canyon Asociation)

Cole, Stephen West, 2006 "Quicksand and Blue Springs: Exploring the Little Colorado River Gorge" (Flagstaff: Vishnu Temple Press)

Diamond, Jared, 2005 "Collapse: "How Societies Choose to Fail or Succeed" (New York: Penguin Books)

Diehl, Richard A., 1983 "Tula: The Toltec Capital of Ancient Mexico" (London: Thames and Hudson, LTD.)

Enciso, Jorge, 1971 "Designs from Pre-Columbian Mexico" (New York: Dover Publications, Inc.)

Ferguson, William M., 1987 "Anasazi Ruins of the Southwest in Color" (Albuquerque: University of New Mexico Press)

Friederici, Peter, Editor, 2005 "Earth Notes: Exploring the Southwest's Canyon Country from the Airwaves" (Grand Canyon: Grand Canyon Association)

Hughes, J. Donald, 1978 "In the House of Stone and Light: A Human History of the Grand Canyon" (Grand Canyon: Grand Canyon Natural History Association)

Jones, Lindsay, 1995 "Twin City Tales: A Hemeneutical Reassessment of Tula and Chichen Itza" (Niwot, Colorado: University Press of Colorado)

Kopper, Philip, 1986 "The Smithsonian Book of North American Indians Before the Coming of the Europeans" (Washington, D.C.: Smithsonian Books)

Martin, Tom, 1999 "Day Hikes from the River: A Guide to 75 Hikes from Camps on the Colorado River in Grand Canyon National Park"

(Flagstaff: Vishnu Temple Press)

National Geographic Magazine: November, 1982 and April, 1996, The Anasazi.

Patterson, Alex, 1992 "A Field Guide to Rock Art Symbols of the Greater Southwest" (Boulder: Johnson Printing Company)

Stevens, Larry, 1983 "The Colorado River in Grand Canyon" (Flagstaff: Red Lake Books)

Schwartz, Douglas W., [1988?] "On the Edge of Splendor: Exploring Grand Canyon's Human Past" (Santa Fe: The School of American Research)

Young, John V., 1990 "Kokopelli: Casanova of the Cliff Dwellers" (Palmer Lake, Colorado: Filter Press, LLC)

Colophon

To counteract and subvert the culture of fundamental corruption inherent in the overly politicized and corporatist early 21st high-tech world requires public organizations dedicated to protecting the rights of the individual. Free/Libre Open Source Software (FLOSS) is the Internet equivalent of free speech, it is synonymous with individual rights and freedom of expression.

Many of the people and organizations protecting the right to free speech, and supplying the tools that support the ability to do so, support FLOSS principles. They labor under moral responsibility to the human race, and because it's fun. They ask only for attribution in return when their work is used.

Moonlit Press supports these contemporary freedom fighters and gives attribution to their work with deep gratitude.

The ability to have and use Free Software is supported and defended by the Free Software Foundation; [http://fsf.org/] among others.

Many FLOSS applications were used in the preparation of this book. Most of them are licensed using the GNU Public License of equivalent FLOSS licenses.

The text of this book was prepared using LibreOfficeWriter; [https://www.libreoffice.org/].

The graphics were prepared using GIMP; [http://www.gimp.org/], and Inkscape; [http://inkscape.org/]. Gimp is a high quality continuous tone image editing package, and Inkscape is a sophisticated scalable vector graphics editing package.

All of the standard fonts used in the creation of this book are licensed under the Open Font License (OFL). [http://www.sil.org/about]. The main body of this book was typeset using Gentium typeface. Gentium is a typeface family, from the SIL International Organization, designed to enable diverse ethnic groups around the world who use the Latin, Cyrillic and Greek alphabets to produce readable, high-quality publications.

Thanks to P.D. Magnus for the Belligerent Madness font used in the title [http://www.fecundity.com/].

Thanks to Pablo Impallari for designing the fonts Libre Baskerville and Cabin. More of his work can be found at [http://www.impallari.com/].

The DejaVu font from [http://dejavu-fonts.org] was used in the main cover design. From the web,"The DejaVu fonts are a font family based on the Vera Fonts. Its purpose is to provide a wider range of characters while maintaining the original look and feel through the process of collaborative development, under a Free license."

We offer our humble and sincere thanks to all the hard working, unnamed, and under-appreciated people around the world who build the tools we need to keep freedom and integrity alive in the high-tech world. Moonlit Press supports these dedicated champions of social and technological justice; they are working to ensure that technological advances do not erode our rights.

Moonlit Press